Airborne Ambush!

Jack felt sweat in the palm of his hands as he flew the helicopter toward the enemy gun emplacements. Then he saw the first nest of enemy gunners—they were holding their fire to conceal their position.

A bright orange flash suddenly seared the air, and a strained voice called to Jack over the radio. "Captain, I've got a man hit here." Explosions filled the air and surrounded the helicopter with color, sound and death. Jack heard a frantic but garbled voice—it was one of his men calling him in trouble . . . and in warning.

"Pilot, I can't read you," Jack called back over the mike. The radio crackled and went dead.

"Captain!" Jack's gunner hollered over the noise, pointing at the ground to the right of the helicopter. Jack felt a wave of nausea overtake him, as he stared down at the scene of destruction and death before him . . .

Junglefire

Jonathan Scofield

A Dell / James A. Bryans Book

This book is dedicated to
GOODNATURE 3
and the men who were.

Published by
Dell Publishing Co., Inc.
1 Dag Hammarskjold Plaza
New York, New York 10017

ISBN: 0-440-04163-5

Printed in the United States of America

First printing—May 1982

1

Phu Bien Air Base, Vietnam
August 1969

O<small>N MEETING</small> Captain Jack Hunter for the first time, people generally believed they had seen him before. Not because he looked at all ordinary, but because Jack was a strikingly good-looking man. He had red hair, the color of burnished copper; he was tall, handsome, with crystal blue eyes which reminded most women of Paul Newman's eyes. All these features came together perfectly, so that Jack looked like the type of man Madison Avenue would pick to advertise Marlboro cigarettes. With just a little imagination, one could picture Jack by a campfire, a herd of restless cattle roaming through the rugged desert behind him.

But Jack wasn't on the great Southwest desert. He

was in a small, plywood-enclosed B.O.Q. room, lying on his bunk with his hands behind his head, looking up at the ceiling. The walls of the room were decorated with pictures from magazines, personal photos, and bits and pieces of memorabilia, including the twisted red and white piece of a tail rotor blade which had been taken from a helicopter crash Jack had survived.

It was oppressively hot, as only Vietnam can be. And because the generator had been inoperative for half an hour, the air conditioner wasn't running. Sweat ran down Jack's face and pooled on his back, but opening the door would have meant letting in an army of mosquitoes. For the moment, Jack preferred the heat to the discomfort of the mosquitoes, but he didn't know how much longer he would be able to take it.

A lizard started across the ceiling. It stopped, stretched its neck and turned its head from side to side. "Yuckup. Yuckup," was the sound the lizard made.

"Yuck you too, lizard," Jack muttered. "Why aren't you eating mosquitoes like you're supposed to? Why do you think I let you live in this palatial residence with me, anyway? You think you have a free ride?"

"Yuckup, yuckup," the lizard said again.

There was a knock on the door. "Cap'n Hunter? Cap'n Hunter, are you in there, sir?"

"Yeah," Jack answered without getting up. "Who wants to know?"

"It's me, Springs, sir. I'm the C.Q." C.Q. meant the enlisted man in charge of quarters.

Jack was the commanding officer of Troop A of the Fifth Air Cavalry. When the C.Q. came to his door it generally meant some sort of problem. Jack sighed and sat up, rubbed his sweat-dampened hair back from his eyes, then stood and walked over to open the door. Springs was standing out in the sweltering heat, dressed in a green tee-shirt, fatigue pants and shower clogs.

"What is it?" Jack asked.

"The generator's goin' to be down for a couple more hours," Springs said.

"Two more hours?" Jack groaned. He couldn't take the heat for that much longer. He would have to face the mosquitoes. "Why so long?"

"We've got to replace the brushes and we don't have any."

"What are we doing about it?"

"Creech and his boys are out looking now, sir. They'll come back with 'em."

Despite everything, Jack couldn't help but smile. Creech was Specialist Six Creech, a young man who exhibited a phenomenal talent for scrounging needed parts and supplies—scrounging being the army euphemism for stealing. Creech had two men assigned to him and their full-time job was to expedite the supply system.

"I hope it doesn't take him all night," Jack said.

"Creech'll make out like a champ, Cap'n, don't worry," Springs said. "Oh, by the way, Lieutenant Bostic told me to tell you that the air conditioner's workin' fine over at the Red Bull."

"Bostic would know," Jack said. "I don't know why he doesn't just move his bunk over there."

"You ought to go get cooled off, sir," Springs said. "There's no sense in you layin' in here gettin' et up by mosquitoes, or comin' down with heat stroke."

"You've convinced me," Jack said, reaching for his

hat. "Maybe I'll walk over there and have a couple of drinks after all. If anything comes up, that's where I'll be."

"Roger," Springs answered. He grinned. "Hey, Cap'n, is it true about the round-eyed snatch? Does it really go sideways?" He moved his hand from side to side.

"How the hell should *I* know?" Jack answered good-naturedly. "I've been over here as long as you have. I can't remember either."

"Yeah, but there are round-eyed women at the Red Bull. The nurses from Second Field Hospital go there."

"No kidding? You mean there are *women* over there? I never noticed that. It just seemed pretty much like any other O-club to me . . . a bunch of people all dressed alike, all sitting around talking about the States. The only difference between the Red Bull and a Stateside O-club is that Stateside, everyone is sitting around talking about 'Nam."

"Yeah, it's the same in the NCO clubs," Springs agreed. "Everyone in the States is talking about Vietnam, and everyone in Vietnam is talking about the States. I wish we could switch."

"It all goes toward your twenty, Springs," Jack answered. He covered his red hair with his hat, then stepped out into the night air. It was only a little less oppressive than his room had been, but there was at least a soft breeze.

Jack's room was one of the two dozen which his company had built for the officers. There were twenty warrant officers, three lieutenants, and one captain in A Troop, and all lived in the hastily constructed B.O.Q.s which looked a little like a poor man's version of a cheap motel. The long row of connected cabins was there; only the pink neon lighting was absent. It was far better than the tents and bunkers many had to live in, so Jack never complained.

And there was also the Red Bull Inn. The Red Bull Inn was an abandoned French country villa. When the army built Phu Bien, they leased the villa from its French owners and gave it a new life. Now it was serving as an officer's club with the unlikely name of the Red Bull Inn. It had its own generator, and thus was immune to the frequent breakdowns which occurred within the compound where Jack and the others of his troop were billeted.

The walk between the troop area and the Red Bull Inn was about a hundred and fifty yards through the remains of what had once been an exquisitely beautiful flower garden. Though enlisted men on punishment detail still kept the lawn trimmed and the flower beds weeded, the garden was no longer seen to with tender loving care, and it showed it. The flowers still scented the night air with their fragrance, though, and it was a pleasant walk, in sharp contrast to the filth of the over-crowded village of Long Phu, just two miles down Highway 13 from the American compound.

There was a movie being shown on the outdoor screen at the Red Bull. The movie, *Move Over Darling*, was being shown for the fifteenth night in a row. Less than half a dozen figures were sitting in the dark watching the images on the screen. Jack's shadow passed across the picture as he walked between the projector and the screen, but no one said a word. Graphic evidence, thought Jack, that any diversion—even, or perhaps especially, from the movie—was welcome indeed.

Inside, the club was noisy with the chatter and laughter of nearly one hundred men and women. The men were either pilots or doctors, and the women were nurses. They were all dressed in fatigues, and there was a degree of truth to what Jack had told Springs. There was a sameness about them which caused their sex to blur after a while.

"American Pie" was playing on the jukebox in the corner, though the music was drowned out by the drone of conversation and the laughter and clinking of glasses. Moving through the crowd were small, attractive Vietnamese women, waitresses hired by the O-club. They wore delicate, butterfly-bright *ao-dais*, the traditional Vietnamese flowing silk dresses, and they carried trays of drinks or empty glasses with equal ease.

Some warrant officer was reflying his day's mission at the bar, gesturing with his hands and using a jargon which would be totally unintelligible to the uninitiated. Jack had no desire to join that conversation, so he looked out across the tables until he spotted Bob Bostic.

Bob was a short, nearly bald-headed man who would have looked much older than his twenty-four years had it not been for his constant smile. He was Jack's executive officer and closest friend.

"Jack!" he heard Bob call. "Jack, over here."

Bostic had a place near the billiard room. There were several people sitting around his table, including two nurses. The others were pilots, but they weren't from the air cavalry; they were from the medical evacuation unit at Bien Hoa on temporary assignment to the hospital. They were dustoff pilots, so called because of the radio code which was used to summon them when they were needed.

Jack recognized one of them as a fellow who had gone to flight school with him.

"Greg Fillion! They finally found a place for you, did they?" he teased, shaking Greg's hand.

"Another Cobra jock, just what we don't need around here," Greg answered.

"Gentlemen, I'll thank you to show a little respect for my commanding officer," Bostic said. He lifted his glass. "I propose a toast to the best damned air cav troop commander in Vietnam."

"You're the commander, and you're just a captain?" Greg said. "Damn, I've never seen a commander below the rank of major. How did you swing that?"

"Hell, there's nothin' to that," one of the other dustoff pilots said. "They'll make anyone commander of an air cav troop."

"Jack isn't just anyone," Bob said. He's going to be famous. Some magazine people interviewed him and there's going to be a story out about him."

"Really?" one of the nurses asked. Her name was Jane Goss. Jack had seen her many times and often thought of asking her out, but she was constantly surrounded by the other officers and Jack had no desire to be just another one of the crowd. This was the first time he had even sat at the same table with her.

"Yeah," Jack answered sheepishly. "At least, I was interviewed. I don't know if they'll use any of the stuff or not."

"They'll use it," Greg said. "They used stuff about our outfit. It was called "Dustoff, Lifeline to the States." I saw it in *Reader's Digest.*"

"Yeah, and I'll bet all you guys carry a copy of it next to your hearts," Bostic teased.

"I carry it in my billfold," one of the dustoff pilots said seriously, and Bostic, Jack and the nurses laughed.

"What's so funny?" the dustoff pilot wanted to know.

"You guys are in the wrong branch of the service," Jack answered. "You should have been in the Marine Corps. You're the only outfit in the whole theater that gets as much press as the marines."

"Hell, you're just jealous," Greg said. "Everyone wants to be a dustoff, but only a few are chosen."

"Yeah, well I don't blame 'em," Bostic said. "I wouldn't mind a cushy job like that myself. I'd a whole hell of a lot rather come in and pick 'em up after it's all over and the V.C. have left, than go in beforehand to soften 'em up."

"Sticks and stones," Greg said good-naturedly, "sticks and stones. Hey, look at that just comin' in over there. Isn't that the Black Dragon?"

"Yeah," one of the other dustoff pilots said. "Yeah, I think it is. Do you think he's got his wife with him? Now there's one Vietnamese lady I could leave my wife and kids for."

"Who's the Black Dragon?" Jane asked.

"Colonel Ngyuen, commanding officer of the Lightning Force," Jack said. "Some say he may be the next president of South Vietnam."

"But he's just a colonel," Jane said.

"Batista was just a sergeant when he became president of Cuba," Jack said. "The rank doesn't mean nearly as much as the position of power. And right now, Colonel Ngyuen certainly has the power. He commands the largest undivided army in South Vietnam. The Black Dragon could take Saigon tomorrow if he wanted to."

"You call him the Black Dragon?" Jane asked.

"*He* calls himself that," Jack explained. "He has a flair for the dramatic."

Colonel Ngyuen was dressed in a black uniform with silver accoutrements. He carried a black baton with a highly polished brass point, and he was wearing a chrome-plated, pearl-handled pistol on his hip. He had a closely cropped moustache and flashing dark eyes, and when he laughed he displayed a shining gold tooth.

"Look who's with him," one of the dustoff pilots said, almost reverently.

A woman came in behind Colonel Ngyuen and his entourage. The woman was Madam Ngyuen, the Black Dragon's wife. She was known as the Dragon Lady, partly because of the sobriquet her husband went by, and partly because, like the woman character in *Terry and the Pirates*, she was a beautiful woman.

Jack had often heard of Madam Ngyuen's beauty, but this was the first time he had ever seen her, and he saw at once that the reports of her beauty had not been exaggerated. She had high cheekbones and eyes which sparkled like set jewels, framed by eyelashes as beautiful as the most delicate lace. He guessed her age as under thirty. Her skin was smooth and golden and her movements were as graceful as those of palm fronds stirred by a breeze. It almost took Jack's breath away to see her.

"Oh, oh, look who's brown-nosing the Black Dragon," Bostic said sarcastically. "I hope Colonel Ngyuen doesn't make a hard right turn; he'll break the nose right off the Fly's face."

The Fly was the considerably less-than-glamorous nickname the officers and men of the Fifth Air

Cavalry had given to Lieutenant Colonel Bert Kramer. Kramer was very young for a lieutenant colonel and he was an extremely ambitious officer, one who let his ambition stand in the way of better judgment. He was the executive officer of the Fifth Cav, and he and Jack had already experienced a few run-ins.

Kramer looked around the crowded room. When he saw Jack, he brought Colonel Ngyuen over to the table.

"The son of a bitch wanted to make sure we saw him with the Black Dragon," Bostic muttered under his breath. "Here he comes."

"Well, Captain Hunter," Kramer said. "Since I see you taking your leisure over here, I take it all of your aircraft are ready for tomorrow."

"The 1352 reports were submitted tonight, Colonel. They're on your desk now."

"And what is the status of your equipment?"

"Colonel, you know that's classified," Jack said easily. "I can't tell you, but, as I said, the information is available for you when you return to work."

Bostic smiled into his glass at Jack's response to Kramer, and he punched Greg with his elbow.

Colonel Ngyuen fitted a cigarette into his holder, and Kramer produced a lighter and snapped a flame to the tip.

"Thank you, Colonel," Ngyuen said. Ngyuen looked at Jack. "Captain, I have a feeling you and I will be seeing each other tomorrow."

"Tomorrow, sir?" Jack replied. "Why tomorrow?"

"We've just been given approval to conduct Operation Thunderbolt," Ngyuen said. "Are you familiar with it?"

"No, sir, I'm not," Jack said.

"Ah, well, you'll be given a thorough briefing tomorrow, as will everyone else who is involved," Ngyuen said. "We are going to attack Chat Nhyn."

"Chat Nhyn, sir?" Jack said, surprised by the information. Chat Nhyn was a village about fifty miles northwest of the base. It had an orphanage in its square, and on this tour, as in Jack's previous two tours, it had been considered neutral territory.

"Yes. We have information—very reliable information, I might add—that Chat Nyhn is being used as a way station by North Vietnamese troops. They think that because there is an unofficial agreement not to strike Chat Nhyn they are safe. But the agreement is only unofficial, and I intend to show them the fury of the Black Dragon."

Jack's eyebrow rose at hearing Colonel Ngyuen speak of himself as the Black Dragon, and his surprise was not unnoticed.

"Do you like the name I have selected for myself?" Ngyuen asked.

"It does have a certain degree of élan," Jack admitted.

Colonel Ngyuen laughed. "Élan . . . yes, I like that. But more importantly, Captain, my enemies know of it. That's what makes war exciting, don't you think? When the enemy knows you, it becomes a personal contest, a war of wills and a battle of minds. It is thus reduced to the primeval struggle of good against evil, but on a personal scale."

"As long as we know the good from the evil," Jack commented.

Ngyuen laughed again. "Yes, yes, that is true, isn't it? One doesn't always know. But then, it really doesn't matter which is good and which is evil. Both are needed in the overall balance of things, like the ancient oriental gods of Kwin and Kwan: opposites to maintain a balance."

There was an almost ecstatic cast to Ngyuen's voice and eyes as he spoke, and Jack knew that, for the Black Dragon, war was the most beautiful thing in life. To a man like Ngyuen, it was the war itself, and not what it sought to accomplish, that was the end result.

"I'm afraid I can't enjoy war as you do, Colonel," Jack said. "I'm afraid I find this whole episode tragic. The sooner it's ended, the better off we'll all be."

"Yes, we all know how you feel, Captain Hunter," Colonel Kramer said with sour impatience. "Your interview with Newstime showed us that."

"You have been in Newstime, Captain?" Ngyuen asked. "I have been in that magazine several times myself."

"Yes, sir, I've read the articles." In fact, Jack recalled, Ngyuen had made the cover of the magazine during the V.C. Tet offensive earlier in the year. Ngyuen had been photographed in the act of executing a captured V.C. prisoner. The picture of Ngyuen holding a pistol to the prisoner's head was flashed around the world.

"It would be better if the interview with Hunter never appeared," Kramer said. "The magazine was kind enough to make pre-publication copies available," Kramer explained to Ngyuen. "Captain Hunter, whom they are calling the reluctant hero, has defended the rights of the dissenters to riot."

"No, sir, Colonel Kramer," Jack said easily. "I have not defended the right to riot."

"Did you or did you not say you approved of Larry DeWitt?" Kramer challenged.

"I said Larry DeWitt has the moral obligation to follow the dictates of his own conscience. And if his conscious tells him he is against the war, he has the obligation, and the right, to protest it."

"I know the DeWitt family, and even they are embarrassed by him. Larry DeWitt is one of the most dispicable Americans this country has ever produced. He, Jane Fonda, Mack Burton, Abbie Hoffman, and all those others should be stood up against a post and shot like the traitors they are," Kramer spat.

"Well, that's where we differ, Colonel," Jack said. "I sort of had the idea that we're fighting to preserve basic democratic rights, which include the right of free expression."

Ngyuen smiled. "Gentlemen, gentlemen, who are we to argue philosophy anyway? We are warriors, you and I. We should leave it to the old men of politics to discuss such things. Our destiny is to be warriors, for whatever cause."

"Colonel Ngyuen," Jack said smilingly, "one might almost get the impression that had you been born in the North you would have fought just as willingly for the Communists."

Kramer coughed a warning.

"Of course I would have, Captain," Ngyuen said, obviously pleased. "I'm glad to see that you understand such things, so that I don't have to defend my profession with empty rhetoric, with talk of freedom and democracy and the sort. I'm a defender of democracy by accident of birth. I could as easily be a Communist, a colonialist, or even a royalist."

"I admire your honesty, sir."

"And I admire your frankness. And your courage," Ngyuen replied. "I'm certain it will serve you in great stead in the days to come. And, after this mission, who knows? You may be able to add a Silver Star to your already impressive array of medals."

"I'm not particularly interested in the Silver Star, sir," Jack said wryly. "I'm more interested in staying alive."

Ngyuen laughed. "Spoken like a true warrior! Do your job, but stay alive. Make the other poor son of a bitch die for *his* country. Still, a chest full of ribbons and a form 66 with honorable combat time can only be of value to an ambitious officer."

"I'm sure that's true, Colonel," Jack said. Out of the corner of Jack's eyes he caught a glimpse of Specialist Springs, his C.Q. Springs was standing in the doorway of the Red Bull, looking around the room as if trying to find someone.

"Would you excuse me please, sir? I see my C.Q. and I have an idea he's looking for me."

"Yes, of course," Colonel Ngyuen said. "I'll see you tomorrow, Captain, on the field of battle!"

Jack nodded at Ngyuen, then at Bostic and the others, and then started toward Springs. He had to walk right by Ngyuen's wife. She had been looking at him during the entire conversation, observing him with a cool and appraising gaze. Her look did not waver as he passed, and he felt his cheeks burning. Damn, was he blushing? Angry with himself, he picked up his pace.

2

C AP'N, I'm sorry to disturb you," Springs said. "But I thought you might want to come to the front gate to straighten somethin' out."

"The front gate?" Jack asked, going outside with Springs. "What's happening at the front gate?"

"Well, sir, Creech found some brushes for our generator," Springs explained. "But there's a White Mouse at the gate wantin' to come in and get them back." The "White Mouse" he was referring to was one of the South Vietnamese national policemen, who all wore white uniforms.

"I see," Jack said. "And just where did Creech *find* these brushes?"

"On a generator at the Vietnamese National Police Headquarters," Springs replied. "Hell, Cap'n, they wasn't even usin' it. It was still packed in cosmoline."

"Really? As short as we are of generators, the White Mice have one packed in cosmoline? They deserved to have the brushes stolen. Hell, they should have the entire unit stolen."

"Yes, sir, that's just the way I figure it, sir," Springs said. "But there's a White Mouse at the front gate who don't figure it that way, and he's real belligerent about it."

"I'll talk to him," Jack said. "In the meantime, you get those brushes put on the generator and get the generator fired up again. The way I look at it, possession is nine-tenths of the law. If the White Mouse doesn't like it, that's tough."

Springs grinned. "I figured you would say that. I'll get 'em on it right away."

Jack walked back across the moonlit flower garden, through the company area, and to the front gate. In the distance he could hear the constant rumble of artillery and see the almost continuous flash of light. For the first several nights he had been in Vietnam he had assumed it was thunder and lightning. Now he knew that it was the artillery fire that went on night after night.

The gate was on the other side of the company compound, and by now several G.I.s in various stages of dress were standing around watching the gate guard hold off the White Mouse.

"What's going on here?" Jack asked, approaching the American guard and the Vietnamese policeman.

"Cap'n, will you tell this goddamn gook he can't come in here?" the guard asked. "Causin' if he tries, he's gonna be one dead slope."

"What's the problem?" Jack asked the Vietnamese policeman. "Why are you trying to come into our compound?"

"Three G.I.s come to police headquarters," the White Mouse said. "They steal something, then come back here."

"What did they steal?"

"When I catch, I find out," the White Mouse said.

"Oh, no, now wait a minute," Jack said. "You mean you don't even know *what* they stole? I'm sorry, but we don't work that way. First you must register a complaint with headquarters, United States Army, Vietnam, in which you state *what* was stolen, and then you get authorization to come on base to look for that item. But you're telling me you don't even know what it was."

"They come from depot behind police station," the policeman said. "We have many things there."

"Yeah, I'll just bet you do," Jack said sarcastically. "Truth to tell, I wouldn't be surprised if you didn't have a couple of helicopters stashed away back there."

"I come in now," the White Mouse said, and he made a start for the gate.

"No," Jack replied resolutely.

At that moment, two more jeeps arrived, each with four policemen apiece, and they all joined the first. Now there were nine of them, and they stood there, glaring at Jack, the guard, and the half a dozen G.I.s who had been attracted to the gate by the commotion. The situation was fast becoming tense.

"What will I do, sir?" the gate guard whispered. "Should I shoot one of the bastards if they try to come in?"

"Chamber a round," Jack suggested. "Maybe that will prevent this from going any further."

The guard worked the bolt on his rifle, and the metallic sound of steel heightened the growing tension.

Suddenly, from out of the darkness behind Jack, a new voice was added to the scene. The new voice was soft and vibrant, like the clear notes of a wind bell. It was the voice of Madam Ngyuen.

The policeman who had been the spokesman replied to Madam Ngyuen, but she spoke back to him, this time much more sharply than before. The policemen stood uncertainly for a moment and then returned to their jeeps and drove away. The crisis was over.

Jack looked at her appreciatively. "Well, I don't know what you said, but whatever it was, it worked. I thank you."

"I simply explained that the Americans are our allies and our closest friends," Madam Ngyuen said. She gave a deep, throaty laugh. "I told them that if they needed lessons in how to treat their friends, my husband would be glad to provide such lessons."

"It sure is nice to know someone with pull at times like this," Jack said.

Suddenly the lights went back on in the A Troop area, and there was a long and loud cheer from the men. Dozens of air conditioners kicked on, the power drain dimming the lights and nearly killing the generator again, but the generator held.

"Well, it would appear that things are back to normal," Jack said. He held his arm toward Madam Ngyuen. "Would you care for an escort back to the Red Bull?"

"I would like an escort, yes," Madam Ngyuen said. "But I don't wish to be escorted to the club. I prefer to be escorted back to my home."

"Your home?" Jack asked in surprise. "But your husband . . ."

"The Black Dragon," Madam Ngyuen said, letting the words slide out disdainfully, "insists upon playing cards tonight. I've no wish to stay there while he indulges in such a vice, but I would prefer not to travel without an escort."

"I should be honored to escort you home," Jack said. "Let me get my jeep."

"That isn't necessary," Madam Ngyuen said. "My husband's car is here. We can use it. After I'm safely home, my husband's chauffeur will bring you back. Then he will await my husband's pleasure."

"Very well. If that's what you want."

They walked back through the company street toward the black Mercedes belonging to the Black Dragon. The chauffeur hopped out and held the door open for Madam Ngyuen to enter, then he pointed to the front seat for Jack.

"I'm afraid you'll have to ride in the front seat," Madam Ngyuen said.

"Yes, of course," Jack answered. "That's perfectly all right."

Jack slid into the front seat, and the car pulled away. It left the compound and drove rapidly down Highway 13, with the driver honking impatiently at everyone else on the road. Chickens, children, old men on bicycles and old women carrying bundles had to scramble to stay out of the way of the speeding Mercedes.

Jack watched the low, squat, dimly lighted huts slip by outside the speeding car. He could see the naked children who were playing in the mud puddles in front of the houses, and the old women bent over their unending labor inside. Finally, he turned around to look at Madam Ngyuen, but she was sitting in the far corner of the seat, totally oblivious to everything going on outside. She sensed him looking at her, and she looked up at him and smiled a cool, Mona Lisa smile.

"I must apologize for making you ride in the front seat," she said. "But riding in the back seat of a vehicle with a woman who is not your wife is the same thing as adultery in this country."

"I understand," Jack said.

"Not that I would be opposed to committing adultery with you," Madam Ngyuen said. "What about you, Captain? Would adultery interest you?"

Jack couldn't have been more shocked had Madam Ngyuen suddenly slapped him. He couldn't believe he was actually being propositioned by this beautiful woman. And yet, clearly he was. The question was, why would she do it? Her picture had graced the magazines and T.V. screens of the world, and she was generally considered one of the world's most beautiful and glamorous women. Why would she waste her time with a mere captain in the American army when she could have anyone she wanted?

"You've nothing to say?" Madam Ngyuen asked. "You won't reply to my statement?"

"I . . . I'm not at all certain I understand the statement, Madam Ngyuen," Jack stammered. To be presumptuous with a woman of her standing could be dangerous as well as embarrassing.

"I'll make the suggestion in the form of an invitation," Madam Ngyuen said. "That'll make it easy for you." She smiled sweetly and leaned forward in her seat. "My husband will be involved for the next several hours. We would be totally undisturbed during that time. I want you to make love to me, Captain."

Jack looked quickly over at the driver, who was honking his horn and cursing someone who was attempting to share the road with them.

Madam Ngyuen laughed. "Don't worry about Mr. Mot, Captain. He doesn't speak one word of English."

"Madam Ngyuen, please, don't think I'm not flattered by your interest. But I'm afraid I couldn't do that. I've too much respect for Colonel Ngyuen and for you."

Madam Ngyuen leaned back into her seat and casually glanced out the window, as if she had done no more than offer Jack a cup of tea and had it refused.

"Well, Captain, I must confess that this is the first time I have ever been turned down. However, don't feel as if your refusal has crushed me. I shall survive."

"I'm sorry," Jack said.

"Please, don't apologize," Madam Ngyuen said. "That only makes the situation worse." She handed him a small card. "Please, keep my card. You may find an increase in your sexual appetite someday, concurrent with an increase in your courage. If you do, call me. Ah, we are here!"

They turned off the road and stopped at a locked gate. Two uniformed guards opened the gate, then saluted as the car passed through the gate, inside the high walls which surrounded the place. The grounds of the estate looked like a well-kept park, with wide expanses of grass, flowers and shrubbery. There were several splashing fountains and a man-made stream which wound through the grounds. In the center was a large, beautiful house.

"Be it ever so humble," Madam Ngyuen said, noticing that Jack was looking about in open admiration. The driver stopped under a portico and hurried around to open Madam Ngyuen's door. She reached over the back of the seat and touched Jack on the hand with fingers that were long and cool, and yet inviting, somehow warming, at the same time.

"Good-bye, Captain. I do hope we meet again."

When Jack returned to Phu Bien, Specialist Springs met him as he was getting out of the car.

"The Fly wants to see you, sir."

"The Fly? What about?"

"Who the hell knows what's on the Fly's mind? In fact, who the hell knows if he even *has* a mind?"

Such disrespect for a senior officer in the same command was not supposed to be good for military discipline, Jack knew. But he had a difficult time correcting an enlisted man for saying aloud what Jack himself thought. Besides, it was no secret that there was little love lost between Jack and Bert Kramer, so Springs knew he was on safe ground when he made the comment.

"Thanks," Jack said. "The generator still holding up all right?"

"Purrin' like a Singer sewing machine," Springs said. "Oh, and in case the Fly brings it up, we're one hundred percent readiness for tomorrow. Creech managed to find some filters for 068, so it's flyable too, now."

"Well, thank goodness for the Creech supply system," Jack said. He ran his hand across his hair and squared his hat. "Let's see what the Fly wants."

When Jack went into the headquarters building he found that Colonel Kramer was in Colonel Mayfair's office. Colonel Mayfair was the actual squad-dron commander, though for the moment he was on R and R in Hawaii, leaving Kramer in temporary command.

Kramer was looking at the 1352 report, a daily report issued by all the troops in the command, telling of the status of the aircraft—which ones were flyable, which were not flyable, and why they weren't flyable.

"I see you still have no filters for 068," Kramer said.

"We just got them tonight, sir," Jack said. "068 is up now."

"Oh? Then why isn't it reflected on the 1352?" Kramer took his package of cigarettes and lighter out. Just as Jack had seen him do many times before, he made a stack of his lighter and cigarette package, not drawing one out to light up.

"The filters didn't come in until after the 1352 reports were completed," Jack explained.

"The 1352s are not supposed to be done until after the last supply run. You should have known then whether or not you were going to get 068 flyable. Now we can't fly it tomorrow."

"What do you mean we can't fly it tomorrow?" Jack asked. "Of course we can. I just told you, the repair has been made."

"You know the regulations," Kramer said. "Any aircraft reported down on the 1352 is down until there is an upgraded report."

"Colonel, surely you don't intend to deny us the use of a Cobra on some paper technicality?"

"Regulations are there for a purpose," Kramer said flatly. He shifted the stack of cigarettes and lighter. "Where did you go with Madam Ngyuen?" he suddenly asked.

"What? Oh, I didn't go anywhere with her," Jack said. "She just asked me to ride in the car as an escort for her when the driver took her home. We dropped her off and came right back here. Why?"

"Madam Ngyuen has a reputation for a certain worldliness which you should be aware of," Kramer said. "I wouldn't want to see you do anything that might reflect discredit upon the army."

"I'm sure I don't know what you mean, Colonel," Jack said.

"Yes, I'm sure you don't," Kramer replied sarcastically. "It's just this, Captain. When that article comes out in *Newstime* next week, there are going to be several reporters around trying to get follow-up interviews. I wouldn't want any of them getting wind of your relationship with Madam Ngyuen and trying to make something of it."

"Don't worry, Colonel. There *is* no relationship to make anything over. I just happened to be standing by the gate when Madam Ngyuen walked up and asked me to ride home wtih her. That's all there is to it."

"Perhaps I'm being a bit overly apprehensive," Kramer said. He picked up an advance copy of the article which would be appearing in *Newstime*. "But if I am, it's because this article made me so. I want you to take this back to your room with you, Hunter. I want you to read it, and as you do, I want you to reflect upon the damage you have done to your peers who are over here fighting this war."

"Colonel, I said nothing in this article I wouldn't

say again," Jack said. "The Department of Army hasn't reacted against it. Why should you?"

"Why should I? Perhaps because I have a stronger sense of duty, yes, and loyalty, than those civilian soldiers they have working in the editorial approval section of Department of Army. And because I know you for the sham you are, Captain Hunter, The Reluctant Hero," Kramer said disparagingly.

Jack took the article from him. "What about o68, sir? May we fly it tomorrow?"

"All right, I'll let it fly," Kramer said. "But you better pray nothing goes wrong with it, or it'll be your ass, Captain. The Black Dragon wants a maximum effort, or you wouldn't get it at all, and I mean it. In the future, make certain that your reports are accurate."

"Yes, sir."

Jack saluted, and took the article back to his B.O.Q. The generator was still working, and he could hear the quiet, reassuring hum of the air conditioners as he moved through the billeting area. He walked into the officers' lounge, pulled out a can of beer from the refrigerator and uncapped it with the opener which hung from a wire beside the refrigerator. Then he settled into a green plastic-cushioned chair to read the words America would read about him when the next issue of *Newstime* hit the market.

JACK HUNTER, THE RELUCTANT HERO

"It is not a matter of doing right. It is a matter of perceiving right." So said Army Captain Jack Cavalier Hunter last week. Captain Hunter is the commanding officer of A Troop of the Fifth Air Cavalry Squadron. The air cavalry is to today's army what the cavalry was in the days of the Civil War and in the war against the Plains Indians. They are an elite group, made up of well-trained and highly dedicated specialists.

Captain Hunter fits the mold of the dashing Custer-type cavalryman in all but one very significant respect: he does not follow his country blindly, or without question.

I think there is a legitimate place for questions," he said. "I am thankful for people like Larry DeWitt" (see *Newstime* July 28, "Keeping the Homefires Burning") "for raising the questions which challenge the conscience of the American people. If I am to fight over here, I want to know that I'm doing what all America wants done. I would not like to think I'm merely an extension of a failed foreign policy."

Captain Hunter comes from a long line of warriors. One of his ancestors, John Langley Hunter, fought in the French and Indian War, and the family has had a proud tradition of service ever since. Captain Hunter, a much decorated Cobra (attack helicopter) pilot, seems cut from the same bolt of cloth. Indeed, it may be an act of bravery that he defends the rights of Larry DeWitt and other antiwar activists from his untenable position as a Vietnam commander.

Jack tossed the article onto the small plywood table in front of the chair, and looked at it for a moment. He thought of John Langley Hunter, the man who had fought in the French and Indian War. Somewhere in the blood coursing through his veins there was a tiny piece of that first American warrior. There was a genetic imprint that left a signature on his body, perhaps in the color of his hair or eyes, or in the muscular structure. Was there a memory as well? Did John Langley Hunter look out from the recesses of Jack's mind, and know what was going on? Could he understand war today, with megatons of explosive power, with flying machines and computers and 1352 reports?

And would John Langley Hunter approve of the way Jack was doing things? He would approve, Jack finally concluded. Part of John Langley was in Jack today, and he would approve.

Jack looked at his watch. It was after eleven, and they would have a pre-dawn take-off to the staging area tomorrow. It was time for him to get a little sleep. He stood up, turned out the light in the lounge, then walked down the wooden porch to his own room. When he opened the door and stepped inside, he was greeted with blessed coolness.

Another day in 'Nam had come to an end.

3

J ACK COULD FEEL the C-130s before he could hear
them, and he could hear them before he could
see them. It started as a rumble, deep in the pit
of his stomach, then a roar in his ears, and finally
there were ghostly shapes sliding through the early
morning mist to materialize as giant four-engined
transport aircraft, touching down on the landing
mat of perforated steel planking with a growl of
authority.

Jack sat on the damp ground of staging area
Centurian, sucking on the sweet tip of a blade of
grass. He had brought his troop into Centurian
early this morning, and then sat with Lieutenant
Bostic to watch the morning mist roll in, masking
the coming of dawn. Along the embankment beside
the line of Cobras were the rest of Jack's pilots,

sprawled in various stages of rest, some reading, some talking, some even sleeping.

"Hurry up and wait," Bostic said disgustedly. "I'll bet that's the only military tactic which has remained unchanged since Caesar's legions."

"Don't be in such a hurry to get your butt shot off," Jack said. He pointed to the Vietnamese soldiers who were off-loading from the C-130s. "We couldn't very well start the operation without them. They're the ones who'll be flying in those Hueys, and they're the ones we're giving fire support to."

"I thought the Black Dragon was so anxious to get on the road," Bostic said. He looked toward the milling mass of Vietnamese soldiers. "Geez, will you look at those sons of bitches? They've all got black on. How the hell are we supposed to know them from the V.C.?"

"I don't know," Jack said. "I guess if someone shoots at you, you just shoot back."

"Yeah," Bostic said. "I guess so. Say, did you see the Dragon Lady last night? Wasn't she something?"

"She's an attractive woman," Jack said noncommittally.

Bostic laughed. "What did you say? She's an attractive woman? Man, that's like saying a soufflé is just eggs. The Dragon Lady is—oh, my God, that's right, you went *home* with her, didn't you?"

"Not exactly," Jack said. "I rode in the car with her because she asked for an escort."

Bostic let his head fall back and his eyes close. He smiled softly. "Ah, such is the stuff of the most delightful fantasy. If I were closed up in a car with her for just five minutes, I'd be horny for the next three months. I've got to hand it to you, friend.

You're more of a gentleman than I am. I'm not sure I could have kept my hands off her."

"I'm sure you would have managed." Jack smiled as he thought of what Bostic's reaction would be if he knew the *real* story of last night. What would he say if he knew that Madam Ngyuen had propositioned him?

"Cap'n, are we about to get this show on the road?" one of his warrant officer pilots asked.

"It looks that way, Mike," Jack replied. "There are enough troops here now to take Hanoi, I would think."

Jack couldn't help but be impressed with the array of equipment the Black Dragon was bringing in for the mission. There were hundreds of troops in full battle gear, helicopters stretching from one end of the field to the other, and a steady train of C-130s coming in at three-minute intervals.

Mike stood up, stretched, and walked toward the edge of the runway to watch the activity. He was wearing a flak vest with a Cobra helicopter painted on the back. The Cobra had eyes and teeth, and was carrying a bloody sword in one of the landing skids, which had been drawn like a hand. Beneath the drawing was Mike's credo in blood-red letters: "*I fly for the only truly nonprejudiced genocide unit in the world. We will kill anyone, anywhere, anytme, regardless of race, creed, color, age, or sex. No questions asked, no quarter given.*"

Another warrant officer joined him, and on the back of his jacket was painted a buzzard, sitting on the top strand of a barbed wire fence and staring out of fierce eyes. "*Patience, my ass,*" the angry buzzard was saying. "*I want to kill something now.*"

"Whatta ya think?" the second pilot asked Mike. "I think we're gonna have us a ball game, Dan."

Dan pulled out a plug of chewing tobacco, sliced off a long, thin piece, then handed the plug to Mike. Mike also cut off a piece, then, in unison, Mike and Dan stuck the tobacco in their mouths, barely discernible beneath the heavy moustaches each of them wore. They chewed silently, uanware that they were the subject of Jack's observation.

Jack felt he had seen this same scene before, like *deja vu.* Then he knew where he had seen them. The steely eyes, the rackish moustaches, the youthful bravado, had been duplicated in hundreds of Matthew Brady pictures from the Civil War. Perhaps one of his ancestors had witnessed the same scene before Pickett's charge.

Colonel Ngyuen came walking by, laughing and talking with Colonel Kramer. As usual, Colonel Ngyuen was followed by an entourage of newsmen, and as usual he cut a dashing figure. For this operation he was dressed in khaki, trimmed in red and gold. The baton he carried today was made of ivory. He was wearing the same chrome-plated pearl-handled pistol he'd worn the previous night.

"Follow close behind me, gentlemen," Colonel Ngyuen was telling the reporters, "and you will never miss the action. I go to the sound of the guns and bathe in the wash of battle."

"Colonel Ngyuen, there's been some talk in high levels about your political ambitions. Is there any foundation to this talk?" one of the reporters asked.

"I am not actively seeking any political recognition," Colonel Ngyuen answered. "In fact, it is quite the opposite. Serving in any political position less than the presidency would cause me to fail in my duty to give my country my utmost."

"Then may I quote you, Colonel?" the reporter asked. "May I say that you would be interested in the president's job?"

"You are presuming a great deal," Colonel Ngyuen said with a small smile. "But in answer to your question I would pose another. Who wouldn't be interested in the job of president?"

"Do you intend to open a campaign headquarters soon?" another reporter asked.

"Gentlemen, gentlemen, please," Colonel Ngyuen said. "Can't we confine this discussion to the mission we are about to conduct? It is far too early to be seriously concerned with my political aspirations, whatever they might be." He smiled, then saw Jack, Bob, and the pilots of Jack's company. He pointed to them. "You should interview men like these. Truly, these men are the samurai of our cause," he said. "Captain Hunter, how are you today?"

"I'm fine, Colonel," Jack said, standing as he answered Ngyuen.

"My wife sends her regards. She was most impressed with you, as am I. I look forward to our exercise today."

"Colonel, the briefing tent is set up and ready for you," Kramer said, trying to get Ngyuen's attention back from Jack.

"Very well, Colonel. If you would call your officers, I shall call mine and we'll get started."

Jack, Bob, and all the pilots of his company moved toward the tent, following the pilots of the airlift companies, and the dustoff and helicopter recovery pilots. The Vietnamese infantry officers also joined them and the briefing began.

The first part of the briefing was for the aviators. They received weather, intelligence, med-evac and helicopter recovery procedures. Then Colonel Ngyuen, speaking in English and in Vietnamese, told of the purpose of the mission. Chat Nhyn, he informed them, was going to be neutralized.

The mist had burned away by the time the briefing got under way, and Jack was surprised to see that the briefing tent had actually been pitched on the edge of the lawn of a large French villa. Two blond-headed children ran laughing through a jungle gym set, the sound of their laughter floating in occasionally to contrast sharply with the continual drone of aircraft engines as the C-130s began leaving. The children played as if they were totally alone, completely oblivious of a strike force which could boast of more fire power in one day than was expended by the entire American army during the whole of the Revolutionary War.

After the briefing, Jack walked back to the Cobra parking area. He felt the same premission tingling he always felt, and he stood beside his helicopter, looking into the cockpit at the familiar instruments and controls, trying to focus on the known quantities so that he wouldn't think of the unknown.

"We about ready to spool up, Cap'n?" Warrant Officer Ed Selfridge asked. Selfridge was Jack's gunner, and, as was required of any gunner of a Cobra, also a qualified pilot.

"Looks that way," Jack said. Jack and Selfridge climbed in and strapped themselves down. They left the canopy open to catch what breeze they could.

In the distance, toward the briefing area, a green flare arced through the sky. That was the signal to start engines, so Jack pulled the starter trigger and heard the igniters popping through the sidetone of his earphones. Within seconds the jet engine, which was nestled in the sleek cowling behind him, was a roaring inferno of white-hot flames, spinning a turbine tens of thousands of revolutions per minute and transmitting that power to the rotor blades overhead. As the auxiliary systems kicked in, the warning lights winked out, and the Cobra sat poised, ready to leap into the air.

"This is Centurian control," a voice said over Jack's earphones. "Cobra element is clear for immediate departure, via prearranged vector."

"Up," Jack said over his microphone, and he lifted up, made a slight pedal correction for torque, then departed over the large French villa with the kids still playing unconcernedly below him. He twisted around in his seat to stare back through the blue-tinted canopy, and saw the line of Cobras stretching back, all the way to the tail end, which was just breaking ground.

"Lead, this is Trail. Your flight is up," the trail helicopter said.

"Snake Five, break left," Jack said.

"Roger, Snake Six," Bob answered.

Snake Five was Bob Bostic, Jack's executive officer, and Bob took one half of the flight of twelve Cobras to form an echelon to provide cover to the left side of the Hueys, while Jack's six helicopters flew echelon right, on the right side. The rich green canopy of the Vietnam jungle passed beneath them.

The Hueys were lifting off then, moving into a flight formation of Vs. Suddenly there was a moment of horror.

Jack didn't see it, and of course the engine noise

and his earphones and APH-5 flight helmet drowned out the sound. But over his earphones he did hear sudden exclamations of surprise and shock from those who did see, and he looked around quickly to see two H-model Hueys, loaded with fourteen human beings each, tumbling to the ground like a pair of giant, spastic birds. One of them had no rotor blades at all and the other had only one, slapping at the air desperately, but ineffectively. There were also other pieces of debris falling and Jack saw with a sickening sensation that some of those pieces of debris were human bodies.

"Jesus God," someone breathed over the radio. "Their rotors meshed."

"They never said a word, did they?" someone else said.

"What the hell did you expect them to say, you stupid son of a bitch?" someone swore.

"This is Centurian Six. Cease all unnecessary radio traffic at once!" an authoritative voice said, and Jack recognized Colonel Patterson, one of the senior officers of the aviation brigade.

Jack forced himself to push the accident out of his mind and for the next several moments he flew the ship mechanically. His skin felt tingly all over and a knot of nausea tore at him. He concentrated on the things he would have to do during the mission.

"Aren't those funny-looking little clouds up there?" Ed asked a few minutes later, pointing to little black puffs which hung in the air before them.

"Yeah, I guess they're—" Jack suddenly broke off his answer when he saw a brilliant flash appear to be replaced immediately by one of the clouds.

"Air bursts!" Jack said. "My God! They've got antiaircraft bursts at 3500 feet!"

"Snake Six, do you observe alpha-alpha?" Centurian Six called.

"Roger," Jack answered.

"I'm going to hold the insertion flight on station to give you a chance to neutralize the fire."

"Thanks loads," Jack said. "Break, break. Snake Flight, this is Snake Six. Deploy as fire teams. Approach the target on the deck."

The other pilots in Jack's company acknowledged, then the flight broke up into fire teams of two helicopters each. They dropped down to a few feet above the trees in order to take advantage of terrain concealment and coverage as they approached the antiaircraft guns.

Jack knew that nothing frightened a helicopter crew as much as the sight of air-bursting rounds from an antiaircraft gun. Helicopters were highly vulnerable to antiaircraft fire. There were many critical areas which, when hit, could bring them down abruptly. Also, helicopters were slow and, relatively speaking, poor at maneuvering. Their only advantage was in the fact that they were seldom employed in areas where there would likely be an air-bursting antiaircraft gun.

Jack felt sweat in the palms of his hands as he approached the gun emplacements. Then he saw the first one. He actually saw it by chance, because it hadn't even begun firing yet. The crew was purposely holding back to conceal its position. But when Jack rounded a slight hill, hung his Cobra on the rotor tip for a second and flattened out, the gun was almost dead center in his sight. Ed thumbed off a short burst of rockets, and the gun pit went up in a cloud of exploding dirt, gun parts, and smoke.

"Good shooting, Ed," Jack called to his gunner. Jack whipped the helicopter into a violent side flare to change his flight path and thus throw off any potential gunners. The wisdom of his move was proven by a bright orange shower of tracer rounds which slipped through the sky where his aircraft would have been in but a second more, had Jack not taken evasive action.

"I've got a man hit here," a strained voice called.

Jack punched his mike button. "Who's hurt?" he called. "Pilot making the call, break off the attack. Dan? Was that you?"

The radio came alive again, but the reply was garbled in static.

"Cap'n!" Ed suddenly called, pointing out the right side of the aircraft. Jack looked in the direction of his gunner's finger just in time to see one of the Cobras knife in under the trees, then explode immediately.

"It was Dan," the gunner said.

Dan was Dan Lumsden, one of the two Cobra pilots Jack had been observing prior to the takeoff. He was the one with the buzzard painted on his flak jacket.

"Whoooee, lookee here what I found, guys!" someone called excitedly. "Their entire ammo dump is back here."

"Snake Flight, concentrate on the ammo dump," Jack ordered.

The Cobras made several more passes, firing rockets toward the ammo dump. Half a dozen fires were started, then several small explosions.

"We'd better get the hell out of here, Cap'n! The secondaries are starting!" Ed said.

"Let's go!" Jack called, turning away sharply. The secondary explosions came almost immediately, and they began spreading out, following the trail of ammunition stores until soon smoke and fire covered a large portion of the area.

"Well done, Snake Six," Centurian Six called. "The AA bursts are gone. I'm bringing them in."

"Roger, Centurian Six. We'll provide landing cover."

"Snake Six, what is your station time?"

"Thirty minutes."

"Suggest you break station as soon as the last Huey is off-loaded, return to Centurian staging area."

"Roger, Centurian Six," Jack answered.

Jack flew back and forth along the tree line until the final Huey was off-loaded, then he led his flight back to the staging area, dropped low over the French villa, and settled down in the parking area which had been assigned to them earlier. His job now was merely to remain on standby, to be called back out immediately if needed.

Jack and his pilots left the aircraft and watched as fuel and ammunition were fed back into them. There was a lot of activity for a while, and exclamations and shouts every time a new bullet hole was found. Jack saw four in his own craft, but they had caused virtually no damage at all and required little more than minor sheet-metal jobs.

Jack lay down beneath a tree and luxuriated in the soft breeze which blew across him. He felt very drowsy and allowed himself to drift off to sleep.

He was awakened several moments later by rifle fire. The shots cracked out sharply, and echoed through the trees so no one could tell where they were coming from. The word was passed down that a Viet Cong patrol had been contacted, and that everyone in the staging area was to stay behind cover. Jack moved even closer to the tree and stared out into the foliage, but he could see nothing. The firing continued sporadically for several moments more, then it abruptly ceased.

There was silence for a moment, then some shouts and Jack saw the dustoff crew running for their helicopter. By the time they had it started there were some people running from the trees, carrying wounded on a stretcher. One of the wounded was an American G.I. and the other was a V.C. At least Jack thought he was a V.C. He was wearing the black pajama-type uniform normally associated with the V.C. But as Bostic had pointed out that morning, the Black Dragon's South Vietnamese forces were also dressed in black.

"Friendlies," he heard someone say. "They're wearing black, and some new guys mistook them for V.C. There are two of them dead back there."

"Damn!" Jack answered. "What the hell do they wear black for anyway?"

There was an American major standing nearby, who was assigned as an adviser to the Vietnamese troops. He heard Jack's question, and though Jack hadn't asked it of anyone in particular, the American major answered it.

"Black is the color of the people," he said. "That's why Colonel Ngyuen chose it for his special strike forces. It's psychological."

"Yeah?" Jack said, watching the bodies being

brought in, now that the more urgently wounded had been taken care of. The dustoff ship was just taking off with a whine of its engine and pop of its blades. "Look at those people, Major. They aren't psychologically dead, they're *really* dead. They're dead because they were wearing what appeared to be enemy uniforms."

"It's part of the price of war, Captain," the advisor answered. "People are killed in war."

"Yeah," Jack said. "Tell me about it. So far today there have been thirty-two people killed. Two of them in actual combat, twenty-eight in accidents, and two . . . psychologically. It's a hell of a war, isn't it?"

4

THE RAIN which fell on Washington, D.C., on the night of August 14 was not a hard, cleansing rain. It was a soft spray that carried trapped within its fine mist some of the ash of the burned buildings from the riot earlier in the day.

Despite the rain, flames licked at the sky and a diffused orange glow underlit the low-hanging night clouds. The streets echoed with a wail of sirens, and frightened citizens huddled in their homes and listened to the sporadic rattle of gunfire and the occasional muffled thump of an explosion from those rioters and looters who continued.

The orange light of the city's night glow disclosed a pile of rubble and charred, smoking timbers from a building which had burned, earlier in the day. Where the fire still smoldered, the falling rain hissed and popped like the sputtering fuse of a live grenade. Scattered pockets of tear gas hung in visible clouds, and the occasional person who ventured into the streets could do so only with a handkerchief clutched against his nose and mouth.

A small bit of bread, wet and sodden, lay in a gutter of black, rushing water. A rat, beady eyes alert for danger, darted out to the prize, grabbed it, then bounded back to the comparative safety of one of the tenement buildings.

Even the White House did not escape completely from the effects of the riot. It was tightly encircled by a barricade of busses, and armed soldiers stood on top of the large vehicles, looking out at the smoldering city. Great banks of floodlights lit up the ellipse, washing out all color and painting a stark scene of harsh white and featureless black.

Across the Potomac River from Washington, in an empty warehouse, a lone young man waited anxiously for his contact to return. The young man's name was Larry DeWitt, and his name, like the names of other antiwar activists, had become a household word. In fact, Larry DeWitt was so well known that he had to spend most of his time in hiding now, for he was a wanted man, having been placed on the FBI's most wanted list just one week earlier, for questioning. In that list, Larry joined with four other political fugitives, so that for the first time in history as many political criminals as regular criminals occupied the FBI most wanted list.

Larry DeWitt was small and slender, with long blond hair and anxious gray eyes. He had slender hands and long, delicate fingers. He was a brilliant pianist, and in another and more gentle era he might have been known for bringing beautiful music to the world, rather than as an urban guerilla.

Lights flashed on the wall of the warehouse and Larry rushed to the window. A vintage station wagon rolled to a stop in front of the loading platform and a young girl got out.

"Dess, I'm in here," Larry called from the shadows.

Dess rushed over to greet him and they embraced on the rickety ramp which had once served to handle truckloads of tobacco.

As Larry held Dess against him he could smell in her clothes and hair the smoke of fires and a faint but unmistakable odor of marijuana.

"You shouldn't have done that, you know," another voice said from the station wagon. The voice was that of Mack Burton, a black man who had been an All Big Ten football player at Ohio State, and who had turned down a pro draft in order to carry on his protest against the war. He was co-chairman, along with Larry, of the American Dissenters League, the ADL.

"Shouldn't have done what?" Larry asked.

"Given away your position like that," Mack said. He, too, got out of the car and walked over to stand at the edge of the wooden platform. He had a fearsome appearance, and when he played football he had been known as "Mack Truck" because of his jarring tackles. But Larry and Dess knew him as a quiet person with some terrible, unshared hurt in his past.

Larry walked over to the edge of the platform and stuck out his hand to Mack. It wasn't exactly a handshake—it was what the brothers called the dap—but it expressed the bond that existed between the two men. Mack turned and looked at the surroundings. The street in front of the warehouse was brick, and running down the middle of the brick street was a spur from the B&O Railroad. The track ran to the far end of the buildings, glistened wetly, then curved off toward the main line. At the place where the tracks curved, a street lamp, surrounded by swirls of cloudlike mist, barely managed to push away the darkness. Larry watched as Mack studied the scene for a moment.

"I'm sorry," Larry said. "I didn't think there was any danger. I recognized the car."

"You didn't know who was with us," Mack scolded.

"No harm done. You two were alone."

"But suppose we weren't alone?" Mack asked. "Suppose we had been arrested and we had no choice but to lead the police to you? You would have fallen right into their trap."

"Aren't we being a little melodramatic?" Dess asked with an uneasy laugh. "Come on, let's toke up." She pulled a marijuana butt from her purse, lit it, took a drag, held the smoke inside for a moment, then passed the joint over to Mack as she exhaled.

"You know I don't do that shit," Mack said.

"Me, me," Larry said. "Give it to me." He reached for it before Dess could take another drag.

Dess giggled. "You make me feel like we're part of the Free French Underground fighting World War II."

"That's the way you should feel," Mack said. "We are fighting an underground war here, and we shouldn't forget it."

"I get it," Dess said, joking. She pointed to Larry. "He's Bogart, I'm Bergman, and you're Sam." She giggled. "Play it again Sam." She was already feeling the effects of the pot.

"I have something to show you," Mack said to Larry. "You know the story that was in *Newstime*? The one where that soldier in Vietnam defended you?"

"Yes," Larry said. "Captain Jack Hunter. What about him?"

"Some congressman has said that Captain Hunter has made all Americans take a second look at their ideals. He's calling for a congressional investigation as to why the FBI has put you on their most wanted list."

"Well, all right," Larry said, beaming. "If we can get Congress to looking into this war, we're halfway home."

"There's only one problem," Mack said sullenly.

"What?" Larry said.

"It's Congressman Benton Powers, and he's already known as an antiwar congressman."

"Yeah," Larry said sourly. "There's very little chance he can even get his hearing organized, much less do any good with it."

"There is one way," Mack suggested.

"What's that?"

"What if you gave yourself up?"

"What? You mean just go down to the police and turn myself in?"

"Why would he do that?" Dess asked. "They'd take him off to jail so fast his head would swim, and then we'd lose him entirely."

"Maybe not," Mack said. "They only want him for questioning. Maybe there's a way we could use the hype on it. What if we made an event out of it?" Mack suggested. "You know, a media event.

We could call Jerry and Bill and have them meet us at the ADL House. Then we'll call the police and tell them where you are, but not until after we've called the T.V., the radio, the newspapers, and all the national magazines. When are you going to get another chance to get an audience like that?"

"True," Larry said thoughtfully. "And it beats having to hide out. But . . . I don't know. Are you sure about it?"

"Look, man, I'm not sure about anything," Mack replied. "I'm just telling you that you ought to play this for as much as it's worth. If they had me on the most wanted list, I'd do it. Now, what do you say?"

Larry looked at Mack for a long, anxious moment, then smiled. "Hell," he said, "let's try it."

Larry walked over to the station wagon and got in, glancing at the front page of the evening paper, at the story about Congressman Powers' attempt to get a new committee appointed.

The ADL House, as it was called, was actually just an ordinary three-bedroom frame house, located in a lower-middle-income residential section of the city. Ostensibly the house was being used as living quarters for Jerry and Bill; therefore all the rent and utility bills came addressed to Jerry or Bill, and not to the ADL.

It was nearly midnight by the time Larry, Dess and Mack pulled into the driveway of the house. The rain had stopped, but the night was still dark, velvet textured. As they walked from the car up to the front porch, Larry could feel the night reaching out for him, wrapping around him like a blanket. He wished he could just lose himself in it.

The door opened before they had a chance to

knock, and Jerry motioned them inside. Once inside, they saw that Bill was there too.

"Good," Mack said. "This saves us the trouble of having to get everyone together."

"Get everyone together for what?" Jerry asked.

"Larry is going to give himself up," Mack announced.

"What? Are you out of your mind?" Jerry exclaimed. "Larry, why would you do a crazy thing like that?"

"Mack talked me into it," Larry said. "And if you think about it, it does make sense."

"Hell, it don't make no sense at all. How can getting arrested make sense?"

"Because it will bring the spotlight on ADL," Larry explained. "And anytime the ADL gets publicity, it helps our cause."

"I still think it's foolish," Jerry said, but his last words were cut off by a blaring loudspeaker from outside.

"In the house!" the loudspeaker said, its metallic voice cutting through all the conversation and laying a chill down Larry's back.

'What's that?' Dess asked in a frightened voice. "What's happening?"

"I'll tell you what's happening," Jerry said grimly. "The pigs are on to us."

"In the house! This is the police! We have you surrounded. Come out with your hands up!"

"It doesn't look like we have much choice now," Bill said. He walked over to the window and pulled the shade to one side. "Yeah, they're out there all right. Looks like a whole—"

There was an explosive crash of glass, and Bill spun around. Larry felt something warm and wet splatter him in the face, and he realized with a sickening feeling of horror that it was Bill's blood, spewing from a bullet hole in his forehead.

Dess screamed.

"They're going to kill us all!" Jerry said. "Get down on the floor!"

Instantly a barrage of shooting began. The windows came crashing in with a shower of bullets, and the curtains and shades were ripped from their rods. After several seconds of sustained shooting, the room was bathed in a wavering yellow light, and Larry saw that the entire porch was a mass of flame.

"We're on fire!" he shouted. He looked at the others, then gasped, and it was all he could do to keep from blacking out. His friends were sprawled in grotesquely twisted heaps, all with bloody wounds. Only Mack Burton still lived, though Mack had been hit several times and was bleeding profusely. Amazingly, Larry had not received a scratch.

"Come out now!" the metallic voice said. The shooting had stopped and only the crackling of the fire invaded the silence of the night.

The roof of the porch suddenly caved in, and pieces of it fell to one side, causing a screen of fire to spread from the house to the hedgerow alongside. With a presense of mind and calmness which Larry was unable to comprehend, he saw that a shielded escape route stretched from a side window to the hedge alongside the house. Larry ran over to the window and raised it, then returned for Mack Burton.

"Come on, Mack, we've got to get out of here!"

"You go," Mack said, his voice rasping with pain. "Leave me. I'll just slow you down."

"No," Larry said. "Come on, you're going with me."

Larry pushed and shoved and cajoled, and Mack managed to get on his feet, then crawl through the open window. Larry crawled right out behind him, and, hidden by the burning porch, they were able to crawl over to the hedge.

"Lieutenant, I think they're all dead in there," Larry heard a voice say. The voice was no more than three feet from him, but the hedgerow was thick and it shielded them well.

"Call Fisher and tell him to be sure to watch the back of the house," the lieutenant said. "I don't want any of the little bastards sneaking out."

"Right, I've already done that."

"Where the hell is the fire truck, anyway? They should have been here by now, shouldn't they?"

"They're just getting here," the lieutenant answered. "See, they're coming now."

"Who would have thought that house'd go up like that?"

"Well, it was one of those old frame houses. The tracer rounds just set it on fire. Anyway, it did its job, didn't it?" he laughed. "Look at that son of a bitch burn."

"The rescue squad is here, Lieutenant," a voice shouted. "You want them up there?"

"It's too late now," the lieutenant said. "I don't think there's anything left in there but barbecue."

"Yeah?"

"Look, the fire has already taken over the front two rooms of the house."

"I hope to shit that DeWitt bastard is in there then," one of the men said.

* * *

Mack had passed out and Larry couldn't move him. He lay quietly while the flames consumed the house, too sick at heart and too terrified to move. Behind him he could hear the roar of the fire. The flames completely engulfed the house where he had lived . . . the house that now contained the bodies of his friends.

"The house is about to collapse," someone shouted, and almost immediately there was a crashing sound as the walls tumbled inward.

The crowd that had gathered stared as if hypnotized at the leaping flames. When the house collapsed, Mack came to and groaned, and Larry knew that this was the best time to leave, while everyone was still concerned with the fire.

"Come on, Mack," he said, urging his friend up. "Come on, we've got to get out of here now."

When Larry was able to get Mack up, he found it unexpectedly easy to walk through the crowd. There were several hundred people gathered in the streets to watch the fire. Police cars and fire trucks blocked the roads and fire hoses snaked across the sidewalks and lawns. The dancing flames of the fire were reflected in the eyes of the policemen, firemen and civilians, whose faces were slack with morbid fascination.

Mack somehow summoned the strength to walk upright, showing no signs of the wounds he had received. Larry and Mack passed through the crowd unseen, as if they were walking through a landscape of frozen time and movement.

"There's our car!" Larry said, seeing the battered old station wagon. Miraculously, it was not blocked in by fire trucks or police cars. "Do you have the keys?"

Mack was walking, but he was almost in a stupor. "Keys?" he answered, as if unable to comprehend what Larry was saying.

"Mack, the keys to the station wagon! Do you have them?"

"Keys . . . ?"

Larry sighed and stuck his hands in Mack's pockets, rifling through them until he found the keys. He let out a small sigh of relief, then he opened the back door, let the seat down, and helped Mack in. Larry started the car, backed slowly out into the street, and was even helped through the crowd by police officers, who were keeping the traffic flowing.

A few moments later the car was taking the on-ramp for I-95 north. Larry turned in his seat to look at Mack, lying stretched out behind him.

"Mack, are you all right?"

Mack didn't answer.

"Hang on, Mack. I'll get you help somewhere, I promise."

Larry hoped it wasn't just empty encouragement. He knew of a small farmhouse in Pennsylvania where they might stay. The husband and wife who lived on the farm were sympathetic to the cause, and Larry had visited there a few times before. But whether they could help Mack was another story. If they couldn't, Mack might die. As Dess had died, and Jerry and Bill . . .

Larry gave a short, humorless laugh. He was against war and he was protesting it, yet his protest had already become a war in itself. How could he continue to claim that he was against war if he was one of the principals in the urban war that was now developing in the United States?

Larry thought of his family, and of their reaction to his commitment to the antiwar movement. Larry was a cofounder of ADL, yet his father was the very antithesis of the ADL. Larry's father, Howard DeWitt, was a wealthy architect, living in White Plains, New York. He was an architect by choice, not by necessity, for the DeWitt family wealth was based upon several generations of successful businessmen, with each generation adding more to the family fortune.

The DeWitts had been in the same part of New York since America's Revolutionary War, and Larry's DeWitt aunts, as well as his mother, in her own right, had traced their lineage and could claim to be proud members of the Daughters of the American Revolution. The Tories in the DeWitt background were of course, conveniently overlooked. Although Larry's father was not qualified to be a member of the American Legion or the V.F.W., he supported those two organizations in every way he could, and he got as much mileage as possible out of the World War I service of Everett DeWitt, Larry's grandfather. Howard had missed World War II entirely, due to poor health.

Larry continued to think of his family and his family's history, so that he wouldn't think of Dess and the others dead in the burned-out house, or Mack, nearly dead in the back of the station wagon. Even though Larry managed to keep his mind busy, it still seemed like an eternity before he turned off the small twisting, blacktop road in the Pocono

Mountains to follow an even smaller, more twisting, dirt road, deeper into the hills, to find the Delleses' place, which they called Sky Meadow.

This was not the part of the Poconos with the tourist lodges and vacation homes. This was where the residents could claim half a dozen generations of kinship with the mountains. This was as isolated an area as one could find in the great northeast population base of the United States.

Larry pulled the station wagon into the front of the Delleses' cabin. The cabin was small, with unpainted, weathered clapboard sides and a shake roof. The walls of the cabin were decorated with old advertising signs, many of them showing the style and logos of products from the twenties and thirties. It made interesting decoration, and it also served the purpose of covering cracks or holes in the walls. An old jeep was parked near the spring house.

Larry turned off the ignition and just sat there for a few moments, listening to the metal pop and tick as the engine cooled down. It was still very early in the morning, and he was certain the Delleses were not yet out of bed. A million sparkling drops of dew glistened in the meadow, and a bird called for its mate from somewhere in the woods. A weather vane on top of the cabin answered the breeze, swinging around with a squeaking sound. The leaves and branches of the trees moaned and sighed with the wind.

"Mack," Larry called quietly. "Mack are you all right?"

"Yeah," Mack said. "At least the bleeding has stopped."

"Listen, we're at the Delleses'. I'm going to wake 'em up now. Maybe Papa will know what to do."

"Yeah," Mack said. "Yeah, that would be nice, man."

5

THE ORPHANAGE at Chat Nhyn was run by a sect of Buddhists who had declared themselves neutral in the war between the Communists and the government in Saigon. For a long time they were able to carry off their policy of neutrality. Then, repeated rumors reached Saigon that the orphanage was a way station and a temporary storage warehouse for guns and ammunition coming south down the Ho Chi Minh trail. But now, two weeks after the attack, Colonel Ngyuen had found no weapons or evidence of their existence. However, to be safe, Ngyuen decided that the orphanage and the pagoda had to be burned.

The orphanage and pagoda were on a square in the middle of the town, and as they burned, the fire created a glowing circle of light in the black of night. Just beyond the wavering flames the people of the town gathered in a large crowd and stood in the protective cloak of darkness. They watched in fearful silence as the soldiers methodically destroyed the relics of the pagoda. Some of the relics were more than a thousand years old.

"Colonel Ngyuen, no one seems to know the location of Binh Du Doung," one of the Black Dragon's senior officers reported. Binh Du Doung was the patriarch of the pagoda, and Ngyuen was convinced, though without real evidence, that he was also a high-ranking officer in the Viet Cong army.

"Have you asked the villagers?" Ngyuen asked.

"Yes, sir. We have questioned them at length."

"Bring three of them to me," Ngyuen ordered.

"Yes, sir," his officer answered, then hurried off.

Ngyuen was standing in the center of the square, watching the fire devastate the orphanage and pagoda. He slapped the side of his leg absently with the highly polished baton, and followed a tumbling paper with his eyes as it rode a column of heat and smoke high into the orange-lit night sky.

"Here are the three villagers you asked for," Ngyuen's staff officer said a moment later.

Ngyuen didn't answer his officer, or even look around. Instead, he continued to stand rooted to the spot, watching the fire. His staff officer opened his mouth to speak again, but Ngyuen cut him off.

"Thank you," he said.

The three villagers, an old man, a young man and a young woman, stood behind Ngyuen, looking at his back. All three had their hands tied behind them, and their faces, lit by the orange glow of the fire, seemed to radiate their fear. The neck of the young man twitched uncontrollably.

"Your Excellency, why are we here?" the young man finally asked.

Ngyuen didn't answer.

The young prisoner cleared his throat and spoke again. "Honorable sir, why are we here? Why have we been brought to you?"

"Where is Binh Du Doung?" Ngyuen asked, without turning around.

The three villagers looked at one another, then looked back toward the back of the man who had asked them the question. No one answered.

Ngyuen turned around, and saw for the first time that one of the three was a woman. She was young and pretty, and during the struggle of her capture, the buttons had been torn from her blouse so that it hung open, exposing her young, firm breasts. Ngyuen walked over to her and slid his hand in under the blouse, cupping a breast. He could feel the heat of her body, and the rapid beating of her heart, brought on by her fear, was sexually exciting to him.

"Do you know where I might find Binh Du Doung?" Ngyuen asked the young woman. He smiled at her. "If you cooperate with me, my dear, you may find that I can be most generous. Yes, most generous indeed," He squeezed her breast harder, then pinched her nipple.

The woman spat on him, hacking it up from deep in her throat.

Ngyuen felt the spittle hit his face, then run down his cheek. His smile vanished and his eyes grew cold. Ngyuen pulled his chrome-plated ivory-handled pistol from his holster and pointed it at the young woman. He pulled the trigger without saying another word, and the pop of the .38 echoed through the square. The young woman pitched back, dying with the expression of contempt still on her face.

The next villager Ngyuen turned to was the old man, who had a narrow white beard, so long that it reached down to his chest.

"Where is Binh Du Doung?" Ngyuen asked.

The old man said nothing. He merely closed his eyes and prepared to die. Ngyuen accommodated him, shooting him without another word.

The third villager was the young man, younger even than the woman had been, and he began shaking convulsively.

"He is in the café!" he shouted. "The master is in the café! Please don't kill me!"

Ngyuen looked at the young man evilly. "So, to save your life, you have betrayed your master," he said in a silken-toned voice. "I am Christian, and in our religion one of Christ's own betrayed Him, too. The betrayer's name was Judas."

Ngyuen nodded, and a soldier cut the binding on the young man's hands. The young man gingerly rubbed his wrists, as if unsure that he was actually free.

"Go, Judas," Ngyuen said quietly. "Take your thirty pieces of silver and go."

The young man turned and ran quickly, melting into the night. Ngyuen pulled a handkerchief from his pockets and wiped his hands as he waited for his soldiers to find Binh Du Doung and bring him to him.

A moment later, a group of Ngyuen's men returned, laughing and yelling at the old man they had. They had a rope tied around his neck, and they were leading him as a lamb is led to slaughter.

The man was very old, of years impossible to estimate. His skin had the texture of dried leather, and the hair of his beard was as fine as threads of silk. His eyes were wide open and clear, and he was totally devoid of fear. He was brought before Ngyuen.

"So, old man, you would make war against your government, would you?" Ngyuen asked. He pulled out his pistol and pointed it at the old man. "I will use you as an example for others who would be so foolish."

The old man's face was composed in a look of absolute peace, and he smiled. Ngyuen looked at the old man in shock. The old man *wanted* to die. This old man actually wanted Ngyuen to shoot him!

Ngyuen put his pistol away with an oath of disgust.

"No," he said. "I will not give you the honorable death you seek." Ngyuen nodded impatiently to one of his soldiers. "Strip him naked," he said. "Strip him naked and tie him to a post in the middle of the village. Leave him here for all to see his humiliation." Ngyuen glanced down and saw a strand of barbed wire from the defensive barricades around the city. He laughed. "No," he said. "Not a post. Make it a cross. And make a crown of the barbed wire," he said. "Put the crown on his head, and make a sign, and put it there too."

"What shall the sign say?"

"King of the Cong," Ngyuen said, laughing at his own fiendish sense of humor.

Seventy miles to the south, Madam Ngyuen stretched on silk sheets, watching the shadows on her wall, projected there by the silver light of the

moon. It had been two weeks, but she was unable
to get the American captain off her mind. He had
refused her invitation, and his refusal had made
him all the more desirable to her.

Could he refuse a second invitation? Surely not.

Suddenly Madam Ngyuen got an idea. Perhaps
it was the location which had caused the handsome
American to balk. Maybe he would be more cooperative if the location for their rendezvous were
more discreet. If she had an apartment in Saigon,
perhaps he would come to her then.

She smiled, sat up, then pulled a note pad from
her bedside table. As erotic thoughts drifted
through her mind, she composed a letter of invitation. Captain Hunter would not turn her down this
time—she was absolutely positive of that. . . .

Jack Hunter was surprised when he received the
letter the next day. He had thought his refusal of
Madam Ngyuen's offer would make him an enemy,
but just the opposite was true. She admitted in the
letter that she was now more intrigued by him than
before, and she asked him to meet her in an apartment in Saigon.

On the day appointed by Madam Ngyuen, Jack
found himself, almost against his wishes, walking
down Tu Do Street in Saigon. Tu Do is a very
broad boulevard that runs from the Saigon River
to a square in the heart of the city. The sides of the
avenue are lined with flowering mimosa and mag-
nolia trees, and the street is divided by a wide
ribbon of palms and grass.

There are numerous flower stalls along the center
island where the shopkeepers sell cut flowers, and
indeed, Tu Do is known as the Street of Flowers.
But it is not the plant life which gives the street

its name. The flowers which give the street its name are its prostitutes. By some unique tradition lost in antiquity, Tu Do is the only street in Saigon where the girls make an open appearance and proposition customers themselves. Throughout the rest of the city, contact must be made through a pimp, a taxi driver, or some other intermediary.

Like the cut flowers after whom the girls are named, the prostitutes appear in all styles. Many have had cosmetic surgery to build out their noses and make their eyes look round—an extremely drastic step, for it marks the girls for the rest of their lives as having been "American whores". Many of the girls wear the latest in western dress, but many others, realizing that the Vietnamese girls are among the most beautiful in the world, accent their fragile, graceful native beauty rather than hide it. They wear the traditional *ao dai*, a free-flowing dress in brightly colored silk. They allow their hair to hang long and luxuriously down their backs, rather than cut it short in the western style.

Though there are many shops and stores in Saigon, the market is controlled by the sidewalk vendors. They spread blankets on the sidewalk, then load the blankets with blackmarket goods and compete for the customer's piastres.

Jack picked his way through the propositioning "flowers," and around the vendors' blankets. His nostrils were assailed by the smells of dozens of restaurants, and even the cooking of the small, portable, soup kitchens. The Vietnamese have a wonderful blend of French and Chinese cuisine, so the aromas which Jack smelled were delightfully stimulating to his appetite.

It was not only the senses of sight and smell

which were stimulated. The street was a cacophony of sound, with whirring cyclos and motorbikes, honking taxis, and roaring army trucks, and calling vendors. There were also transistor radios all along Tu Do, all tuned to Vietnamese radio stations, playing the strange half-note and minor chord music, generally sung by a female with a hauntingly sweet voice.

Jack turned off Tu Do onto Le Loi, and found the address he was looking for. He had to climb a set of blue tile stairs which led up between two buildings, until he reached a landing, off which opened four doors. The door he wanted was number 35.

Jack looked around, then walked over and knocked lightly on 35.

Madam Ngyuen opened the door after one knock, and Jack stepped inside. She smiled at him and he grabbed her to kiss her.

"*No,*" she said, struggling away from him.

"I'm sorry," Jack said, stung by the unexpected rebuke. "I must have misunderstood."

"You didn't understand," she reassured him, "but why rush? Patience is a virtue which you westerners should master. Have a drink with me, Captain. Absinthe, perhaps?"

Jack followed Madam Ngyuen across the room, subconsciously aware of a soft fragrance, tantalizing, but not overpowering.

As Madam Ngyuen settled into a chair, her hemline rose along her thigh, and Jack could see the smooth expanse of leg, cool-looking and exciting. She poured the smokey liquid into two small glasses and handed one to Jack. They touched glasses briefly, then Jack drank the liquor, feeling it burn throughout his whole body and bringing heat to his loins.

The door to the bathroom opened, and an old lady padded out, moving quietly on bare feet. Jack looked at his hostess in surprise.

"Don't be alarmed," Madam Ngyuen said, a trace of amusement coloring her voice. "Haung was merely preparing our bath."

"Our bath?" Jack asked.

"Yes," Madam Ngyuen said, standing. She walked over to the bathroom and pointed inside. Steam was rising from an enormous sunken tub, and the scent of bath perfume filled the air.

"I've never seen a bathtub so large," Jack said. "It looks like it was built for two people."

Madam Ngyuen smiled. "It was. This is apartment 35."

"Meaning what?"

Madam Ngyuen laughed. "Don't you see the significance?"

"I'm afraid I don't."

"Thirty-five is a very special number," Madam Ngyuen said. "It is the number of sexual power."

"You mean like 69?"

"No," Madam Ngyuen said. "Sixty-nine is significant to the Americans, only because of the juxtaposition of the numbers six and nine. Such a juxtaposition is suggestive of oral sex. Thirty-five has a deeper, more mystic significance, based on numerology, and not on a superficial coincidence." Madam Ngyuen picked up a purple robe and handed it to Jack.

"Here," she said, pointing back into the room. "Remove your clothes and put on this robe, and don't enter the bathroom until you hear me call.

Notice that the robe is purple? The color purple, like the number 35, denotes sexual power. The color purple works a spell upon your sex."

Jack smiled.

"Don't be too quick to discard a truth about something which you can't understand," Madam Ngyuen said, reading his smile.

"I promise, I will not prejudge," Jack said. He couldn't explain it, but he did seem to sense a vitality about himself. Whether it was related to the number 35 and the color purple, as Madam Ngyuen suggested, or merely to the fact that he was in the presence of one of the world's most beautiful women and he knew he was about to go to bed with her, he couldn't say. But he did feel a certain virile power.

Jack stepped into one corner of the room and removed his clothes, then put on his robe. He was a little self-conscious about the pile of clothes on the edge of the bed, so he folded them neatly and put them on the floor beneath the bed. He already had an erection, and as he moved its contact with the robe sent tiny electric shocks coursing through him.

"Captain, would you come in now, please?" Madam Ngyuen called softly.

Jack opened the door and saw Madam Ngyuen standing beside the tub. The robe she wore also purple, was delightfully short, revealing her long, golden legs.

"I hope to teach you many things, Captain," Madam Ngyuen said in her low, throaty voice. "One of the things I want to teach you is the sexually invigorating properties of the bath. Now, if you would be so kind as to turn your back, I shall step into the water."

Jack wanted to ask why he couldn't watch, but he kept silent and turned his back as he had been instructed. He heard the soft rippling of water as she settled into the bath.

"Now, if you would step in, please?"

Jack allowed the robe to drop to the floor, then he stepped into the tub. The water was very hot, but not so hot as to make him wait before sitting down.

"Turn to face me," Madam Ngyuen said.

When Jack turned, he could see the golden gleam of her breasts, adorned but not covered by the bath suds. One of her nipples peeked through and it was maddening to his senses. He reached for her.

"No," she said sharply. Then, more softly, "Please, don't be impatient. Enjoy your bath."

As they bathed, Jack noticed that he was gradually able to see more and more of her body. At first he thought it was an accidental exposure; then he realized that it was a studied exposure as she wiped away more of the soap suds. Each minute after tantalizing minute, she opened more of herself to his view until every delightful curve was finally laid bare. But only briefly, because as soon as she had removed the last of the suds and was completely exposed, she stepped out of the tub and covered herself with a large towel. For one maddening instant, she had been totally nude. And then, once again, her body was protected from his gaze.

"Would you?" she asked, holding up a flask of oil. The oil was an amber color, and the glow shining through it made it appear as if it had an inner fire.

"Yes," Jack said. His tongue was thick and his throat dry and he found it extremely difficult to talk. He took the flask, half expecting it to be hot from its brilliance, and followed Madam Ngyuen into the other room. Then, with her back still to him, she removed her robe.

Jack took a short breath of appreciation at the sight of her nudity. The smooth flow of her skin continued in an unbroken line from her shoulders down her gently curved back, across the soft mounds of her buttocks, split by the fold between the cheeks, and on down her thighs and calves, ending in perfectly proportioned ankles and feet.

Madam Ngyuen lay on her stomach, and Jack poured some of the oil on her beautiful golden skin and began rubbing. The sensuousness of it moved through his fingers and enflamed his whole body until he was consumed by sexual desire.

"Now, my beautiful American captain," Madam Ngyuen said in a voice that was low with her own passion. She turned over and held her arms up in invitation to him, beckoning him down to her. "Make love to me now."

Jack moved over her and Madam Ngyuen put her arms around his neck and pulled him to her, taking his tongue deep into her mouth, then pushing it back with her own tongue thrusting into his mouth.

Jack abandoned himself then, subject to the whims and dictates of this beautiful creature. He returned her kisses and caresses, and felt every inch of her soft, pliant body as it surged against his, urging him on.

When the moment was exactly right, he moved into her, helped by her cool hands and long, supple fingers. He pushed against her unbelievably wet softness. Madam Ngyuen raked his back with her nails and for a moment Jack was afraid he would lose control, but he managed to hang on, to match his rhythm to hers, allowing her time to reach her own pinnacle. Then, as he felt her melting into white-hot fire beneath him, he allowed his own body to erupt into a shattering climax.

Afterward they lay together for several moments, neither moving nor speaking. But the feel of her skin and the scent of her musk reawakened his ardor, and he went to her, and they made love a second time.

This time Jack had no difficulty in controlling himself, and it was slower, more sensual lovemaking. When they finished, they lay in each other's arms and Jack thought of how it had been with her. It was exotic and exciting, and his head spun with the dizziness of it. They had asked nothing from each other, save the momentary truth of sexual pleasure, and in that they had given as much as they had received.

Darkness came, and Madam Ngyuen's quiet, even breathing told Jack that she was asleep. Jack got up and walked over to the window to look out on *Le Loi* street. The street crawled with lights, but the noise seemed much more subdued than it had been during the day. Somewhere below, a young girl was singing, her voice clear and sweet and soft as velvet. In the dark sky on the far side of the city, he could see the rotating red Grimes light of a Huey over Tan San Nhut, and his spirit leaped the time and space between this musk-scented room and the glowing cockpit of that helicopter. And for a moment, he felt a great guilt.

6

Mike Delles, known to his friends as Papa, was about six feet tall, with long silver hair which joined a full silver beard to frame his face. He had twinkling brown eyes and a friendly smile, large shoulders, a slight belly-rise, and legs which looked too small for his upper torso.

"I knew that book I read about veterinary medicine would come in handy one day," Papa said. "Hell, you're as healthy as a horse."

Papa had been examining Mack Burton, who was lying in a hammock between two trees outside the Delleses' cabin. Mack's upper torso was criss-crossed with bandages, and they looked starkly white against his black skin.

"What the hell are you trying to do out here anyway?" Papa teased. "Get a suntan?"

"Don't you know how that works?" Mack replied. "Whiteys get darker in the sun and black folks get lighter. One of these days all the white folks are going to turn black and all the black folks are going to turn white, then we aren't going to let any of you black sons of bitches drink out of our water fountains."

"What the hell is a water fountain?" Papa asked, taking a swig of beer from the can he always seemed to have. "What the hell is water?"

"Listen," Mack said, seriously. "You saved my life. I'll never forget that."

"It wasn't me," Papa said. "It was that little shit in there." He pointed to the cabin with his can of beer. "You were more dead than alive when he brought you here. But if he hadn't brought you anyway, you'd be gone now."

"I know," Mack said. "I owe him, too. What's he doin' in there anyway?"

"He's in there showing Joanie how to cook. Or, for all I know, he and Joanie may be up in the loft, playing with his dork." Papa took another swallow.

Mack laughed. "You don't seem too concerned."

"Well, I don't think the little runt could hurt her any," Papa went on. He pointed to the notepad. "Writing your autobiography, are you?"

"No," Mack said. "I'm writing a letter to Stacey."

"Stacey?"

"My sister," Mack explained. "She's in Vietnam."

Papa was taking a swallow of his beer and he coughed and gasped, then laughed aloud as beer spewed out.

"Damn! You're one of the biggest antiwar dissidents in the country and you have a sister in the army?"

"She's not in the army," Mack said. "She's a civilian, working with the State Department, assigned to the marines in Vietnam. I'm sure that she's heard about the shooting and the fire in Washington by now, and she may be afraid that I'm dead. I want to reassure her."

"Yeah, well, I hope you aren't foolish enough to put a return address on the letter," Papa said.

"No way."

The front door of the cabin opened and Larry and Joanie came out. Joanie, who was Papa's wife, was in her late forties, nearly twenty years younger than Papa. She was thin, with some black left in her hair, and clear blue eyes which were filled with compassion for all living things. It was a joke among all who visited the Delleses that Joanie couldn't kill anything. Spiders, snakes, frogs, flies— Joanie thought all such creatures should have equal right to life, though she did occasionally, as she put it, speak harshly to mosquitoes and other biting things."

"Are you finished?" Papa asked, as they sat down on the porch to join him and Mack.

"Finished with what?" Joanie asked innocently.

"Cooking supper, or playing with Larry's dork."

"Oh," Joanie said. "Well, we finished supper, but we didn't get a chance to play with Larry's dork. What do you say, Larry, shall we play with your dork?"

"I'm willing," Larry said, grinning at the game.

"Hold it," Papa said, holding out his hand. "If you haven't already done it, it's too late. Besides, why would you want to do that, when you can sit out here in the presence of a sage and be blessed with pearls of his wisdom?"

"A sage?" Larry said, laughing. "What makes you a sage?"

"Well, I do what a sage does," Papa said. "Therefore, I am a sage."

"And just what does a sage do?" Larry asked.

"Oh, that's just it," Papa said, chuckling his answer. "A sage doesn't do much of anything. That's all part of his charm, you see."

Papa spoke with an expression of merriment that Larry and Mack had seen before. He was a man who took very little about himself seriously, they suspected, and yet at times there was the hint of a profound wisdom beneath his jokes and smiles.

"Listen, that sounds like good work," Mack said from the hammock. "How would I go about becomin' a sage?"

"The easiest way is to get really old," Papa explained. "Anyone over eighty years old is automatically a sage, and the people will listen to what he, or she," he said, deferring to Joanie, "says, as if he, or she, really knew what they're talking about. I'm only sixty-seven, so I've taken the next easiest way. I *look* like one and I *act* like one. I have a distinctive beard, I wear old clothes, I smoke an old pipe, I live in a quaint mountain cabin, and I talk in riddles. It seems to work quite well."

"Well, sage," Joanie said, "let's go in and eat, what do you say?"

Papa and Larry helped Mack out of the hammock, and then they followed Joanie into the cabin. The inside of the cabin was as cluttered as the outside. Two walls were filled with paperback books, and a homemade desk sat in front of one of the walls. The desk was covered with papers, magazines, notepads and folders. The other two walls were decorated with deer antlers, old posters, pop bottle caps, antique tools, and one shelf was loaded with patent medicine, circa 1890.

"It smells good, whatever it is," Mack said.

"It's the cheapest cut of beef, cooked in the cheapest dago wine," Joanie said. "The combination generally turns out surprisingly good, however. Larry, get four bowls, will you?"

"Hey, look," Larry said. "Here are two that match." Larry and the others laughed, for Joanie's "china, crystal and silverware" were actually plastic, crockery, tin and wood, random pieces picked up over the years. Larry thought of the tablesettings in his parents' home. There was enough china, crystal and silverware to have a different setting for every meal. And yet never, in all the time he had been at home, had he enjoyed a meal as much as he had enjoyed the meals here, with the Delleses and Mack.

Papa went over to the small stove and raised the lid on a bubbling pot. An enticing aroma came from the pot, and Papa stirred and sniffed knowledgably. "Hmm, it needs a bit more marjoram," he said, and he began applying liberal portions of the spice without consulting anyone else.

"Let's eat it before Papa decides to brew some witches' stew," Joanie teased, and she scooped out generous portions in the bowls.

"Uhm, this is delicious," Mack said. He looked around the cabin. "I'm glad Larry knew about this place," he said. "How did you come to be here, anyway? I mean, you don't seem like farmers or anything."

"Oh, we're farmers," Papa said. "Or at least, we're gardeners. We don't raise anything to sell, just to eat."

"Did you raise this beef?" Mack asked. "I've seen goats here, but no cows."

"Heavens! Do you think I would kill one of my babies?" Joanie asked. "No way."

Papa laughed. "When we first moved here, we were going to raise chickens, cows and pigs. The pigs started eating us out of house and home, because Joanie would never let me slaughter any of them. We finally had to sell them. We kept the chickens, and we eat their eggs, but she won't even let me kill one of them."

"What about the goats?"

"Well, cows were too expensive, so we got goats for the milk."

"What did you do before you came here?" Mack asked.

"I was chief engineer for Baker Aviation Incorporated."

Mack whistled. "That's a big company!"

"With a big defense contract," Larry added. "Several big defense contracts."

"Oh, I know what happened," Mack said. "You got fired because of your views on the war, didn't you?"

"No," Papa said. "My pacifist views were well known then, and I used to wear the peace button on my lapel for all to see. Only in those days, it wasn't the peace symbol, it meant 'ban the bomb.' I used to get a little ribbing over it. People would tell me that I was helping to design machines to use in war, that I had no right to call myself a pacifist—you know, that sort of thing. But the war wasn't going yet, and the feelings weren't running so high, so I could do that and just be considered eccentric."

"Then came the Doomsbuggy project," Joanie said.

"The Doomsbuggy project?" Larry said. "I've never heard of it."

"It was what we called a new fighter aircraft that Baker was working on," Papa said. "It was the most advanced, most efficient killing machine ever conceived of by man. That's where the nickname came from. As far as I know, the machine is still under development. At least I haven't heard anything about it yet."

"So you quit rather than work on the Doomsbuggy?" Larry prompted.

"Yeah," Papa said. He smiled. "We were in a plans meeting one afternoon and I said I was going to step out for a cup of coffee. I went over to the machine, bought a cup, then stood there looking out the window. I saw a couple of kids out on the highway, carrying backpacks. I thought, 'That should be Joanie and me.'"

"He came home and got me," Joanie said, taking over from there. "He just came in the door and said, 'Honey, let's go.'"

"She never even asked me where," Papa said, smiling at her and reaching over to take her hand in his. "She just walked out the door with me. We didn't take a thing with us. We left the furniture, television, and stereo."

"And china," Joanie put in, holding up her cracked bowl.

"All we took was the car, and we traded it for the jeep you see parked out front, and one thousand dollars cash. We found Sky Meadow here, cleaned out our savings account by paying cash for this cabin and the 120 acres of land, then we wrote a letter to the bank telling them they could have our house and everything in it."

"How do you stay alive?" Mack asked. "How do you make enough money to live?"

"You'd be amazed at how little it takes to live if you put your mind to it," Papa said. "Last year I sold seven articles and two book reviews—total income: seven hundred and ten dollars."

"And I sold two quilts for thirty-five dollars apiece," Joanie put in proudly.

"Our biggest expense is beer," Papa said. Then he burped, and laughed. "And I'm workin' on a deal where I'm going to audit a distributer's books for him once a month, in return for ten cases of beer a month. That'll set me up for life."

"I envy you," Mack said. "I envy both of you, being able to just drop out like this. I wish I could do it."

"No," Papa said. "You don't really want to do it. You're doing what you want to do, and what the rest of the country needs you to do. If we didn't have a few brave souls like you to stand up and fight for what is right, then it would be impossible for old farts like me ever to become sages. You'll always have a place here, Mack, and you, Larry, and anyone else who fights the brave fight, and who needs it. It's a quiet way of registering my protest, but it's the strongest statement I can make."

"I'll tell you, if it hadn't been for you and Joanie and Sky Meadow, we'd be up shit creek right now," Larry said.

"Come on, guys, keep this up and we're going to

start singing ballads and crying in our beer," Papa said. He finished his stew, then stood up. "Give me that letter, Mack. I'm going down to gas the jeep. I'll drop it in a mailbox for you."

Da Nang, Vietnam

"Hey, Frank, you going over to mail call?"

Frank Bell, the marine lance-corporal to whom the question was addressed, sat up on his bunk and pushed his hat back from his eyes. His eyes were cobalt blue, staring out from beneath coal-black brows and hair. His face and body were darkly tanned after several months of exposure to the Vetnam sun.

"I don't know why I bother," he said. "I've got no one in the States writing to me."

"Oh, spare me the blues," said the other marine, a youth as blond as Frank was dark. His name was Jeff Stewart, and he and Frank had come to Vietnam together. "Get my mail, anyway. I've got duty driver tonight."

"All right," Frank agreed. "But if you get another perfumed letter from Ginger, I'm just going to have to open it and read it," he teased.

"You do and I'll bust your head," Jeff promised. Jeff made the threat easily, but he was probably the only one in the entire division who *could* make that threat. Frank was the division heavyweight boxing champion and not even a close friend was about to threaten him except in jest. "Oh, Stacey wants you to check her mail, too."

"Why didn't you say so in the first place?" Frank asked. "Where's Stacey?"

"She's in the orderly room, typing out gook reports."

"Don't let her hear you calling them that," Frank warned. "She takes this civic action program seriously."

"I know I'm a southern boy, but I'll tell you what. She may be a black girl, but if Stacey wanted to take *me* seriously, I'd walk right down the middle of Capitol Street in Jackson, Mississippi, with her on my arm and a sign tellin' the KKK to kiss my ass."

"With your mama and papa lookin' on, huh?" Frank teased. "I'll just bet you would."

"Listen, that Stacey's one beautiful woman."

"And her brother's one big dude," Frank said. "Did you ever see him play football?"

"No, did you?"

"I saw him on television once, when Ohio State played Michigan. Old Mack Truck cleaned some plow, I'll tell you."

"You reckon he's dead?" Jeff asked.

"They didn't identify the bodies."

"That don't mean he ain't dead," Jeff said. "It just means they didn't identify the bodies."

"Hey, Stewart!" someone called. "The ol' man needs a driver!"

"Don't forget my mail!" Jeff called, as he trotted out to the jeep.

Frank wandered down to the end of the barracks and pulled a paper cup from the water jug, then thumbed himself a cup of water, watching as the bubbles gurgled up. He wished there was some way to take this jug of ice-cold water with them when they went into the field. In the field all they had was the lister bag—when they were lucky. Sometimes they had to use water rationing and go two or more days just on the water they had in their canteens. When that ran out, they started getting water anywhere they could find it, sometimes even dipping into rice paddies. They had the chlorine tablets, which were supposed to purify the water, but the chlorine made the water taste so bad that many didn't even use them.

Frank drank two cups of water, then crushed the cup and pushed through the screen door to walk across the sun-baked red dirt to the mail room. Frank's barracks was in the line of barracks right next to the runway, where an F-4 Phantom jet was just starting its take-off run, less than fifty yards away. The jet was laden with bombs and rockets, and it roared down the runway, pushed along by two horizontal pillars of fire. The pilot rotated, then kicked in his after-burners, sending the explosion of their ignition rolling across the base, shaking the stomachs of all who were nearby. With afterburners the Phantom went up like a rocket, so that by the time Frank reached the mail room the jet was little more than a brilliant point of light, high in the northern sky. By the time mail call was completed, the jet would be making its first bombing run over North Vietnam.

"Bell!" the mail clerk was saying, just as Frank arrived. "Is Bell out there?"

"Yeah," Frank answered, surprised to hear his name called. "Yeah, I'm right here."

The mail clerk tossed the letter disdainfully, and hands grabbed it, then passed it along until it reached Frank. Frank took it, wondering who it was from, then saw that it was from his sister. He smiled as he thought of her. She was four years younger than he, and an absolute beauty. One of his friends once teased him by saying he learned to fight so well by fighting the boys off his sister.

Claudine, who preferred to be called Deena, was the exact opposite of Frank in many ways. She was blonde and svelte, while Frank was dark and muscular. Deena was very outgoing, and because of her cute, saucy ways she made friends easily. She had been captain of the cheerleading squad and president of her class in school. Frank, who had always been quiet and reserved, went to work as a truck driver after school, but Deena went to nurse's training. Frank had joined the marines as an enlisted man, while Deena went into the army with a commission.

Dear Frank,

How does it feel, knowing that I can tell you what to do now? That's because I am a first lieutenant, dear, dumb brother, and you are only a lance corporal. (What's a lance corporal? We don't have such a rank in the army.)

I'm teasing, of course. You are still my big, and I do mean big, brother, and whatever you say goes for me. Except for one thing. You told me not to come to Vietnam, and there, dear Frank, I'm going to have to disobey you. Sorry brother, it's not my doing, it's the doing of the United States Army. Just when I thought I was going to do my entire tour right here at Fort Benning, I up and get orders sending me to RVN.

I've already received my assignment, too. I'm going to the Second Field Hospital at Phu Bien, which I understand is not too far from Saigon. Maybe you'll get a chance to come see me sometime. That doesn't mean to go out and do anything stupid like get wounded or something just to get down there, though, you hear me?

Did you hear? Uncle Gilbert is in the country now. He's a full colonel in the marines. How about that? I'll bet he could get you a cushy assignment if you wanted one.

I know, I know, you don't play the game that way. You always have been Jack Armstrong, the All-American boy. The strong, silent, All-American boy. Take it easy, brother, and I'll be seeing you.

Love,

Deena

Frank folded the letter, then looked up and saw that the others were leaving. The mail clerk was about to close his window.

"Hey," Frank called. "How about Stewart? Did Stewart get any mail?"

"I didn't call his name, did I?" the clerk answered.

"What about Stacey Burton?"

"Come on, Bell, where you been?" the clerk asked irritably. "I called Burton's name about four times, and no one answered for her."

"I'm sorry," Frank said. "I was reading my letter and didn't pay any attention. Give it to me, will you? I'm supposed to take it to her."

"I wish you guys would get your heads out of your butts," the mail clerk complained as he looked through the pile of mail he had been unable to deliver. "You think all I have to do is hand out letters. This isn't my only job, you know. I've got half a dozen other jobs around here."

"Yeah, I know you have it rough," Frank said.

The mail clerk was one of the few men in the company who didn't go into the field during combat operations and he was very defensive about it. Frank didn't hold it against the clerk that he didn't go out, but the clerk couldn't know that.

"Here it is," the mail clerk said. He looked at the envelope. "It's a good thing it got here. It doesn't have any return address. It would have been dead-letter city."

Frank took the letter, then walked back through the compound, passing a listless volleyball game, then a couple of guys tossing a baseball back and forth, and finally coming to the orderly room. The orderly room was a building constructed of plywood at the bottom half and screen wire at the top. Like all the other buildings in the company area, it was unpainted and drab looking.

Frank pushed the screen door open and stepped inside. Stacey was sitting behind a desk, working on some papers in a manila folder. She looked up and smiled brightly as Frank came in.

"Hi, Frank."

Stacey was indeed a beautiful woman. She had soft blue-black hair and large brown eyes, the beautiful characteristics of her race, but her skin was actually no darker than Frank's deep suntan. Her teeth were brilliantly white and perfectly formed, and she had a smile that could make a person dizzy with its radiance.

"You got a letter," Frank said.

"Who is it from?"

"I don't know. I hope it's not some guy. I'd hate to have to go break his arm to keep him from writing to you."

"Oh, now, you wouldn't do that, would you?"

"Yeah," Frank said. "I'd do it if it was needed to teach the fella a lesson." Frank walked over to Stacey's desk, looked around quickly to make certain they weren't being watched, then kissed her.

Stacey returned the kiss, and for just a moment, Frank felt her lips quiver under his. He put his hand in her hair and held her face to his for a bit longer. When they finally separated, Stacey let out a long, slow sigh.

"You ought not to do things like that to a girl when she's working," she teased.

"How about when she's not working?"

Stacey smiled at him. "I'll be in my room around ten," she said. "I won't be working then."

"I'll be there," Frank promised, and he felt a quick, building heat as he thought of what lay ahead. He had been visiting Stacey's room for a month now, always in secret because they were both afraid of the talk that would get around if anyone knew.

"Who's the letter from?" Frank asked, as Stacey opened it.

"I don't know," Stacey said. "There's no return address, it's all very mysterious, it could be—oh!" Stacey gasped, then she put her hand to her face and began to cry.

"Stacey!" Frank said. "Stacey, what is it? What's wrong?"

"Wrong?" Stacey said. "Oh, Frank, baby, nothing's wrong. He's alive!"

"What?"

"Mack, my brother," Stacey said. "This letter is from Mack. He's alive!"

Stacey was so happy over the news that she ran into Frank's arms, and Frank held her close to him for a long moment, feeling her sobs of joy and glad that he was here to share the moment with her.

In the shadow of the bulletin board just outside the orderly room, a lone figure stood looking through the wire screen at the scene inside. He took a deep drag of his cigarette, then pinched it out and butt-stripped it before he discarded it.

"So," he said under his breath. "Frank Bell is gettin' himself a little nigger poon-tang, is he? How the hell does *he* rate? If anyone is getting in Miss Burton's britches, it should be me." He chuckled to himself. "But I'll get you, little darlin'. I'll get some of that or my name isn't Sam Morrow, and I'm not a captain in the United States Marine Corps."

7

JACK KILLED THE ENGINE and remained in his seat, filling out the "dash twelve" of the logbook while the blades and the gyros coasted down. Ed Selfridge opened the canopy and climbed out, then stepped back to talk to Jack.

"Son of a bitch," Ed swore. "Jack, we've got to do somethin' about those guns at Parrot's Beak. Those two Loaches from the Sixty-eight never had a chance."

"Yeah, I know," Jack said. He slipped the log book into the pocket, then took off his flight helmet. His sweat-dampened copper hair was plastered to his forehead. "I wonder when those guns moved in there? They weren't there last week."

"Cap'n Hunter! Cap'n Hunter, she got 'em, sir! Charlene got the tickets! She 'n the kids are going to meet me in Hawaii!" Springs shouted, running toward the helicopter, waving a letter over his head.

"Hey, Springs, that's great!" Jack said. Springs was due to go on R&R to Honolulu, and he and his wife had been saving for it ever since he had arrived so she would have enough to take the three children and meet him there. Springs had been keeping Jack abreast of the progress—the lawns Gary Junior had mowed, and the fact that the entire family had cut back on Christmas and birthday presents. Once, Springs even read a part of one of Charlene's letters in which she told him they were eating meat only once a week to save on the grocery bills.

"God, I just can't believe it's true," Springs said. "Tomorrow night I'll be there. Tomorrow night! Hey, Mr. Selfridge, you just got back from Hawaii last month, didn't you?"

"I sure did," Ed said.

"Did you like it?"

"It was fantastic."

"Listen, have you got any idea about things to do? You know, for the family?"

Ed grinned at Springs. "Well now, Springs, the things *I* did, you wouldn't exactly want to do with a family."

"I don't think you'll have any problem figuring out something to do," Jack teased.

"Oh, I almost forgot," Springs said. "Colonel Mayfair wants to see you. He asked me to tell you as soon as you could get away."

"Ed, tell Lieutenant Bostic I'm going up to squadron, will you?" Jack said. He carried his flak jacket and helmet over to the jeep, which was parked near the flight line, then got in and drove across the clanking PSP toward the squadron headquarters.

There was a row of cut-down fifty-five-gallon oil drums along the edge of the runway, and half a dozen Vietnamese women—called "mamasans" by the G.I.s, whether they were mamasans or not—were pouring diesel fuel into the drums. The drums had been pulled from the outdoor toilets, and they were called honey-buckets. Everyday the honey-buckets would be burned off and the foul-smelling smoke would drift over the compound. No part of the camp would escape the odor; not even the flower garden at the Red Bull was safe.

Beyond the mamasans was the Fifty-sixth Maintenance Company. This was where the helicopters were brought for repair, and there were several sitting there now in various stages of assembly. It was this company that would send a helicopter into the field to recover those helicopters which had either crashed or been shot down. The recovery crew was known as Goodnature 3, and Jack had a lot of respect for them. The V.C. knew that any downed helicopter would bring the recovery crew in, so the V.C. often waited in ambush for them.

The squadron headquarters was just on the other side of the field hospital, and as Jack drove by the hospital, he saw two dustoff Hueys sitting on the pads out front. Both had been used on this day to evacuate the aircrews of the two helicopters which were shot down by antiaircraft fire from Parrot's Beak. There were a couple of bikini-clad nurses lying on a blanket in front of the hospital, sunning themselves, and Jack saw a ¾ truck loaded with E.M. turn around and drive back slowly to enjoy a second look.

CLEAR YOUR WEAPONS HERE, the sign outside the headquarters building read. An arrow pointed to a fifty-five-gallon drum full of sand. Jack emptied the cylinders of his .38, spun it to make sure it was empty, then slipped the pistol back into his shoulder holster before he went inside.

"Oh, Cap'n Hunter, sir," Sergeant Kincannon greeted him. "Just a minute, I'll tell Colonel Mayfair you're here."

"Thanks," Jack said. He stepped over to the water cooler to thumb himself a cup of water. Two years earlier, when Jack had first come to Vietnam, an article had appeared in a national magazine, telling Americans how bad all the water tasted. "If you want to do something nice for your loved one in Vietnam," the article suggested, "send a packet of dry fruit-punch mix." As a result of that article, nearly every women's club in America took it on as a project, and for months it was impossible to find water to drink in Vietnam, because every cooler had been converted to hold fruit punch. Jack didn't believe he could ever drink another glass of fruit punch as long as he lived. It was good to be back to water.

"Cap'n?" Sergeant Kincannon called. "The colonel will see you now."

Jack liked Colonel Mayfair. Colonel Mayfair was serving his last tour, and would be retiring when he returned to the States. He had no axes to grind, and no ambitions to fulfill. He was easy-going with his officers and with his men, and he delegated authority without jealousy or intimidation. He had sparse gray hair and was a small round man, but without any of the complexes which so often affected small men. Colonel Mayfair didn't have to prove anything and he knew it.

Colonel Mayfair wasn't alone in the office. Colonel Kramer was there also.

"Hi," Colonel Mayfair said when Jack reported. He pointed to a chair. "Sit down. I heard about the two ships from the Sixty-eighth. Do you know what happened?"

"Only what I heard," Jack said. "The Sixty-eighth was using armed LOHs to fly cover for the first lift element, and we were flying cover for the second element. The guns opened up on 'em, and got two of them. It was a complete surprise to everyone. There was no mention of the guns in the briefing."

"What did you do?" Colonel Kramer asked.

"Well, sir, when we heard about the guns, we went around the mountain and came in from the back side."

"That gave the V.C. about fifteen minutes more warning that there was an operation on," Kramer said accusingly. "The whole idea of coming by Parrot's Beak was to make an insertion before the V.C. knew what hit them."

"Colonel Kramer, we were in the *second* lift element. The initial element had already landed. We had no surprise to protect," Jack said.

"Nevertheless, I'd hate to think that the V.C. are going to start dictating our flight paths for us now."

"I'd say Jack's move was prudent," Colonel Mayfair said quietly. "We didn't sustain any damage did we?"

"No, sir. Charley left the back door wide open," Jack replied.

"Well, we won't be able to count on that indefinitely," Mayfair said. "My guess is that they'll leave those guns there and make us go around every time. That way they can move troops into the valley guarded by Parrot's Beak, and turn it into a regular staging area."

"We've got to take those guns out," Kramer said.

"Take 'em out? How?" Jack said, eying Kramer incredulously.

"The same way we took out the guns at Chat Nhyn," Kramer said. "Take 'em head on."

"Colonel Kramer, if you'll forgive me for saying so, sir, that's the worst idea any cavalry officer has had since Custer thought he'd kick the ass off a few Indians."

"You took out the guns at Chat Nhyn," Kramer said. "You can do it again."

"Look," Jack said, getting up to walk over to the wall map. "Here is Chat Nhyn, and here were the guns, here, here and here. We had all kinds of maneuverability against those guns. We could have come at them from any direction we wanted, and we could evade their fire." Jack demonstrated by moving his finger around the board.

"Now, look at Parrot's Beak," he went on. "The guns are right inside the valley mouth here, and the only way you can hit them is straight on. That means they know where you're coming from, and they know how high you'll be. They also know how fast we'll be flying—which, believe me, isn't fast enough."

"And what would *you* propose, Captain?" Kramer asked. "That we just detour around the mountain forever, just give up and say, 'Here, Charley, the valley is yours. Do anything you want with it.'"

"I'd ask for air force strikes," Jack suggested.

"Oh, that would be fine, wouldn't it?" Kramer said sourly. "We've preached the concept of air cavalry for years. Hell, Colonel Mayfair, you, more than anyone, should know how much trouble we had convincing the Defense Department to let us arm our aircraft."

Colonel Mayfair laughed. "Don't I know, though? I remember strapping 30 caliber machine guns on the skids of H-13s back at Fort Rucker in '56. Everyone thought we were crazy."

"Well, we've come a long way since then," Kramer went on. "And I don't intend to give the air force the satisfaction of coming to our aid the first time we have an air strike that's a little tough."

"Colonel, that's what the air force does for a living," Jack said.

"God damn it, Captain, I'm trying to get it through your head that it's what *we* do for a living, too."

"If we try that, some of us are going to wind up dying for a living," Jack said.

"Colonel Mayfair, I'll lead the strike," Kramer said.

Mayfair leaned back in his chair and put his hands behind his head, then looked at his two officers.

"Damn it, will you two quit bickering like a couple of ten-year-old brothers? Bert, you've got as much on the ball as any officer I've ever known. Here you are, a lieutenant colonel at an age when I was still trying to make captain. And Jack, you're one of the few captains in Vietnam with a command. Hell, you'd think with two such outstanding officers my last days in the army would be a picnic. Now, I'm not ready to call in the air force yet."

Colonel Kramer beamed broadly.

"But I'm not ready to authorize a strike, either. At least, not yet. For the time being we'll do just what Jack did . . . we'll avoid it."

"We can't avoid it forever, sir," Kramer protested.

"I know we can't avoid it forever," Mayfair said with the patience of a weary father. "But neither do we have to worry about it at this very moment. I'm going to get some photo-recon before I make up my mind what to do."

"Yes, sir," Kramer said, subdued.

"By the way, Jack, there's a replacement for 068 at Tan San Nhut," Colonel Mayfair said. "You can take my ship down there in the morning to pick it up. You'll have to take someone to fly the new Cobra back."

"I'll take my gunner, sir," Jack said.

"Fine, fine. Listen, would you take Lieutenant Goss with you, too?"

"Goss?"

"Jane Goss, the nurse. She's rotating back to the States tomorrow, and I promised her C.O. I'd get her there."

"Sure," Jack said.

"As a matter of fact," Colonel Mayfair said, looking at his watch, "I imagine her bon voyage party is starting over at the Red Bull right now. What say we call it a day and go tell her goodbye?"

"Sounds good to me," Jack said.

"Bert?" Colonel Mayfair asked.

"No, thank you, sir. You go ahead," Bert said.

"I'm inspecting Delta Troop's property book to-night."

"Why?" Mayfair asked. "Is Delta Troop short some equipment?"

"Not that I know of, sir," Bert said. "But I want to keep it that way."

"If you'd rather look at little numbers in little squares than come to a bon voyage party, then you go right ahead," Mayfair said. "Come on, Jack, is your jeep outside?"

"Yes, sir."

A moment later, they were getting into Jack's jeep. "You have the best-looking jeep on the base," Colonel Mayfair said. "Perhaps in the country. It looks like a little sports car."

Jack's jeep was the result of Creech's scrounging ability, and Springs's tinkering. The paint was standard olive drab, but the jeep was waxed and buffed to a high gloss every day. The seats were covered in yellow naugahide, and the wheel caps and the inside of the grill slats were painted yellow. There was also a yellow cover over the mounted spare tire, and, as yellow was the color of the cavalry, there was nothing unauthorized about the color combination. The jeep had yellow floor carpeting, and highly polished brass knobs and switches, and though that was a departure from regulations, no one but Colonel Kramer had ever made a negative comment about it.

"It's not my jeep, sir," Jack said. "I just drive it. It belongs to Creech and Springs."

"I guess it does give them something to do," Colonel Mayfair said, patting the polished dash-board appreciatively. "Damned if I wouldn't mind having this sitting in my driveway in Tampa when

I retire. You think Creech could . . ." Mayfair stopped, then laughed. "I know damn *well* he could have one sitting there when I get back. That's why I'd better be very careful and never mention it to him, not even as a joke."

Jack parked in front of the Red Bull, then pulled a chain up to lock it through the steering wheel and thus prevent the jeep from being stolen. The party was already under way when they went inside.

"Hey, Jack, I hope you didn't mind us starting without you!" Bostic called, laughing. Then he saw that Jack was with Colonel Mayfair. "Oh, uh, good evening, Colonel," he said, more seriously.

"It's thirty minutes until the end of the official duty day," Colonel Mayfair said sternly. "You haven't drunk anything yet, have you?"

"Oh, no, sir," Bostic said quickly, his words ending in a noticeable—and probably deliberate—hiccup.

Mayfair glared at him sternly for a moment, then he couldn't sustain it and he broke into a laugh. "Why the hell not?" he asked. "Have you found a better way to get drunk?"

"No, sir," Bostic said. "Drinking is just fine." He took a long drink to prove his point, and then, realizing that the colonel had only been teasing all along, he joined in the laughter, though uneasily.

"Jack," a woman's voice called. "Jack, come over here and say good-bye."

Jack looked toward the voice and saw Jane Goss sitting on a wooden bench which ran along the wall. He smiled and walked over toward her.

"What are you doing over here all alone?" he asked. "Why aren't you mixing with the others and celebrating?"

"What's to celebrate?"

"Why, hell, I thought you were going home tomorrow."

"Yeah," Jane said. "I put in for retention and was turned down. Did you know that?"

"You wanted to stay?"

"Why not?" Jane answered. "What's there to do in the States? I'm going to Fort Leonard Wood, Missouri. Can you believe that? That's right in the middle of nowhere, and I do mean nowhere."

"What's there for you here?" Jack asked. He smiled. "Except a lot of men, I mean."

"That's not a bad reason," Jane admitted with a little laugh. "But it's not the only reason. I don't know, I can't explain it, but it seems like people are more alive over here. It's like this is the real world, and everything in the States is phoney. I mean, how can everyone go on with business as usual when there's a *war* on, for chrissake? There ought to be bond drives and war rallies, parades, that sort of thing. Why aren't the people getting behind us?"

"You've seen too many World War II movies," Jack said easily. "But the John Waynes and Clark Gables and Gregory Pecks aren't fighting this war. No one cares about this war and no one cares about the people who are fighting it."

"I know," Jane said. "And that's why I don't want to go home. I don't want to be around people who don't care."

"Ah, give yourself six months and you'll be just

like everyone else," Jack teased. "When someone asks you about Vietnam you'll swear you've never heard of it."

"You've been home between tours," Jane said. "Did you forget all about the 'Nam?"

"No," Jack admitted. "I never forgot."

"Then what makes you think I will?"

"I don't know. I guess I was just trying to make you feel better."

Jane looked at him a moment before asking, "How come you never cared about how I felt before?"

"What do you mean?"

"You never asked me out."

"I never figured you had the time," Jack said. "From what I could tell, you were always pretty well attended by men friends."

"I would have made room for you," Jane said, looking at him intently. "We could have had some . . . interesting times." She let the word *interesting* slide out slowly, suggestively. "Although from what I've heard, you've been pretty occupied yourself."

"What have you heard?"

"I've heard that Madam Ngyuen has the hots for you," Jane said.

Jack blushed.

"Damn, it's true, isn't it?" Jane said in surprise. "I wasn't ready to believe it until this very moment. Tell me about her."

"I'd rather not talk about it," Jack said.

Jane put both arms around Jack's neck and pulled his face to hers, then planted a long, deep kiss on his lips. When she finally pulled away, she looked at him with an intimate smile. "I wish you would've had a chance for a comparison," she said. "I'd like to know how I would stack up in the bed department against an internationally famous beauty like Madam Ngyuen."

"I imagine you'd stack up very well indeed," Jack said, a little surprised by the unexpected kiss and by Jane's sudden forwardness.

"Hey, he's not the only one you're leaving behind, you know!" one of the men shouted, and he came over to plant a kiss on Jane's lips. Jane, laughing good-naturedly, accepted his kiss, then saw that the others were lining up.

"I wish I'd thought of this earlier," she quipped. "I'd have made a kissing booth, and charged two dollars a kiss."

"What could we get for twenty?" someone called, and his ribald question was met with general laughter.

Jack stayed with the party until a little after eleven. Then, after making sure that Colonel Mayfair had a ride back to his quarters, he returned to his own room, sprayed it with insecticide, and took his shower. By the time he finished the shower the smell of the insecticide had receded enough for him to be able to breathe comfortably, and there were more than half a dozen mosquito carcasses on the white sheet of his bunk.

Jack fluffed up his pillow and went to sleep, listening to the rhythmic booming of the nightly artillery barrages.

8

Y OU'D BETTER close your eyes, Jane, or you're going to bleed to death," Ed Selfridge commented, teasing Jane about her bloodshot eyes. Jane threw her bag into the back of the Huey, then climbed onto the red nylon seat which ran along the transmission tunnel.

"Oh," she groaned, leaning her head back against the netting. "Truly, drink is the devil's brew. I feel terrible. How do you men manage to do this night after night and still fly?"

"Because we're a bunch of hairy macho bastards," Ed said.

The crew chief stepped out of the helicopter. He was wearing an extra long cord to his headset, so he was able to walk around the ship to watch the engine as it was started.

"Clear?" Jack asked.

"Clear, sir," the crew chief answered.

Jack pulled the starter trigger and the turbine began to whine. The blades started around, slowly at first, then faster, until the tips became a blurring halo.

"Clean start, Cap'n," the crew chief said, looking through the inspection ports of the engine. "Wait a minute, here comes Springs."

Jack looked around and saw Springs running toward him, dressed not in his usual fatigues, but in khakis, complete with ribbons and polished brass.

"Cap'n, how about a ride to Saigon?" Springs asked.

"Hey, that's right, it's R&R day for you, isn't it? Sure, get in. But don't sit too close to Lieutenant Goss. She bites."

"I can't have any of that," Springs teased. "If Charlene sees someone's bite on my neck, it'll be my ass."

Springs got in just ahead of the crew chief and strapped himself in.

"Up," Jack said, as he pulled pitch.

Jack flew out over the roof of the Red Bull, keeping the nose low to build up airspeed, then he pulled up on the collective to gain altitude. He leveled off at 2500 and called Paris Control, the central flight controller at Tan San Nhut.

"Paris Control, Snake Six out of Phu Bien for Tan San Nhut, 2500, in a UH1-B."

"Snake Six, we have artillery firing in Tango-Zulu and Mike-Papa coordinates, rounds at 4500 feet."

"I'll give those fellas all the room they want," Jack said. "Snake Six out."

A lush green jungle unfolded below them, split

by the winding and shining Saigon River, and interspersed with flooded rice paddies and fields of all hues, from black through brown, yellow through green. Little villages sat clustered along the banks of the river, or along the concrete ribbon which was Highway 13. Dozens of yellow and blue buses moved antlike along the highway, competing with the trucks and jeeps for right-of-way. From up here it seemed impossible that the peaceful-looking land they were flying over was at war. Finally the sprawling, teeming city of Saigon came into view, and Jack released the friction lock to lower the pitch. The blades began popping as they spilled air, and the helicopter started a very gradual descent, until they were about two hundred feet above a cluster of antennas and heading straight for the helicopter landing area.

"Paris Control, Snake Six over antenna farm," Jack said.

"Snake Six, clear to land."

Jack terminated his approach about three feet off the ground, then hovered to set down on the landing pad indicated by one of the flight line personnel. He killed the engine, then twisted around to look at Jane.

"Have you got time for lunch?"

Jane laughed. "Finally, you ask me out. Where to?"

"There's a Mexican place on base here called Casa Grande. It's pretty good, if we can hitch a ride."

"I got a friend here, he can take you over in his ¾ if you don't mind ridin' in a truck," Springs suggested.

"Sounds good enough to me," Jack said. "Come on."

Jack and Jane followed Springs to find his friend, while the crew chief tied down the blades and Ed went in to arrange for the new Cobra.

"That's his truck there," Springs said. "You two get in. I'll get him out here."

"Thanks," Jack said.

Springs's friend came through for him, and a few moments later Jack and Jane were walking through the door of the Casa Grande. The Casa Grande was a restaurant operated by the air force N.C.O. club, but open to men and women of all ranks and of all branches of service. It was long and narrow, with red and white checkered table clothes and authentic Mexican food.

Jack was halfway through the meal with Jane, wondering why he had never asked her out before, when a thin man wearing a doctor's insignia and the oak leaves of a major came over to the table.

"Excuse me," he said. "But by your patch I see you are with the Fifth Cav. Aren't you at Phu Bien?"

"Yes," Jack replied, surprised that the doctor had recognized the patch. Most military doctors, he felt, could barely recognize their own rank.

"There's a young lady dining with me who just arrived in the country. She's going to the field hospital at Phu Bien, and she needs a ride. You wouldn't be returning soon by any chance, would you? And, if so, would you have room for her?"

"Sure," Jack said. "Why don't you bring her over and the two of you join us?" He pointed to Jane. "This is the person she's replacing."

The doctor smiled and thanked Jack, and stepped back to the rear of the room. A moment later he returned, leading the new replacement.

Jack liked what he saw of the new nurse from the first moment. Her legs and hips moved in a loose-limbed way that was subtly provocative. She had blonde hair, worn as long as the army would allow, and she had a way of brushing it back from her face that Jack found appealing. Her eyes were blue and wide. She tilted her head and smiled, and looked right at him as the doctor introduced her.

"I'm sorry, I hurried off before I could get your names," the doctor said. "I'm Tom Smith, and this is Claudine Bell."

"But I prefer Deena," the nurse quickly put in.

"Deena, this is Jane Goss, and my name is Jack Hunter. I'll be taking you up to Phu Bien."

"Jack Hunter! Yes, I know you now," Deena said. "I read about you in *Newstime* magazine. You're the Reluctant Hero."

"You don't *know* how reluctant he is," Jane said, referring to Jack's reluctance to date her in the past. It was a statement that meant nothing to the others, and Jane made no effort to explain it. "Anyway, I'm beyond it all," she went on. "I'm going back to the States today, leaving the torch for you to pick up and carry forward."

"How is the duty at Phu Bien?" Deena asked.

"The staff is good," Jane answered, "the facilities are more than adequate and you certainly have the feeling of being needed. You couldn't ask for any more than that, I don't suppose." Jane smiled as she added, "Of course, we *do* have to share the base with a bunch of crazy men."

"Crazy men?"

"The Cobra jocks," Jane explained. "Anyone who would fly a Cobra is just plain crazy, if you ask me."

"What's a Cobra?"

"What?" Jack gasped in mock horror, clutching both hands over his heart. "Did you just say what I *thought* you said?"

"All I asked was, what is a Cobra," Deena said innocently.

"Madam, I'll have you know that a Cobra is the most noble steed any cavalryman has ridden since the days of the old west. A better name than Cobra would be Pegasus, for she is indeed a flying horse."

"Does he always talk like this?" Deena asked Jane.

"A Cobra is a helicopter," Jane explained. "But it isn't an ordinary helicopter. It's narrow and sleek, like a fighter airplane. Only instead of having wings, it has a rotor. And it carries rockets and guns and all sorts of nasty things like that."

"Heavens, you mean I have to fly to Phu Bien in one of *those*?" Deena asked, screwing her face up anxiously.

"No," Jack said. "I'm down here in the standard dustoff-type buggy. I'm here in a Huey."

"Oh, I know what dustoff is," Deena said. "They're the guys who go in on the battlefield and pull out the wounded."

"Yeah," Jack said. "Yeah, you would know that."

"Hey, the officers' club bar is open now," Jane said, looking at her watch. "Come on, let's go over to the club and have a farewell drink."

"I've got to fly back," Jack said.

"That won't stop you from coming with me, will it?" Jane asked.

"Doc?"

"I've got to get back to work," the doctor said. "But take the lieutenant with you so she won't get lost."

"I'd better not have a drink, either," Deena said. "I'd hate to report to my new commander with alcohol on my breath."

"Believe me, honey, Major McGee will never notice it. She gargles in formaldehyde every day," Jane said.

"Major McGee?"

"She's the chief nurse," Jane said. Then, when Jane saw Deena's look of apprehension, she softened. "She's a tough cookie, but she's fair. Do your job and she'll stay off your back, believe me."

"Thanks," Deena said.

The main officers' open mess was just across the street, and when the three of them stepped into it a moment later, it was so dark, compared to the bright outside sun, that it took a moment for their eyes to adjust to the dark. Jack was surprised to see two captains sitting at the bar. He had seen the club officer unlock the door as they walked across the street and he had thought they would be the first ones in the club.

"How'd you guys beat us?" he asked as he and the two ladies joined them at the bar.

"We jus' didn't leave las' night," one of them answered. His tongue was thick from drink, and he and the other captain looked at Jack and the two ladies for a long time, trying to make their faces come into focus.

"Are two of you girls?" the other captain asked.

"Can you tell which ones?" Jack asked with a little laugh.

The two captains consulted for a moment. "The soft ones," one of them finally said.

The officers were dressed in khakis, but the uniforms didn't have the telltale markings of a Stateside press. They were obviously waiting to go home.

"You jus' got here, didn't you?" one of them—Butler, his name tag read—asked of Deena.

"Yes," Deena answered. "How could you tell?"

"It's easy," said the other one, Captain Fox. "We can see the look on your face. You're eager to go out and do battle with the wily jungle foe. Besides, I can tell that you're admiring our ribbons with secret though covetous, glances."

The breast pockets of both captains were bare.

"Hey, dumb-ass," Butler said. "We ain' wearin' our ribbons."

"Oh," Fox said. "Well, pretend, if you will, fair Lieutenant . . . what are you, a nurse?"

"Yes," Deena said.

"I love nurses," Fox said. He cleared his throat. "Imagine, if you will, the Silver Star."

"You don't have any Silver Star," Butler said.

"What the hell difference does it make?" Fox answered. "We're just pretending, aren't we? I can pretend any damn medal I want."

"Go ahead," Deena said, amused by the two captains.

"The Silver Star is followed by a Bronze Star, followed by an Army Commendation Medal with the V device for bravery." Fox hiccuped and splashed some of his drink over his pocket. "And in the next row down we have the Purple Shaft."

"What the hell did you get the Purple Heart for?" Butler asked.

"I caught a burst of clap in the groin while making a combat recon against the belly of a whore in 500 P alley."

"Oh, yours is genuine then," Butler said with respect. "Mine came from a sprained ankle while waiting in line to hump a Red Cross girl. Excuse us, ladies, if we offend."

"That's all right," Deena said, laughing.

"You shouldn't be ashamed of your Purple Heart," Fox said consolingly. "You also serve who only stand and wait."

"Especially if our cause is just," Butler added soberly.

"So there you have it, ladies and gentlemen," Fox concluded. "The standard nine-ribbon package, the basic load of our division."

"What was your division?"

"The fightin' Big Red One," Butler said.

"The valiant here-we'll-stand mother-lovin' sons of the cannon, fire-breathin', Commie-killin' First," Fox added.

"Course, I see by your patch you're a Cobra jock," Butler went on. "You tear up ol' Charlie's ass some yourself, huh?"

"I'd rather be where I am than pounding around on the ground," Jack said. "I wouldn't want your job for anything."

"I don't blame you," Fox said. "We don't want it, either. Now that we're goin' home, you can take the Big Red One and stuff it—"

"Butler, remember, two of them are soft," Fox warned.

"Yeah, I almost forgot," Butler said.

"You men sound almost bitter," Deena said.

"Bitter? Why should we be bitter? We're going back to the world. Right, Fox?"

"Right, Butler. And I'm going to love that little bun that's been in my wife's oven for four months now just like he was one of my own kids."

"Right, and so what if the college I was accepted into won't be opening this fall because the administration office was burned down in an antiwar riot? There are other schools, arent' there?"

"Right. And look at our accomplishments over the last year. Do you realize that I had five new buildings constructed in my company this year?" Butler boasted. "I was the building projects officer."

"Right," Fox said. "And do you realize that I tore down five buildings during my year here? I was the grounds utilization officer."

"That's a coincidence," Deena laughed. "You tore down the same number of buildings he built."

"Not really a coincidence," Fox said. "They were his buildings."

"I'll bet you didn't care much for that," Deena said to Butler.

"No it had to be done. Besides, I needed the lumber. So when he would tear the buildings down, I would get the lumber from the old one to build a new one."

"Captain Hunter? Is there a Captain Hunter in here?" someone called from the brilliant splash of sunlight which fell in through the opened door.

Jack looked around, and through the glare made out Springs's friend, the man who had driven them to the restaurant in the ¾ ton truck.

"Yes, I'm over here," Jack said, realizing the specialist couldn't see them in the dark room.

"Cap'n, you'd better get back down to Phu Bien quick, sir," the soldier said with an anxious note to his voice.

"Why? What is it? What's happened?"

"It's Gary, sir."

"Gary? You mean Specialist Springs? What about him? His R&R flight has already left, hasn't it? It was supposed to leave at 11:30."

"That's just it, sir," the soldier said. "The plane left, but Gary wasn't on it."

"He wasn't *on* it? What do you mean he wasn't on it? There was no way Springs was going to miss that plane."

"He didn't miss it, sir. They wouldn't let him on. His orders had been pulled."

"Pulled? Why?"

"Colonel Kramer revoked 'em, sir, and gave the slot to a bird colonel up at headquarters."

"What? Why would that son of a bitch do that?" Jack asked in a loud, angry voice.

"I don't know, sir. I only know one thing."

"What's that?"

"If you don't get back to Phu Bien before Springs does, you're going to have one dead lieutenant colonel on your hands. Springs is going to kill him."

"Ah, he'll calm down before he gets there," Jack said.

"No, sir, that's what's so frightening about it," the soldier said. "Springs is real calm now. He's just calm and cold. He's going to frag him, sir, sure as I'm standing here. He's going to waste that son of a bitch all over Phu Bien."

9

As Jack approached Phu Bien, he saw that a crowd of people was gathered around the perimeter bunker in the northeast corner of the field. Jack adjusted his landing approach so that he could sit down very near them. He hopped out of the helicopter as soon as he had killed the engine, then ran beneath the blades which were still swooshing rapidly and pushed his way to the front rank of the crowd.

"Ed what is it? What's happening?" Jack asked, when he saw Warrant Officer Selfridge standing in the crowd with the others.

"It's Springs, Cap'n," Ed said. "He's got Colonel Kramer in the bunker with him."

"He's got a grenade," someone else explained. All he has to do is let the spoon go and . . . kabloom!"

"Damn, how did he get back here so fast?" Jack asked.

Ed sighed. "That's my fault, Cap'n," he said. "He came over and asked me if he could ride back in the new Cobra."

"Didn't you think that was strange?"

"Well, I asked him about the R&R and he said his orders had been cancelled. But he was calm about it. I thought he just figured he couldn't do anything about it."

"Has anyone tried to speak to him?"

"Hell yes. The M.P.s, the ol' man, the duty officer."

"Any of his friends?" Jack asked.

"I tried to talk to him sir, but the provost marshal wouldn't let me," Specialist Creech said.

Jack looked over at the tall, thin soldier who was so adept at scrounging. "Come on," Jack said. "Let's go talk to him."

About fifteen yards in front of the crowd, between the crowd and the bunker, was a line of armed M.P.s, all wearing flak jackets and helmets.

"Sir, you can't go any further," one of them called out as Jack started through their line.

"That's one of my men in there," Jack said, pointing to the bunker.

"I'm sorry, sir, but you can't go any further," the M.P. said again.

"Who the hell says I can't?"

"Major Morris, sir." The M.P. called, "Major Morris, come here, quick!"

And M.P. officer, the provost marshal of the field, responded quickly to the M.P.'s call. Jack knew Morris, though not very well. They had seen each other in the Red Bull a few times.

"Sir, this captain says he's going to go in there and talk to Springs."

"We're keeping everyone out," Major Morris said to Jack.

"You're not keeping Creech and me out, Major, unless you intend to do so by force," Jack said.

Morris pushed his helmet back and scratched his head for a moment, looking at Jack and the specialist who stood with him. "Do you think you can do any good?"

"We'll never know until we try."

"I don't know," Morris said. "He seems like a crazy man to me. Anyone who would pull the pin on a grenade and take a hostage like that . . . he's liable to go off the deep end any moment. If you two were in there when he did that, the grenade would get all four of you."

"Do you know the story?" Jack asked.

"I heard he had his R&R orders cancelled," Morris said.

"It's not just that," Jack said. "He and his wife have been saving for ten months so she and the kids could meet him there. Now she's there, and he's here."

"Geez, that *is* tough," Morris said. "Did Colonel Kramer know that?"

"I'd like to think that he didn't know," Jack said. "But whether he knew or not, that's what prompted Springs to this."

Morris looked around, then he spoke quietly so that no one beyond them could hear. "A bastard who would do something like that almost deserves to be fragged," he said. "But why didn't Springs just come back and shoot him? Why all this?"

"Because I don't thnk he really wants to do it," Jack said. "If he did, he would have already done it. Major, I think he *wants* someone to talk him out of it."

"All right," Morris finally agreed. "Go ahead."

"Thanks."

Jack and Specialist Creech approached the bunker.

"Gary?" Creech called. "Gary, it's me, Nick."

"Who's with you, Nick?"

"It's me, Gary. Jack Hunter," Jack said. "May we come in and talk to you?"

"Captain Hunter, you order this crazy man to put down this grenade at once!" Colonel Kramer shouted. "At once, do you hear me?"

"You'd better shut the hell up, you son of a bitch, or I'll shove this grenade up your ass and let it go," Springs said harshly.

"Did you hear what he said to me, Hunter?"

"Colonel, I think you'd better do what he says," Jack called back. "He's in command right now."

"I always knew the cap'n had more sense than you," Springs said to Kramer.

"Gary, may we come in?" Jack called.

"Yeah," Springs answered. "Yeah, come on in."

Jack and Creech walked between the outside row of sandbags, toward the large steel box in the center. The box was called a conex container, and it was actually used to ship containerized cargo, but, when reinforced with a double wall of sandbags, it made a satisfactory bunker against mortars and small arms fire.

It was dark inside the bunker, and Jack had to stand there for a moment, letting his eyes adjust to the darkness.

"Do you see us now?" Springs asked quietly. "We're over here in the corner."

Jack could see them. Kramer was sitting in the corner and Springs was standing very near him, with the grenade tightly clutched in his hand. His fingers were wrapped around the firing spoon, so the grenade was not yet armed. But the moment he relaxed his grip, which might happen if he were rushed, the spoon would deploy and the grenade would go off.

"Gary, why are you doing this?" Jack asked.

"Why? Why am I doing it?" Springs wiped his eyes with his free hand, and Jack saw that he was crying. "Can you imagine the picture in Honolulu tonight when the plane lands? Charlene, Gary Junior, and the two girls, all standing there, waiting for me, probably . . ." His voice broke and he took a deep breath. "Probably holding one of those leis, you know, to put around my neck. They'll be so excited, so happy, then I won't be there." He turned and looked at Kramer. "I won't be there because of this low-assed son of a bitch!" He shoved the grenade toward Kramer, and for one brief terrifying instant, Jack thought he was going to arm it.

"No!" Kramer screamed, his voice going up in fear.

"Gary no!" Creech shouted.

Springs stopped with his hand right in Kramer's face, then he let his arm drop again.

"Colonel Kramer, why did you do that?" Jack asked. "Gary is eligible for R&R, and his service has been outstanding. Why did you cancel his orders?"

"Colonel Kleuver needed to go to Honolulu," Kramer said. "There were no more slots for brigade, so I gave him Springs's slot. I was going to let Springs take the next slot."

"Didn't it occur to you to check with Springs before you did that?" Jack asked.

"Why the hell should I check with him?" Kramer retorted. "I am acting commander, and R&R slots are my prerogative. I am the one who says who can go and who can't go. They're a privilege, not a right."

"But all the plans he made . . ."

"Colonel Kleuver had made plans as well," Kramer said. "Very important plans."

"Wait a minute," Jack said. "Kleuver came here from Honolulu. His family *lives* there! He could have gone anytime. In fact, if I'm not mistaken, he's already been there once during this tour."

"That's just it," Kramer said. "If I hadn't given him one of our slots, he wouldn't have been able to go a second time."

"So your brown-nosing Colonel Kleuver is what caused all this," Jack said.

"Captain Hunter, I don't like the way you're talking to me," Kramer said.

"Colonel, it doesn't seem to me that you're in much of a position to have a complaint about anything," Jack said. He sighed, then held out his hand. "Give me the grenade, Gary."

"Cap'n, why don't you and Creech just back on out of here now and let me set this thing off?" Springs asked. "I don't want you two to get hurt."

"Come on, Gary," Jack said. "You know you don't really want to do this. If you did you would have already done it. Look at him. Is he worth it?"

"Yes," Springs said resolutely.

"Really? You just told me how hurt your family is going to be in Honolulu," Jack said. "How sad they would all be when they discovered you weren't on that plane. But how would they feel if they got a telegram from the army telling them that you had killed yourself? At least now, they'll get over their disappointment as soon as they see you again. If you do this, it's forever. They'll never see you again."

Springs looked at Jack for a long time. Then, with a sob, he held the grenade toward Jack.

"Thank God," Kramer said, standing up. "Let's get the hell out of here!"

"Sit down, Colonel!" Jack shouted. At the moment Kramer had started up, Springs nearly changed his mind, and in that instant he lost his grip and the handle sprung off. The fuse popped, and the grenade was armed.

"Oh, my God!" Kramer said, sitting back down and looking at the sputtering grenade with an expression that was a cross between sickness and horror.

"Give it to me!" Jack shouted, and Springs, as shocked as everyone else, handed it to him.

Jack had about four seconds left when the grenade was placed in his hand. He stepped to the door of the bunker, then tossed it outside, between the walls of the conex container and the sandbag walls surrounding the bunker. "Get down!" he called, and everyone in the bunker lay flat on the ground.

The grenade went off with a stomach-jarring thump. The people who were standing outside the bunker saw the smoke rise and heard the explosion, and thought that Springs had carried out his threat.

"Jesus, God!" Ed said, more of a prayer than an oath.

Deena, who had stayed outside with Ed, let out a short scream when the grenade went off.

"We've got to get in there," Ed said, starting toward the bunker. "Let's just pray that someone is still alive."

Ed started toward the bunker and Deena, as if moving without will of her own, went with him. But before they had gone more than a few steps, they saw all four people walking out through the sandbag barrier, amazingly, unhurt.

"Jack!" Deena said, and so overjoyed was she to see her most horrifying imagination had not been true, that she ran to him and put her arms around his neck and kissed him full on the mouth.

Jack was taken completely by surprise, and when the kiss ended he looked at her and grinned. "Damn, I'd disarm one grenade a day for that," he teased.

Deena realized then what she had done, and she blushed and took a couple of hesitant steps backward. "I'm sorry, Captain Hunter. I don't know what got into me. It's just that I was so . . . so *scared* and—"

Jack laughed. "Listen, don't worry about it," he said. "I appreciate your concern, and I promise not to hold it against you."

Two M.P.s put handcuffs on Springs then, and started leading him away.

"Gary!" Jack called, and Springs looked around. "I'll get you out of here," he said. "I promise."

"Yeah," Kramer muttered. "He'll get out of here, all right. Straight to Leavenworth for twenty years."

"Colonel Kramer, could you stop by my office and give a statement?" Major Morris asked.

"I'd be glad to, Major," Kramer said. Kramer looked at Jack with eyes which flashed in anger. "You've an accounting too, Captain," he said. "I didn't appreciate the way you talked in there."

"Back off, Kramer," Colonel Mayfair suddenly said, and Jack looked around to see his commanding officer for the first time since returning from Tan San Nhut. "Whatever he said worked. He got the grenade, didn't he?"

"Colonel," Kramer said, "you don't know what all—"

"I don't want to know, either," Colonel Mayfair interrupted. "He said whatever he had to say, and no one is going to question it."

"Yes, sir," Kramer said sullenly. Kramer walked off with Major Morris, and the rest of the crowd began to disperse now that the excitement was over.

"Did you hear why Springs went after him?" Jack asked Colonel Mayfair.

"Yes," Mayfair said. "I don't know what the hell ever possessed Kramer to do such a thing. Believe me, if I had known he'd done that, none of this would have happened."

"Colonel, what's going to happen to Springs?"

"I don't know."

"I wouldn't want to see anything drastic happen to him," Jack said. "Listen, if you knew how much this meant to him—the months of planning, the letters they exchanged, the scrimping—it had to have an effect on his mind."

"Maybe we could get him sent home on a psychiatric," Mayfair suggested. "Combat fatigue."

"I don't think there *is* any such thing as combat fatigue in this war," Jack said.

"Damn, I can't keep up with it. First they called it shell shock, then combat fatigue. What are they calling it now?"

"Nonspecific stress reaction," Deena said.

Colonel Mayfair looked at the pretty young nurse, surprised to hear her join in the conversation.

"Colonel, this is Deena Bell," Jack said. "I picked her up at Tan San Nhut and brought her back as Jane's replacement."

"Well, it looks to me like we replaced one pretty lady with one who's even prettier," Colonel Mayfair said. "Welcome to Phu Bien."

"Thank you," Deena said. She looked toward Springs, now riding away in the M.P. jeep. "Do you suppose you can get him transferred to the hospital?"

"I think so," Colonel Mayfair said. He smiled. "He can't be charged unless the squadron commander signs the charge sheet. And I am the squadron commander."

"Kramer will have those charge sheets on your desk by the time you get back to your office," Jack said dryly.

"You let me handle Bert Kramer," Mayfair said. He pointed to the helicopter. "Are you going to leave my helicopter sitting over here, or are you going to take it back to my pad where it belongs?"

"Oh, I'll take it back," Jack said.

"Can I drop you off somewhere, young lady?" Colonel Mayfair asked Deena.

"She's with me," Jack said. "I'll drop her off."

"You're going to fly her over to the hospital pad?"

Mayfair asked in disbelief. "It's less than a mile away.

"I've got to move the helicopter anyway," Jack said. "Come on, Deena."

Deena started toward the helicopter with Jack.

"Young lady, surely in some orientation course somewhere you learned the difference in rank between a colonel and a captain?" Mayfair teased.

"Not only that, but she can probably tell the difference between a young handsome warrior and an old used-up fart," Jack called back good-naturedly.

"Vipers!" Mayfair said. "I've taken vipers to my bosom!"

"Won't you get into trouble talking to him like that?" Deena asked as she climbed into the helicopter.

"No. He's one of the finest men I've ever known." Jack pulled the shoulder harness down over Deena, and as he did so the back of his hand brushed briefly against her breast. It seemed to him that he could feel it leap at the contact, that the heat of it came through the thin blouse she wore.

"Do you give everyone such service?" Deena asked.

"No, not everyone," Jack admitted.

Deena watched, without appearing to watch, as Jack started the engine, scanned the instruments, and then lifted the ship up. He was a handsome man, to be sure, but there was more than that about him. There was a dynamic energy about him that she felt whenever she got close to him. The touch of the back of his hand to her breast, for example, had been such a small, fleeting thing. And yet it had brought an instant heat, not only to her breasts but to her entire body, dampening her loins and enflaming her desire.

Deena closed her eyes, then looked out the window, down onto the roof of the hospital. This was ridiculous. How could she let one man affect her so? She was not some innocent young high-school girl with a crush on a handsome teacher. She had been through crushes, and even one semiserious affair in which she lost her virginity. And yet the mere physical proximity of this man seemed to stir her more than any man she had ever met.

The helicopter landed on the H pad in front of the hospital, and Jack pointed through the windshield.

"Right in there and to the left you'll find Major McGee," he said. "She's the chief of nurses. She'll take care of you."

"Thanks," Deena said. "For the ride, and for everything."

"Maybe I'll catch you at the Red Bull," Jack said.

"The Red Bull?"

Jack laughed. "You'll find out about the Red Bull."

Deena got out, closed the door, then stepped back and held her hat down on her head while the helicopter lifted up and started over toward another part of the field.

When Deena went inside the hospital, she saw an orderly making circles on the floor with a barely damp mop.

"Excuse me," Deena said. "Could you—"

The orderly pointed toward a door before Deena could finish her question, and then went right back to mopping without saying a word.

"Thanks," Deena said.

Major McGee was a large woman. She wasn't exactly fat, she was just large, with broad shoulders, practically no waist, and big, muscular arms and legs.

"We just lost our post-op nurse," Major McGee said. "I'm going to put you in there."

"Jane Goss?"

"Yes," McGee said. "Do you know her?"

"Not really," Deena said. "But I met her in Saigon. Captain Hunter took her to Tan San Nhut and he brought me back."

McGee smiled. "Jack Hunter?"

"Yes. Do you know him?"

"Honey, what nurse doesn't?"

"Oh?" Deena said, with a note of disappointment in her voice. "You mean he's a ladies' man?"

"Well, not exactly," McGee said. "There isn't a nurse in the hospital who wouldn't welcome a tumble from him, if you know what I mean. But he's taken property, all locked up."

"Oh," Deena said. She smiled, hoping that it reflected humor rather than disappointment. "Who's the lucky nurse?"

"It's not a nurse," McGee said. "It's none other than Madam Ngyuen herself. Our handsome Captain Jack Hunter is the Dragon Lady's lover."

10

STACEY had no air conditioner in her room in Da Nang. She did have a small oscillating fan which sat on a footlocker beside her bunk, humming and turning slowly from her head to her feet, directing its cooling breeze over her body.

It was dark, and Stacey lay with her head on Frank's naked shoulder, feeling his even, steady breathing as he slept. The air still hung heavy with the smell of their lovemaking, and she carried his wetness deep in her womb. She allowed her hand to slide down across his body, over his flat stomach, into the brush of hair, and then stopped on that part of him which was now slack and spent, but which had a short time earlier thrust her up to the stars with pure rapture. She squeezed it once, and even in his sleep Frank reacted, twitching where she held him.

It was at moments like this that Stacey knew she was in love with Frank Bell. She knew that Frank loved her, too, because they had spoken of it to each other, and cried over the impossibility of it, and swore that they were going to stop seeing each other before anyone got hurt. But both knew that it was already too late for that.

Stacey didn't know if Captain Morrow knew about them or not, but a few remarks he had made had started her to wondering. Captain Morrow wasn't all that tactful in his remarks, either. He started talking to Stacey about the differences between her life-style and his, the differences in their backgrounds. Then he tried to "soften" his remarks by saying that Frank Bell, just as a very coincidental for-instance, was a low-ranking enlisted man, while Stacey, as a State Department employee, enjoyed the rank and privileges of an officer. But Stacey knew that Morrow didn't mean that at all. Morrow was talking about the fact that Frank Bell was white, and she was black.

Stacey knew well all the subtle inferences a bigot used when trying to couch his prejudice in other words. Stacey knew, because Stacey had felt the fullest possible brunt of racial discrimination. Frank couldn't have realized how much of a joy it was to Stacey when she discovered that her brother was still alive, because Frank didn't realize that Mack was the only member of Stacey's family still alive. All the others were gone now, victims of unbelievable bigotry and brutality.

Stacey had never really known Mack well, not until the last five years. That was because Mack was actually Stacey's half-brother. Mack's mother had left Stacey's father when Mack was just a baby; she was a Negro from Cleveland, Ohio, who couldn't take the treatment that was standard fare for the *niggers* of Alabama. She had begged Mack's father to come back to Ohio with her, but Mack's father insisted that Alabama was his home and he would never leave.

Two years after Mack's mother left, she got a divorce and Mack's father married again, this time to the half-white woman who was to become Stacey's mother. There were four more children born of that marriage, but Stacey was the oldest. Five children, coming as quickly as they did, wore Stacey's mother out, and she died when Stacey was just fifteen-years-old. Stacey's father told her then that he was counting on her to be the woman of the house.

For the next three years, Stacey tried as hard as she knew how. She completed her high school education because her father wouldn't let her quit. But neither could she leave after that. She kept house, fixed supper for the children every night, tucked them into bed, and heard their prayers.

Stacey's father worked as a cutter on a sawmill gang for a decent white man named George Sims. He had to leave before sunup and rarely got home before sundown, even in the long daylight hours of summer.

Fixing supper hadn't been too hard for Stacey. There wasn't much to choose from; most of the time they had fatback and dry beans. When it was in season, Stacey would gather the poke salad greens which grew wild along the fence row. They had a bit of a garden out back in a cleared patch.

Keeping the kids clean was harder. Sometimes when money was short, Stacey would walk down to the service station on the highway. She'd wait for her chance to slip into the restroom and fill a Mason jar with soap from the liquid dispenser. If there were any extra rolls of toilet paper or paper towels and she had a coat to hide them under, she'd take those, too.

Beside her, in the bed, Frank rolled over, and Stacey had to move her arm. It had gone to sleep and she sat up, working at the tingle which traveled from her wrist to her elbow. Her aching arm reminded her of the pain of that night five years ago. She didn't like to remember it. Most of the time she kept it blanked out of her mind, but it kept coming back.

It was on Saturday night in the fall, and she'd just laid supper out on the table for the children. They didn't have a television, but they did have a radio, and she had heard the score of the Ohio State game. The sportscasters were talking about the brilliant play of her half-brother, and she had been very proud. Mack had come to Alabama on four or five occasions to visit his father, and he had become somewhat of a hero to Stacey.

Suddenly Stacey's father came bursting through the front door, his face a mask of terror.

"Stacey, girl. I'm goin' to have to get runnin'. They's twenty dollars hid 'neath a loose board in the outhouse. I'll try and get some more to you when I can. See Mister Sims. He'll help you if you need it."

"Daddy!" Stacey said, her voice bordering on hysteria. "What's wrong?"

"They's a bunch of white men got it in their heads I done raped a white woman," he said. He yanked rubber boots out from under the bed and began pulling them on. "I'm goin' through the swamp," he added.

"Why would they think such a thing, daddy?" Stacey asked. She gripped the handle of the iron skillet, holding on to it as tightly as she could, as if it would help her hold on to the very fabric of life.

"They caught us together. But it wasn't rape, girl. We been sportin' off 'n on now for near on to a year."

"Oh, God, daddy!" The skillet fell with a clatter to the stove. "You should have known better!"

Stacey heard the sound of pick-up trucks, then the cursing and calling of men from outside. Ten-year-old Albert darted inside as a sudden flood of light spilled into the shack. There was more cursing and calling from outside. The younger children gathered around Stacey and her father.

"It's too late," Stacey's father said fearfully.

"No, daddy! Run! Go out the window!"

"Hey! You! Nigger in there! Get your black ass out here, boy, or we'll burn down that shack with you 'n all them little snot-nosed kids you got running around."

"Daddy!" Stacey pleaded. "Run, please run!"

"It's too late, girl. They're probably all around the house."

The unbelievingly loud report of a gun shattered the front window. Glass crashed into the house and scattered all over the floor.

"Get down!" Stacey's father ordered, slamming the two youngest to the floor himself.

"That's just a warning, nigger!"

Stacey stared into her father's face. It was a horrible ashen color, and his hands were shaking.

"I've got to go out there. The young ones, they'll—" He gestured toward them, then, before Stacey could move, he had the front door open.

He stood silhouetted in the beams of light from three pick-ups. Crouched low, Stacey scurried to the smashed window and tried to see out. She could see only the glare of light and shadows.

The door to one of the trucks was open and the radio was playing loudly. Stacey could hear the ending strains of Nancy Sinatra singing "These Boots Are Made For Walking."

"All right," the announcer said. *"You are listening to the big bam, WBAM in Montgomery. Time now is eight o'clock. Time for the news, brought to you by Tube Rose Snuff. If your snuff's too strong, it's wrong. Use Tube Rose."*

"Oh, Jim, Jim, Jim, Jim," one of the white men said in a singsong voice coming from the darkness. "What for did you want to go 'n stick your black pecker into a white lady for? You should'a know'd better."

"It weren't rape, you can ask the lady," Stacey's father called out in a quivering voice.

"She tried to tell us it weren't rape," the white voice replied from the darkness. "But after we knocked her aroun' a bit, why it come to her that it prob'ly was rape after all."

Stacey stood frozen in fear, not even conscious of the fact she was standing bare-footed in broken glass.

"Yaaaahoooool" a voice broke in, thrusting incongruously into the proceedings. "War Eagle!"

"What the hell got into you, Harley Mack?"

"I just yelled War Eagle! Didn't you hear the

man on the radio? Auburn just beat the piss out of Vanderbilt."

"Well, who the hell *don't* beat the piss out of Vanderbilt? Turn that son of a bitch off."

"*Governor Wallace stated today that if he cannot succeed himself, his wife, Lurlene, will run—*" The radio went dead. The one called Harley Mack slammed the door to the truck and walked over to stand with the others.

"Well, come on. We gonna kill a nigger, or ain't we? You made me turn off the radio, so let's get on with it."

"We gonna do it. We gonna do it," the one who had just been talking to Stacey's father said. "I just ain't figured out how yet."

"Well, shit! Let's just shoot the son of a bitch and get it over with," Harley Mack grumbled.

"No!" Stacey screamed. She ran out of the house and slid to a stop in front of her father.

"Well, lookie here, just lookie here now," Harley Mack said. He licked his lips. "Lord, ain't you a purty 'un for a nigger! Looks to me like Mary Lou ain't the only white woman ol' Jim's been with. Lessen I miss my guess purty good, this here girl's got a white mama. Or at least, a high yella. Your mama a white woman, girl?"

"Please," Stacey begged. "Please, just go away and leave us alone. My daddy's an honest man."

"Girl, get back in the house," her father said, shoving her aside. "Get!" Stacey fell to her knees. A man roared with laughter.

"Hey, with that good-lookin' little piece of high yella stuff, why you reckon ol' Jim had to go and mess aroun' with a white woman for?"

"This here is his daughter."

"Since when does that matter to niggers?" Harley Mack roared, and they all laughed. Stacey stood up as rage and humiliation filled her.

"You bastards!" she yelled. "You rotten bastards!"

"Hey, she's a wildcat," one of the men snickered. "Listen, I jus' got me 'n idea. Why'nt we just tear us off a little o' this while we're out here?"

"Run, Stacey," her father urged. The fear in his voice reached her and she turned quickly, but got no more than four steps when she was caught by two of the men. She fought and bit, but they managed to rip her dress off. She felt the sudden blast of late autumn air on her naked body.

"Look at that," someone said, and there was almost a reverence in his voice. "You ever seen anyone that purty?"

"You gonna talk or screw?"

"Yeah, let's get on with it."

"You leave my daughter alone, you white sons of bitches," Stacey's father called, yanking at the arm of one of the men, trying to break the circle of staring men.

Harley Mack turned, gave Stacey's father a violent shove, then raised his shotgun. Stacey's body jumped with the gun blast that echoed through the Alabama woods. In the brief silence that followed, she looked in horror at the bleeding body of her father, twitching in the dirt.

Rough hands suddenly grabbed her and threw her down. She felt the forceful invasion of her flesh, once, twice, three times. She stopped fighting and lay there in a kind of helpless stupor, waiting for it all to end, for death to come to her too.

As the last man crouched over her, she smelled

burning wood. Then she felt the heat of licking flames. The kids! The house! She screamed, raking the man's face with her fingernails as she fought to get out from under him.

"Shut up! You didn't fight the others none. Why are you fighting me?"

"The kids," Stacey sobbed. "The kids are in the house."

"What the . . . ah, Jesus God! They's kids in there. Get up offen her, you stupid son of a bitch!" someone shouted.

The man released her and Stacey ran to the house, but the children, in their fear, had locked the door. She clawed at the weathered timbers. She pleaded with the men to help her, but no one came.

Only the terrified screams of the children answered her, then those too dwindled into silence and there was only the sound of the fire as it ate at the dried wood.

The intense heat drove Stacey backward. She turned and looked into the faces of the men. One cleared his throat. Another stared at the toes of his work-scarred brogans. Guns were picked up, there was a scuffling of feet as they climbed into their trucks. As they drove away, Stacey sat on a tree stump in front of the burning house. It was the smooth-topped stump the little ones used for a table when they played house. . . .

George Sims, the owner of the sawmill where her father had worked, found her there the next morning, sitting naked in front of the burned-out house. Her body was shaking, but she didn't feel the coldness of the weather. The weather was outside her body, but Stacey was frozen inside.

George took Stacey home with him, and finally

managed to get through to Mack. He told Mack what had happened, and asked him if he could bring Stacey up to Columbus, Ohio, where Mack was a senior in college. Mack agreed at once, and George drove Stacey up to Columbus in his own car.

Mack helped Stacey find a job, and got her enrolled in the university. Stacey buried herself in her studies, and resolved to dedicate her life to change society. She was recruited by the State Department after graduation, and was sent to Vietnam to work with the people of Vietnam, to help the refugees of the war-torn country build new lives for themselves.

Stacey's brother Mack had been so impressed with Stacey's dedication to reshaping society that he had become active in the antiwar movement in the States, and Stacey was never prouder of her brother than she had been when he turned down a pro-football contract in order to carry on his antiwar work. Stacey had cried bitter tears of anguish when she thought that he had died, perishing in a fire as had her other brothers and sisters. The realization that he was still alive had made her supremely happy.

Only Frank was complicating her life now. For beyond the racial differences and the problems that could eventually cause them was the feeling that she would be abandoning her resolve to change society. For when Stacey was with Frank, she could think only of Frank, and nothing else. He filled her mind and her being, and she would have been jealous of his total domination of her had she not loved him so.

Stacey nudged Frank in the darkness to wake

him up. It would not do for him to spend the entire night there.

Frank moaned once, then, grudgingly, he sat up. He reached for his clothes.

"What time is it?" he asked.

"About two in the morning."

"Stacey," Frank said as he pulled on his socks. "Has Captain Morrow said anything to you?"

"About what?" Stacey asked, feeling her heart leap in alarm.

"About us."

"Not exactly . . ."

"But he has said something?"

"Yes," Stacey said.

"That explains it."

"Explains what? Frank, baby, what are you talking about?"

Frank reached for Stacey and put his arms around her. "I didn't want to have to tell you this," he said, "but there's no way to avoid it. You're going to find out sooner or later."

"Find out what?"

"I'm leaving, Stacey. I've been reassigned."

"Reassigned! Where to? Where are you going?"

"I'm going to remote Team Alpha," Frank said. Stacey gasped. "Oh, Frank, no!"

Remote Team Alpha was the name of a special patrol which spent up to ninety days at a time in the jungle. Though there were no regulations against assigning anyone to the team against their wishes, it was, by tradition, composed only of those men who volunteered.

"I'm leaving tomorrow," Frank said.

"Frank, you didn't volunteer for it, did you?"

"God, no! Honey, in the first place, I've seen enough field duty to satisfy me. I don't feel like I have anything to prove by spending three months tramping around in the bush. And in the second place, I wouldn't want to go anywhere where I'd be unable to see you for three months."

"Then why don't you try to get out of it?" Stacey asked. "You know, go see the colonel or someone. I mean, you didn't volunteer for it and—"

"You don't have to volunteer for it. If you get assigned, you're assigned, and that's that."

"But you could *try* to get out of it!"

"No, Stacey, I can't," Frank said. He looked at her with an intense expression in his face and in his eyes. "You know me better than that now for sure, don't you?"

"Yes," Stacey said sadly. "Yes, I know you better than that."

Frank finished dressing as Stacey sat on the edge of her bunk. She was crying, but she wasn't crying aloud. Tears were tracking down her cheeks, falling in silence.

"I'll be gone when you wake up in the morning," Frank said. "It'll be a while before we see each other again."

"I know . . ."

Frank came over and kissed her once on each cheek, stopping the tears in their tracks.

"Be good," he said. Then, quickly, he slipped through her door and out into the soft Vietnamese night.

11

THE BLACK DRAGON conducted another operation flawlessly, hitting a V.C. strongpoint with sudden brutal and unexpected fury. The body count of V.C. dead was very high, although Colonel Ngyuen also lost several of his own soldiers; he had committed them without corps artillery support because he didn't want to share any of the fruits of his victory. There were no American losses.

The pilots came back from the mission that night in good spirits, and they stood around the Red Bull reflying the missions with their hands. They laughed and talked and the tensions and the fears they had held in check for the whole day escaped in the nervous animation of their conversations.

Jack was late coming to the Red Bull, because it was necessary for him to sign the final papers authorizing a "compassionate reassignment" to Specialist Six, Gary Springs. That meant that Springs would be returning to the States, after only ten months of a normal twelve-month tour.

Springs had been released from the hospital after an overnight stay and confined to the company area. Despite the fact that he was going home earlier than expected, he hadn't fully recovered from the trauma of missing the R&R, or from the incident with Kramer, and he avoided the others whenever he could. Springs became a shadow, eating alone, spending time reading or attending to the light duty to which he was assigned. Not even his old friends Creech, nor Jack himself, seemed to have access to him. Jack was afraid that Springs was going to be one of the silent casualties of the war, with problems which might surface years after the fact.

Over in the Red Bull, Deena sat at a table nursing a gin and tonic, looking for Jack. She hadn't told anyone that she was looking for Jack, and indeed had not fully confessed that fact to herself. She searched for him among the men at the bar. They still wore their momex flight suits, now unbuttoned for comfort. Their shoulder-holsters yawned emptily because most of them had taken their pistols to their rooms, though they continued to wear their holsters and belts. The belts were lined with loops that were filled with .38 caliber cartridges, so that the men looked something like pictures Deena had seen of Pancho Villa's banditos.

"Hey," Bostic said, sucking the foam off the top of a beer, then wiping his mouth with the back of his hand. "Did you see what kind of form the ol' Black Dragon was in?"

"I never saw him once we got started," one of the other pilots said.

"Well, let me tell you," Bostic said. "The son of a bitch set up a command post on hill 232, and he stood there in *dress whites* watching the operation through binoculars."

"Damn, like watchin' a parade or somethin'."

"Yeah," Bostic said. "And he was flanked by his color guard, carrying not the South Vietnamese flag, but his own."

Jack came into the Red Bull then, and Deena watched him as he took his hat off and ran his hand through his hair, looking around the room. His hat, which had a pair of black wings sitting atop the two black bars of his rank, got stuffed into one of the many leg pockets of his flight suit. He saw Deena and smiled at her, then came to join her at her table.

"You're sitting all alone?" he asked. "How did that happen? I would have thought half the squadron would be over here with you."

"They're still too busy flying," Deena said, indicating the group at the bar.

Jack looked toward them. "Yeah, this is the kind of mission that you can enjoy reflying. Everything went by the book—lots of excitement but no one was hurt."

"Would you rather be up there with them?" Deena asked coyly.

"Instead of here with you? Are you crazy? Besides, I don't get the opportunity to refly the missions. Their job ends when we land; mine is just starting." He put the back of his hand against his forehead. "The rigors of command, you know," he said, affecting a put-upon air.

"I've heard it's most unusual for a captain to be a commander over here," Deena commented.

"There are plenty of grunt captains who are company commanders," Jack said. "Grunt" was the word for infantry. "To have a combat air command as a captain is a bit unusual."

"How did you get it?"

"I'm senior captain in the squadron, and so far Colonel Mayfair has managed to avoid taking aboard any majors to shoot me out of the saddle," Jack said.

"You like Colonel Mayfair, don't you?"

"Yes," Jack said. "I like him a lot. And I give thanks every day that his DROS is just one month before Colonel Kramer's, because they won't give Kramer the squadron for only thirty days."

"What about the soldier with the grenade? Is he going to be okay?"

"Springs will be departing Tan San Nhut tomorrow for the land of the big P.X.," Jack said.

Deena laughed. "I take it you mean the States."

"You got it, baby, the place where door knobs and women's eyes are round."

"Hey, Jack," Bostic called from the bar. "Jack, come up here and kick the shit out of this obnoxious warrant officer for me." Everyone laughed at Bostic's suggestion.

"I'm your commanding officer, Bob, not your slack man," Jack answered. "If you want the shit kicked out of a warrant officer, you're going to have to do it yourself."

Bob looked at the big officer who was standing beside him, smiling down at him from behind a large handlebar moustache.

"Listen, didn't you used to play for the Oakland Raiders?" Bob asked the big warrant.

"They wouldn't let me play with them," the warrant said. "They were afraid I'd hurt some of their little boys."

"That's what I thought," Bob said. He cleared his throat. "Let me buy you a beer, and let's talk about you being my slack man."

The bar laughed, and Deena, laughing with them, turned back to Jack. "What's a slack man?"

"When you run into more than you can handle, your slack man comes in to take up the slack for you. Listen, you want to go out to the bunker with me?"

"The bunker?" Deena asked. "What do you mean?"

"Come on, I'll show you," Bob said. He walked over to the bar and got a cold six-pack of beer, then led Deena through the door and out into soft night of the flower garden around the Red Bull.

"How are you going to open those?" Deena asked.

"I've got a P-38 hanging from my dogtag chain," Jack said, pulling his dogtags out and dangling them, showing her the small but very effective army can opener known as a P-38. "You know, there have been a lot of words written about the best piece of equipment to come out of World War II. Some say it was the German .88 howitzer, some say the Sherman tank, and some say the B-29 bomber." He held up the little P-38. "My vote would have to go for this little piece of equipment. It's the only thing that's still being issued in the exact form of its World War II design."

"Are you a military historian?" Deena asked.

Jack laughed. "No, not really," he said. "But I'm a family historian, and in my family that's almost the same thing. There was a Hunter in the French and Indian War, and there's a Hunter in this one.

For a country which espouses peace, we've seen one hell of a lot of war in our history."

"Do you think we've been wrong?"

"Who can tell?" Jack said. "Sometimes I think maybe the Black Dragon is right. Maybe the warriors should leave such philosophical questions to the politicians. The only thing is, when the politicians fail they call on the warriors to take up the slack."

"Is that why you're known as the Reluctant Hero?" Deena asked. "Because you have views like that?"

Jack laughed. "The Reluctant Hero is the title some magazine writer dreamed up. I wish I'd never granted that interview. I either get teased about it, or find that it was totally misunderstood, and some people get downright hostile."

"I guess you heard about Larry DeWitt?" Deena asked. "The very week that article came out about you, DeWitt, Burton and a girl were trapped in a house. The house burned and everyone inside was killed."

"Yeah, I read about that in *Stars and Stripes*," Jack said. "But they haven't identified the bodies, have they?"

"No, but it has to be them. Who else could it be? They were both seen driving to the house with a girl. That fits, doesn't it? Two men and a girl?"

"I guess . . ."

"The only thing," Deena went on. "The station wagon they drove up in drove away. The police think someone stole it during all the commotion, but there's always the chance that someone from the house could have escaped some way. I don't know. I think the whole thing is so tragic. I mean who would honestly believe that the United States would ever have political fugitives, like in Russia, or Germany before the World War?"

"There's the bunker," Jack said.

"Why, it's right in the middle of the flower garden," Deena said. "It's not even a bunker. I thought you were talking about one of those ugly conex containers with sandbags and barbed wire."

"Yes, it is a bunker," Jack said. "Or at least, it *was* a bunker. It was a French bunker."

"French?"

"Remember them? Before it was the Vietnam war, it was the French–Indo–China War. They fought over here for ten years. This is the remains of one of their bunkers."

The bunker was no more than a grassy rampart, forming four sides to enclose a depression in the ground. Flowers were now growing all over the rampart, and an old fountain was in the middle of the depression. The fountain was a statue of a young boy holding a fish on his shoulder, with water spilling from the fish's mouth. It was green with corrosion and algae was growing in the fount, but compared to everything else about Phu Bien it was as lovely as the loveliest garden of Versailles.

"I had no idea this was here," Deena said as she and Jack sat down on the grassy knoll.

"I think the people who owned the villa came up with this as the only way to utilize a bunker. After all, how many homes need a bunker in their back yard?"

"But it's lovely," Deena said. "And down in here, shielded by the sides, it's almost as if we managed to shut ourselves off from the rest of the world. You can't see the barbed wire fences, or the sandbags, or the guns."

The skies flashed with light, and they heard the distant rumble of artillery.

"You can sure hear them, though," Jack said. He opened two cans of beer and handed one to Deena.

"Do you like Vietnam?" Deena asked, taking the beer.

"Do you mean do I like being here, fighting?"

"No, I mean the country, the people, the culture."

"I think it's a beautiful country," Jack said. "It's a damn shame it's been torn by war for nearly forty years. As for the people and their culture, I'd like to see them have forty years of peace to develop a culture, and to show the world what kind of people they might be."

"What about Madam Ngyuen?"

Jack looked up quickly. "What do you mean?"

Deena wished she could retract the question, but it was there now, hanging between them like a block of ice, and she had to go on with it.

"I've heard some things," she said. "I've heard that—"

Jack interrupted her by putting his fingers to her lips. "I'm not sure what you've heard," he said. "And I don't know how the story got around. I've never told a soul about anything."

"Will you tell me?"

Jack took a long, thoughtful drink, then discarded the empty can. "Yeah," he finally said. "I don't know why I should, but I will."

Jack told of the first time he had ever seen Madam Ngyuen, and of her proposition to him when he escorted her home. Then he told of receiving the letter from her a while later when she again propositioned him, this time giving him an address in Saigon.

"I went," Jack said. "And she was there. We met, and . . ."

"You made love?" Deena asked quietly when he didn't go on.

"Yes," Jack admitted. He looked at Deena with a pained expression in his face. "Deena, you can't believe how guilty that made me feel. I remember lying there in bed, listening to the clack of the soup vendors' sticks, and thinking how wrong I had been. I've never been back."

"Has she contacted you again?"

"She's sent me two or three letters, but I haven't answered her."

Deena broke into a smile. "Then you aren't what one would call her lover, are you?"

"No," Jack said. "Why are you so—"

But Jack's question was interrupted by Deena's lips, for she put her arms around him then, and pulled his face to hers in a consuming, almost urgent kiss.

"Well," Jack said, when at last the kiss ended. "What was that all about? Not that I mind, mind you," he added with an easy smile.

"I guess you could just say that I'm happy still to be in the running."

"What do you mean, in the running?" Jack asked. "I'd say you're a front runner." Jack kissed her again, this time as the aggressor, and as he kissed her, he gently pushed her back until they were both lying on the mattress of grass. Jack's lips traveled from her mouth down along her throat, and down to the top button of her fatigue shirt. He unbuttoned it, and kissed her flesh behind the button, then proceeded down the shirt, opening a button and kissing, opening a button and kissing, until Deena was lying there with her shirt fully unbuttoned, and Jack's kisses falling from her shoulder to her belly button.

Jack moved his hands beneath her, and Deena positioned herself to help him, so that the bra was removed, freeing her breasts. Jack tenderly stroked the nipple with his thumb until it stood swollen and straining to be loved.

He kissed each nipple, feeling her body jump with the sensations he was causing her and listening to the soft moans of pleasure which escaped from deep in her throat.

"We should have a bed with silk sheets, and a door to close," Jack said.

"No," Deena said, her voice was choked with passion as she spoke. "Oh, no, what could be better than to be here, among the flowers, under the stars? This is perfect, absolutely perfect."

Deena removed her pants then, and Jack looked at her moon-silvered body, with the small though well-formed breasts, topped by straining nipples, and eager thighs beckoning him on. At that very moment they were right in the middle of a helicopter airbase which included nearly one thousand soldiers, out in the open air, less than fifty yards from the hustle and bustle of the crowded officers' club. And yet, Jack felt as if they were alone on the white sand of a South Pacific island, the only two people left on earth.

His blood turned to liquid fire, and he quickly took off his own clothes, now abandoning any thought that they might be seen—in fact, stimulated by the very danger of it. He lowered himself over her, feeling her softness, her moistness, as he went into her.

Jack thrust into her again and again, blotting out all the world save this tiny corner of paradise, and she rose against him, giving him all that was hers to give.

Jack felt her muscles contract, and then the jerking and thrusting of her pelvis, and he knew that it was beginning for Deena. She threw her arms around his neck, trying to pull him into her, nibbling at his ear and whimpering out her rapture, so that he could hear as well as feel her ultimate pleasure. Then Jack let himself go, feeling as if he were somehow receding from the tips of his fingers and the tips of his toes, even from the scalp of his head. He was collapsing in on himself like a gigantic implosion, like a star going supernova, and then, with the energy concentrated in one great mass, exploding outward again, rushing through the jerking, sensitive connection which held him attached to the woman beneath him, pulling him into her so that the two of them became one and their souls intermingled.

And then there was the tenderness. They lay together without talking, looking at the stars and the distant rose-colored lights, and listening to the rumble of a world which was not theirs, but a world gone mad, and Jack wondered if this could be love.

12

HEADQUARTERS
USARV
APO U, S. Forces 96037

SPECIAL ORDERS NO. 282   23 October, 1969

E X T R A C T

17. DA 348. By direction of the Secretary of the
Army, following individual is authorized to accept
the award of the VIETNAMESE CROSS OF GAL-
LANTRY. HUNTER, JACK CAVALIER 02214390
CPT 062B HQ USARV APO 96307

ADMINISTRATIVE DATA
Auth: Para 3-58, Sex XV LTR 14 Jun 1963
HOR: Grafton, Virginia
PLEAD: Ft. Benning, GA

SPECIAL INSTRUCTIONS

Award will be presented by Colonel Ngyuen Thom, CO Presidential Strike Forces (Lightning) ARVN

FOR THE COMMANDER

> T. L. Hanson
> Colonel, GS
> Chief of Staff

OFFICIAL:

GREGG A. LYONS
1LT, AGC
Asst Adj Gen

DISTRIBUTION: 110 AG Gen Mail Bra, 5 AG Orders, 10 Individual indic, 2 CG USARV, 2 HQDA (DAAG-ASO-o) Wash DC 20315, 2 HQDA (DAPO-OPD-INF) Wash DC 20315

C-I-T-A-T-I-O-N

In that Captain Jack C. Hunter, 02214390, did distinguish himself by heroism while participating in aerial flight as evidenced by voluntary action above and beyond the call of duty, to wit: Captain Hunter, on the morning of 5 August, 1969, while acting commanding officer and strike force leader of A Troop of the Fifth Air Cavalry, (Cobra Attack) in an aerial and ground assault against the heavily fortified position of Chat Nhyn, observed air-bursting antiaircraft fire defending the position. With great disregard for his own safety, Captain Hunter proceeded against the antiaircraft emplacements, personally accounting for one gun position, and through his leadership, eliminating all the positions. With the enemy guns thus neutralized, the operation was allowed to continue, meeting with great success. Forces of the Army of the Republic of Vietnam, under the command of Colonel Ngyuen Thom, routed the enemy from Chat Nhyn, and destroyed the command and nerve center, rendering the facilities useless for further activity. Many V.C. and North Vietnamese soldiers and underground operations were killed, and the senior V.C. commander of the district was captured, all made possible by Captain Hunter's heroic action. Captain Hunter's actions were in keeping with the highest traditions of the military service, and of the cooperative counter-insurgent operations of the combined powers of the United States and the Republic of Vietnam, and reflect great credit to himself and the United States Army.

For The Commander

> Creighton W. Abrams,
> Commanding General
> United States Forces, Vietnam

OFFICIAL:

GREGG A. LYONS
1LT, AGC
Asst Adg Gen

Jack was embarrassed by the award of the Vietnamese Cross of Gallantry. If the award was to be given, it should have been given to all the pilots who participated in the operation, but the award singled him out as the sole recipient. He also felt that he had done no more than his duty, and certainly had not gone "above and beyond the call," as was indicated by the accompanying citation.

Jack apologized to the others but there were no hard feelings. The Cross of Gallantry was a Vietnamese medal with a name far more impressive than its actual merit, and Jack hoped that the award, when it did come, would be slipped through distribution, as were the orders which arrived unexpectedly.

But Jack was disappointed. Not only was the Black Dragon going to award the medal personally, he had also requested and been granted a full-scale awards ceremony, complete with a band and a parade. Jack tried in every way he knew to get out of it, but he was unable to avoid it.

"But I think it's exciting," Deena said. Deena and Jack were having dinner at the Red Bull, Jack demolishing his usual steak with an egg, while Deena had the roast chicken special.

"You think it's exciting to be standing out there in front of several hundred men, receiving a worthless medal that you didn't earn?" Jack asked.

"But you did earn it," Deena said. "You did do what this citation says you did, didn't you?"

"Yes," Jack said. "But so did everyone else in the troop. It's our *job*, Deena."

"But you were the commander."

"That didn't mean anything to the V.C. gun crews," Jack said. "They didn't try any harder to get me than they did anyone else."

"Nevertheless, I think you should be proud of it," Deena said. "I know I will be, standing out there watching."

Colonel Kramer stepped into the Red Bull then,

and as it was the dinner hour and most tables were full, he walked over to the table where Jack and Deena were eating.

"May I join you?" he asked. "All the other tables seem to be full."

"Please do," Deena said, smiling up at him.

"Jack, I don't believe I've met this attractive young lady," Kramer said, smiling broadly at Deena.

Jack caught Kramer's use of his first name, a means of ingratiating him with Deena no doubt. He winced, but he said nothing about it.

"Colonel Kramer, this is Lieutenant Bell," he said.

"Oh, we can do better than that," Kramer said. "My name is Bert." He offered his hand to Deena.

"Deena," she said.

"So, have you heard about the award our boy will be receiving tomorrow?" Kramer asked. The waitress came to the table then, and Kramer looked at Jack's steak and egg, made a face, then looked at Deena's roast chicken. "I'll have that," he said, pointing to Deena's plate.

"I've heard about it," Deena said. "I'm coming to the award ceremony. I think it will be very exciting."

"Oh, it will be, I'm sure," Kramer said. He laughed. "You know, Jack, for a reluctant hero you're certainly going to be in the limelight tomorrow."

"Not by my choice, Colonel, as you well know," Jack said quietly.

"Yes, sir," Kramer went on. "T.V. crews are going to be here, newspaper and magazine reporters, maybe even your friend from *Newstime*, and of course, dozens of VIPs. Oh, and guess who else is going to be here?"

"I haven't the slightest idea," Jack said.

"Madam Ngyuen," Kramer said brightly. He looked at Deena. "You've heard of Madam Ngyuen, haven't you, Deena? She's Colonel Ngyuen's wife."

"Yes, I've heard of her," Deena said.

"But have you ever *seen* her?" Kramer asked. "She is a very beautiful woman. Of course," he laughed, "I suppose Jack could tell you more about that than I."

"What do you mean by that?" Jack asked, looking up and staring at Kramer through eyes that were angry and cold.

"Nothing," Kramer said lightly. "I don't mean anything by it, really. It's just that, well, you *do* know her personally, and have a better insight as to what she's really like than any of the rest of us. I'm sure she's coming to the ceremony tomorrow because it involves you."

"Madam Ngyuen seems the type of person who enjoys making public appearances," Jack said. "She attends all such functions with her husband."

"Yes, but the award of the Vietnamese Cross of Gallantry?" Kramer said. "I don't mean to belittle what you did, but the medal itself is of very little consequence. Many get it just by serving as advisors to the ARVN troops."

"Then let's not make it more than it is," Jack said. He pushed his plate aside, and looked over at Deena. "Are you about ready to leave?"

"Oh, there's going to be a band here after dinner," Deena said. "Aren't we going to stay for it?"

"No," Jack said.

"Oh, please do stay, Jack," Deena said. "It's been so long since I heard live music."

"You stay if you want to," Jack said sullenly. "I've got some things to do."

"Listen, this is a pretty good band," Kramer put in quickly, seizing the opportunity to step in. "I've heard them before. I'll stay and catch it with you."

Deena looked at Kramer in surprise, and then up at Jack, hoping Jack would get her off the hook. Instead Jack just looked at Kramer, and then at Deena. "Suit yourself," he said, turning and walking away from the table.

"Jack!" Deena called.

"Let him go," Kramer said. "Don't worry about it, he'll be all right. You haven't been in the country very long, have you?"

"About six weeks," Deena said.

"You'll learn to recognize those symptoms in some pilots who put in a lot of hours each month. They're often quiet and sullen."

"Jack says you put in as many hours as nearly anyone in the squadron," Deena said.

Kramer looked at her in surprise. "He told you that?" Kramer smiled. "I wouldn't have thought Captain Hunter would admit it. He isn't one of my biggest fans, you know. Yes, I do put in as many hours as the others, but I'm a bit more mature, and perhaps better able to handle it than some others. This isn't a put-down, merely an observation."

Deena looked at Kramer, seeing him for the first time as a person in his own right. All she knew of Kramer was what Jack had told her about him. He had pointed Kramer out to her, so she did know what he looked like, and his blond hair, light blue eyes and handsome features had come through, despite the evil picture Jack had painted.

"He was upset about the business over Springs's R&R, I know that," Deena said, wondering how Kramer would react to the subject.

"Yes," Kramer said. "Well, we all were. Believe me, Deena, if I'd known Specialist Springs had made such extensive arrangements, I mean bringing his wife over and all, I would never have pulled his orders. I'll bet no one has ever told you the other side of the story, have they?"

"No," Deena admitted.

Kramer finished his dinner and pushed his plate aside, then took out a cigarette package and lighter. Jack had often described Kramer's odd habit of making a stack with the lighter and package, and then flipping the stack back and forth. It was his only way of staying off cigarettes, Jack said.

Kramer sighed. "Colonel Kleuver's daughter was getting married, and he wanted to attend the wedding. The R&R system over here is designed more for the enlisted men than the officers. Generally, we don't mind that—after all, being an officer entails obligation as well as rank and privileges." Kramer smiled wanly. "This is my third tour in the 'Nam, and I've yet to take an R&R. Kleuver had taken an R&R early in this tour, again because of his daughter, when she and her fiancé broke up. The girl took it hard and Kleuver was afraid she might do something . . . well . . . drastic. So, as you can see, his R&R was not the kind designed to bring him rest and relaxation. He went to Honolulu, got everything straightened out, in fact did

such a good job that a few months later his
daughter and the young man were ready to get
married. But this time, there were no R&Rs available unless an existing slot could be utilized. Kleuver asked me if I could help him. I've served with
Colonel Kleuver in the past. In fact, I owe my
early promotions to him, and he's in a position
now to be the endorsing officer on my current
OERs."

"OERs?" Deena asked.

"Officer efficiency reports," Kramer said. "Even
nurses get those, don't they?"

"I suppose we do," Deena said. "I've just never
paid that much attention to it. I'm only in the
army for a short time anyway."

"Believe me, honey, the career officer lives and
dies by the OER. That's why I felt obligated to
help Colonel Kleuver if I could. I looked at our
schedule and saw that Springs was the next EM
up for R&R. There was another slot just two weeks
later, so I moved him to that one, and gave Colonel Kleuver his."

"Didn't you even tell Springs?"

"No," Kramer said. "Look, I was acting C.O. at
the time, Mayfair was gone, and I made a command decision. That's all. Sometimes it isn't easy
to do. In this case, no matter which way I went
someone was going to get hurt. On the one hand
we had Colonel Kleuver and his family, and a
daughter with a history of instability, and on the
other hand I had an enlisted man who, at best,
would have his vacation delayed by two weeks.
I didn't know about his wife and family, or I
might have acted differently. Of course, the entire

command knew only that I screwed him out of his R&R now, and no one has ever taken the time to hear my side of it."

"Why don't you tell people your side of it?" Deena asked.

Kramer gave another wan smile. "No," he said. "I made the decision, I should have the strength to stand behind it."

"Ladies and gentlemen," someone announced over the microphone on the stage at the far end of the bar. "For your edification and pleasure, the Red Bull Inn, in cooperation with the Australian SEA Club Shows Incorporated, present Debbie Hill and her Outback Mamas!"

The drums and an electric guitar erupted in a volcano of sound then, and a bosomy blond, in a sequined gown which was cut so low that her ample breasts threatened to spill over, grabbed the microphone and began singing into it.

"Because I love you . . . yeah, yeah, yea. . . ."

"Just what the world needs," Kramer said, leaning over to speak into Deena's ear so she could hear over the amplification. "Female Beatles. Maybe we can breed them to the originals, and start a whole race of Beatles."

Deena laughed, and reached over to touch him. She laughed because she thought his statement was funny, but also to cover something. His hot breath in her ear had a disquieting effect on her . . . an effect she didn't want him to know about and that she didn't want to admit.

The concert was about an hour and a half long, and though Kramer invited Deena to have a few drinks with him afterward she begged off, saying that she had early duty the next morning. Kramer reached out and took her hand in his.

"Listen, I don't really care what most of these people think about me," he said. "I only care that I do my duty as it should be done. But I do care about what you think and—"

"Colonel Kramer," Deena interrupted. "Please, don't say anymore. You must know that I've been seeing Jack these last few weeks, and I wouldn't want to upset him."

"Yes," Kramer said, again with a weary smile. "Jack does seem to have a way with women, doesn't he?"

"What do you mean by that?"

"I don't mean anything," Kramer said quickly. "I hope you didn't take it wrong. Captain Hunter and I don't always see eye to eye, but I feel that we do respect each other as officers. I know I respect his ability and his dedication to duty. I just hope that neither you nor I are disappointed if he fails to live up to our expectations."

Deena left the Red Bull and walked back to the nurses' quarters, reflecting over the strange events of the evening. She had seen Colonel Kramer in a new light, and though there were things about his personality which still disturbed her— the way he perceived his duty, for example—there were things about the man that she could admire. That very fixation upon duty, honor and country also marked him as a person of determination and strong will; admirable qualities in a man. And he was handsome, there was no denying that. She had felt the disturbing effect of their proximity for the entire evening, and it was for that reason, even more than the early morning duty, that she left as soon as the concert was over.

Deena's new awareness of Colonel Kramer allowed her some judgment which was independent of Jack's opinions, and Deena thought that independence was probably healthy in their relationship. Her relationship with Jack was growing, and it would be stronger, she decided, if it was a relationship between two separate though bonded identities than if she allowed a blending of personalities to the point that her own identity was destroyed. And yet, despite all that these thoughts, Deena knew that the *best* thing she could do for the relationship, was to see as little of Kramer as she could possibly manage.

13

A S THE BAND played, the echo of the drum and of the bass horn floated back from the walls of the hangar buildings, arriving about one half-beat after the melody so that the music came out in a strange, cacophonous sound in march-time. The warrant officer who was directing the band was aware of the off-beat echo, and he both quickened and slowed the chop of his baton to try and regulate it, though without success.

Behind Jack, dressed in khaki, stood the entire squadron, from Troop A, temporarily under the command of Lieutenant Bostic for this formation, to Troop D at the far end of the formation. Standing nearby, but not actually a part of the formation, were several of the nurses and doctors from the hospital, among whom was Deena Bell, granted an hour off for the occasion.

Jack stood all alone in the middle of the field, sweating profusely under the hot sun, cursing under his breath, annoyed not only that he was having to go through all this, but that he was having to subject his men to it as well. It was especially galling to him that he was singled out when his performance had been no more heroic than anyone else's.

Colonel Ngyuen stopped in front of Jack. Ngyuen was wearing a black satin flying suit, a red neck scarf, and exceptionally dark sunglasses. The sunglasses were American army flight glasses, and his wife, standing behind him, was wearing them as well.

Ngyuen looked over at Colonel Kramer, who cleared his throat and stepped up to a microphone.

"Attention to orders," Kramer read. "Headquarters, United States Army Vietnam, Special Orders number two eighty two. Captain Jack Cavalier Hunter is hereby awarded the Vietnamese Cross of Gallantry, for performance above and beyond the call of duty."

Kramer went on to read the citation, droning through it in such a monotone that if Jack had ever thought he deserved the award, he would have changed his mind after the reading. Finally Kramer finished and stepped away from the microphone, then looked back at the Black Dragon and nodded.

"So, you are the handsome young officer my wife has found so fascinating," Colonel Ngyuen said quietly. His flawless English had the trace of a French accent, and his voice was silkenly smooth.

Jack's eyes darted quickly to Madam Ngyuen,

and then back to the front. He didn't say anything.

"She finds your company quite charming, she has told me. But she has also said that you refuse to so much as answer any of her letters. You had no real intention to be rude, did you, Captain?"

"No, sir, of course not," Jack replied.

"I thought not. My wife has done much for the war effort, and she is sponsoring a small reception this afternoon, in your honor. She asks that I extend you an invitation. Isn't that right, dear?" Ngyuen asked, looking over at his wife, who had yet to utter a word. "Your commanding general told me you would be glad to attend," he added to Jack.

"I shall expect you at two," Madam Ngyuen said.

"That's fourteen hundred hours, Captain," Ngyuen said. "And now, my dear," he said, turning back to his wife, "please open the medal case for me."

Madam Ngyuen opened the box and her husband drew the gold pendant with its red and yellow ribbon from the felt-lined interior. "From a grateful people, Captain," Colonel Ngyuen said, pinning the medal on Jack's tunic.

"You may also be pleased to hear that Warrant Officers Dan Lumsden and Matthew Taylor are receiving this award posthumously," he said, referring to the two crewmen on board the Cobra that was shot down during the operation.

"They are most deserving, Colonel," Jack said.

"As are you, Captain. As are you," Colonel Ngyuen said. He turned to his wife. "My dear, we have a few calls to make, and then I shall get you home in time to host the reception." He turned and smiled at Jack. "The one in your honor, Captain. Please don't forget."

After the ceremony was over, Bostic, Selfridge and some of the other officers in Jack's company walked up to him to congratulate him. They were all aware of how he felt, and the congratulations themselves were a form of good-natured teasing.

"Listen," Bostic said, putting his finger under the medal and pulling it out from Jack's tunic, holding it so that it caught the sunlight and flashed brilliantly. "Where do you think we could get this hero something to drink?"

"The Red Bull?" someone suggested.

"No, let's don't share him with the masses yet," Bostic said. "How 'bout the lounge over at the BOQ?"

Jack looked toward the group of nurses and doctors, hoping for a glance of Deena, but as she was on duty she had already started back to the hospital. He felt someone looking at him, though, and then saw that Madam Ngyuen was standing by her husband's car, staring at him from behind the dark glasses she was wearing.

"Yeah, the lounge," Jack said, anxious to get away. "That sounds good. Let's go have a beer."

"We'll put all the marks by Jack's name," Bostic said, a reference to the fact that a drink tally sheet was kept posted on the refrigerator door, and every time someone got a beer they put a mark by their name, then settled at the end of the month.

"How does it feel to be a hero?" Bostic asked a moment later as he stabbed holes in the tops of the cans of beer, then passed them around. Beer spewed out each time he punched the opener in, and foam bubbled invitingly over the top of the cans.

Jack took a long drink from his can before he answered. "It feels phony," he said.

"Yeah, well, it gave the troops something to do for a while," Bostic said. He looked at Selfridge and laughed. "And it probably saved Ed a little money. He was going to head on down to plantation row and buy a little Saigon tea for the whores."

"Well, bless their little hearts," Selfridge said. "They're friendly little girls, and they're always thirsty."

"There's someone I wouldn't mind buying a little Saigon tea for," one of the officers said, pointing through the window with his beer can. He was pointing at Madam Ngyuen.

"You and me both," Bostic said. "I'll tell you, she is the most beautiful damned dink I've ever seen."

"Hell, go down to Maxim's on Plantation Road and you'll find at least five as pretty as she is," Selfridge said. "Big Boobs, for example, or the Rabbit Girl, or Brandy or even Ammo Bearer."

Bostic laughed. "The chief has this area laid out, doesn't he? Think he doesn't know where to get a steam and cream?"

"What about you, Cap'n? You haven't commented. What do you think about Madam Ngyuen? Is she a good lay?"

The question was asked in fun, but Bostic glared at the warrant who posed it, letting him know that he was coming dangerously close to stepping out of bounds. The warrant realized then that he may have overstepped the line, and he cleared his throat and tried to back off.

"I mean . . . I heard that you . . . uh, well, the talk is—" He realized that he was just getting in deeper and he stopped.

"I don't give postmortems," Jack said flatly. He finished his beer, then flipped the can toward the large box used to collect the empties. "I have to be going."

"You dumb shit," Jack heard Bostic say to the warrant as he left the lounge, but he didn't turn back to get involved. Let them think what they would; it was beyond his ability to control anymore. At least Deena understood, and she was the only one he cared who . . . Deena! Damn, she had the early duty and was getting off at 1300. They were supposed to go to the My Kahn Floating Restaurant this afternoon. He wouldn't be able to take her now. Damn Madam Ngyuen and her reception!

Jack started over to the hospital to talk to Deena, but halfway there he met a doctor that he knew. He decided that it would be easier to send the message to her through the doctor. It was the coward's way out, perhaps, but it would save a lot of questioning and explaining. He sent word that "something had come up," and that he would see her later to explain.

That afternoon, Jack parked his jeep in the courtyard of the Ngyuen villa. From inside the walls of the estate it was impossible to tell that this elegant home was situated in Vietnam, surrounded on all four sides by amazing filth and squalor. Here, fountains splashed and flowers blossomed, and trees shaded a Baroque-style Mediterranean house which would have been in place on the French Riviera.

A servant met Jack and escorted him into the house. The inside of the house was a mixture of French and Oriental decor, but whereas these two schools blended in cooking, they did not blend well in decorating, so that the result was a mishmash of ostentatiousness. Huge, deep blue Ming vases competed for space with Monet originals, and Louis XIV furniture.

"Ahh, Captain, how good of you to come," Ngyuen said. "My wife will be so pleased."

Ngyuen was wearing a white sharkskin suit with a lime-green shirt. It was the first time Jack had ever seen him out of uniform. He was standing at the bar, pouring himself a drink. He held the bottle of Canadian Mist up for Jack, and Jack nodded yes.

"Where is your wife?" Jack asked. "And where are the others?"

"The others?" Ngyuen asked innocently.

"Yes. Isn't there to be a reception here?"

"Yes," Ngyuen replied. "But there are no others, dear boy." He tasted his drink and smacked his lips appreciatively. "There is just you."

"Are you disappointed?" Madam Ngyuen's smooth throaty voice asked.

Jack looked toward the sound of her voice and almost gasped. She was wearing an *ao dai*, but the silk pants which were normally worn beneath the long, free-flowing outer garment were absent. The *ao dai* was split from her waist to her feet on each side, and beneath the *ao dai* there was nothing except a long, lovely expanse of naked leg and thigh.

"Do you like my wife's mode of dress?" Colonel Ngyuen asked, laughing. "She has singlehandedly changed one thousand years of dressing custom by discarding the long silk pants. You must admit, it does do much for the costume."

"Your wife is a lovely woman," Jack said truthfully.

"Yes, well, I'm sure the two of you will have a wonderful time this afternoon," Ngyuen said. He put his empty glass down on the bar. "I must be going."

"What? Where? Aren't you going to stay here?"

"No," Ngyuen said lightly. "It is my wife's reception, not mine."

Jack watched, dumbfounded, as Ngyuen left. Then he turned back toward Madam Ngyuen. "Is this what it appears to be?"

"And what does it appear to be, Captain?" Madam Ngyuen asked in an amused voice.

"It appears to be a setup. It looks as if your husband is procuring for you."

"You may believe that if you wish," Madam Ngyuen said. She reached behind her to release the catch to her bra, then she removed it, pulling it from under the *ao dai* so that the nipples of her breasts now stood in bold relief against the silk of the garment.

"I want no part of it," Jack said. He put his glass down and turned to leave.

"Captain, you cannot tell me you did not enjoy our time before," Madam Ngyuen called after him. "Stop, now, and think of it. Think of the hot blood, and the mingling of flesh, yours hard and driving, mine soft and yielding . . ."

Jack stopped, and put his fingers to the bridge of his nose. Despite himself vivid scenes of their time before came back to him, and he felt a quick, building heat which could easily turn into a fire within if he allowed it to. But he fought it back, and pushed his way through the door to leave.

As Jack waited for the gate to open to allow him back onto Highway 13, which ran by the front of the villa, he saw a jeep pass by on the road in front of him. There were two people in the jeep. The two people were Colonel Bert Kramer and Lieutenant Deena Bell.

At first Jack was shocked, then angry. The anger overtook him, pushing away any explanation behind what he had just seen, dominating his senses only with a feeling of hurt and betrayal. Deena had wasted no time in finding another date for this afternoon, and to make things worse, she was going with the one man Jack disliked most.

Jack threw the jeep into reverse and backed around into a turn, confusing the guards who were opening the gate for him to leave. He started back up the drive toward the house, spinning his tires in the loose gravel as he sped back. He parked under the portico again, and was out of the jeep and in the house before the servant could even meet him.

Madam Ngyuen was still standing at the bar, with her glass now half-empty. When she saw him, she smiled, broadly at first, and then more faintly as she quickly regained control of the situation.

"So, you have come back?"

"I remembered what it was like," Jack said.

"And you want it again?" Madam Ngyuen teased.

"Yes."

Madam Ngyuen walked over to him, then leaned into him, pressing her silk-covered flesh against him.

"How badly do you want me? Enough to accept the fact that my husband knows?"

"Yes," Jack said, his anger with Deena turning with equal force into a mounting desire for Madam Ngyuen.

Madam Ngyuen kissed him, and from the first moment her lips contacted his, he became disassociated from reality. All thought of right and wrong, the idea of vengeance against Deena, the shame of having been procured, were blotted out. Jack was aware of nothing save the white heat of the kiss, and the spreading fire of sexual arousal.

He did not remember leaving the room or actually removing his clothes, although there were bits and pieces of both actions which managed to get through the sexual inebriation. He was aware of a curving marble staircase, of a canopied bed and silk sheets, of air moving across his naked body, and then he found himself in bed with her. He could feel her wonderfully smooth skin, her soft curves and firm breasts. Her passionate, experienced lovemaking beckoned him to the ultimate explosion, and it wasn't until several moments later that Jack realized it was all over, that his system had been subjected to such a heavy charge of sex that all other senses had been short-circuited, withdrawing him from reality.

Colonel Ngyuen sipped his drink quietly and looked through the large window into the bedroom at his wife and the American captain. The glass through which Ngyuen was looking was actually a one-way window, which in Madam Ngyuen's bedroom was the mirror on her large ornate dresser.

Ngyuen felt a fluttering in the pit of his stomach, a slight weakness at the back of his knees, and a dampness in the palms of his hands. His breath was coming in short, ragged gasps, and there was a pounding erection pushing at the front of his pants. It was always this way when he watched his wife having sex with another man or with other women.

Theirs was an accommodating arrangement, he thought. She enjoyed sex, and had been wonderfully cooperative over the idea of having a one-way glass installed in the bedroom so that Ngyuen could watch anytime he wished. He had not been able to see her at the first meeting with the American captain, as it had taken place in a Saigon hotel. It had been he who urged his wife to set up a second meeting, and when the letters failed, it had been he who came up with the idea of the award and the "reception" afterward. And now, it was well worth it.

The arrangement between Ngyuen and his wife wasn't all one way, though. He allowed her to enjoy sex with other men, and an occasional woman, while she allowed him to indulge in his own particular tastes.

"Colonel, do you wish to make love now?" a voice asked from behind him.

Ngyuen turned toward the sound of the voice. There, standing by the bed behind him, was a beautiful young girl. She was totally nude, and her skin was without blemish, and without curves or breasts. The girl was eleven years old.

"Yes," Ngyuen said thickly. He went to the girl's bed and stood there as her experienced young hands removed his clothes. When he was totally naked, the girl lay down, then looked up at him, waiting expectantly.

Ngyuen got into bed with the girl, then, without preliminaries or tenderness, thrust himself into her brutally, getting as much satisfaction from her muffled cry of pain as from the physical stimulation of the act. He pounded against her, thrusting in and drawing out, closing his eyes to see the picture of his wife beneath the American captain . . . and then other equally erotic pictures.

Ngyuen recalled the young woman who had stood at the burning pagoda in Chat Nhyn, and he remembered the feel of her hot breasts, and the rapid beat of her heart. He could see again the fear in her eyes, and then he remembered what it was like when he shot her.

And that was the ultimate sensation for Ngyuen. It left him groaning and twitching as he spent himself in and on the young girl beneath him.

Deena felt guilty. She had accepted Colonel Kramer's invitation to go to Saigon only after she learned that the business which had come up with Jack had been the reception with Madam Ngyuen.

"I'll tell you what came up," she muttered under her breath when she found out. "It wasn't business . . . and it's *come up* between him and that woman before."

Deena didn't want to spend the afternoon brooding in the Red Bull, and an even worse alternative would have been to lie around the nurses' lounge. So when she took a paperback book outside to read on one of the picnic tables by the Red Bull, she was advertising to anyone who saw her that she had absolutely nothing to do. That was when Kramer moved in.

"I thought you were going to the My Kahn."

"My plans were changed," Deena answered.

"Would you like to change them back?"

"What do you mean?"

"Would you like to go with me?" Kramer asked.

Of the two alternatives facing her, spending the long afternoon reading a book she couldn't really get into, or going to the My Kahn with a man she considered handsome and interesting, despite his enmity for Jack, she chose the latter. And it had been fun. Too much fun. So much, in fact, that when Kramer kissed her, just as they stepped through the door of her room upon returning, she had kissed him back.

She more than kissed him back. She expanded it, testing to see how far she could let it go, and only when she felt herself in danger of falling into an abyss from which there was no escape did she suddenly put on the brakes and come back. She broke the kiss off, and then, with her head spinning dizzily and with her blood running hot, she looked at him with a look of surprise and fear on her face.

"No," she said. "Please don't."

"Do you think Captain Hunter is being as strong with Madam Ngyuen?" Kramer asked.

"What?"

"Deena, be realistic," Kramer said. "Don't you know that Captain Hunter is in bed with Madam Ngyuen right now? This very minute? You don't owe him anything, and you know it." Kramer kissed her again, and his hands went under her blouse, then slipped easily under the cups of her bra to grasp her breasts, warm and vibrant. "You don't owe him a thing," he said again.

With an effort of supreme willpower, Deena pulled back, though every nerve-ending in her tortured body cried for her to go on. Kramer might be right, and a part of her soul was injured at the idea that Jack would be with Madam Ngyuen now, after he had been with her, and that part of her cried for revenge as surely as her body cried for fulfillment. Despite all that, Deena found the strength to pull back.

"What about what you owe your wife?" she finally managed to say.

Deena's words froze Kramer in his tracks, and he let her go, then looked at her with eyes which were longing, and strangely sad. He was silent for a long moment.

"You're right," he finally said. "I can't afford a breath of scandal; her father is a general. It could be disastrous for my career. Please, don't say anything about this. I'm sorry, I'm sorry." Kramer turned and nearly ran back down the hallway outside the row of hospital rooms which were serving as nurses' quarters.

Deena pulled the door shut, then walked over to lie on her bunk. Tears stung her eyes, and the pain of Jack's betrayal and of the betrayal of her own body tore at her. Hunter and Kramer be damned. She hated both of them.

14

FRANK BELL returned to consciousness slowly and in stages, floating as a feather caught in an updraft, reaching one level, then gradually climbing to the next. Before he was fully awake his senses began sending signals to his consciousness . . . the strong smell of gasoline, a salty taste in his mouth, the sounds of excited high-pitched voices.

The last sense to return to Frank was the sense of sight, and when he opened his eyes and saw the shattered windshield of the jeep digging into the dirt, he stared at it for a long moment, trying to figure out why the jeep was upside down, and why he was lying beneath it.

"Ambushed!" he said aloud, suddenly remembering the stomach-shaking thump of the command-detonated mine. "Jimmy, come on, we've got to get out of here," he called to the driver of the jeep. "We've been ambushed!"

Frank was in his fifth week as a member of Remote Team Alpha, and he and PFC Jimmy Winsom had been driving from the team headquarters to Boc Sang, a tiny village which was part of the Alpha Team defense plan. They were taking ammunition to the village guards to allow them to defend their own village against any V.C. attack, but they were ambushed before they were halfway there.

Frank finally extracted himself from the wreckage of the jeep, now more than ever aware of the strong smell of gasoline. He saw that the tank had been ruptured, and gasoline was dripping out at a substantial rate.

"Jimmy," he said. "We've got to get out of—" Suddenly he stopped and grabbed onto the jeep to support himself. He closed his eyes and looked away, afraid that he was going to be sick.

Jimmy Winsom was still in place behind the twisted steering wheel of the jeep, wedged into the upside-down seat as if he were a piece of macabre sculpture, glued in place.

The top half of his head was gone.

"Oh, Jesus, Jimmy," Frank said, looking at the young black soldier who was not only his squad mate, but had also become his friend.

The jeep had left the road, flipped over, and slid belly-up down an embankment into the bottom of a deep ravine. Up by the road, Frank could hear the jabbering and calling of the men who had set off the mine. Frank understood enough Vietnamese to realize that they didn't know whether there were one or two Americans in the jeep.

Frank looked quickly up and down the ravine, but there didn't seem to be any way he could run without being in the open. Then he looked at the jeep again, and he got an idea. What he needed was a diversion.

"I'm sorry, Jimmy," he said quietly. "But you're going to have to help me get away."

Frank struck a match and dripped it onto the gasoline-stained ground. The fire flamed up, and he ran, crouching low, for a clump of bushes about thirty yards away.

The jeep exploded, sending a huge fireball and a puff of black smoke boiling up into the sky.

"*Hi! Choi oui!*" one of the Vietnamese shouted, and Frank saw them at the edge of the road, silhouetted against the skyline, looking down at the burning jeep. There were six of them, all armed with AK-47 automatic rifles, and they weren't V.C., but North Vietnamese Regulars.

Frank could get them all . . . two bursts from his M-16, and he could kill all six of them!

Frank raised his rifle up between the clump of weeds and aimed, then he pulled the trigger.

Nothing! The damn rifle was full of mud and dirt, and it misfired.

There were more voices on the road, and then another half dozen North Vietnamese joined the first group. And still more voices indicated that there were many more besides the dozen he could see. Where in the hell were they all coming from? No one in Remote Team Alpha knew about this many N.V.N. in this area.

Now Frank was glad his rifle had jammed.

The N.V.N. chattered among themselves for a while longer, then a couple of them climbed down the embankment toward the burning jeep, carrying on a yelling conversation with those who remained on the road.

Just as the two N.V.N. reached the jeep, there were several shots fired, and they both dived to the ground, as did the ones who were standing on the road. Frank was as startled by the shots as the N.V.N. were, and then he realized that it wasn't shots actually being fired, but rather ammunition cooking off in the jeep fire, the thousand rounds of 7.62 ammunition he and Jimmy were taking to the village.

The N.V.N. figured out what was happening as quickly as Frank did, and they began to laugh. But Frank had the last laugh, because the rounds, even though they were just cooking off, were sending bullets whizzing out indiscriminately, and everyone had to keep his head down until the last round had detonated, or risk being hit by a wild shot. It had the same effect as someone providing covering fire, and Frank was able to use that time to sneak away undetected.

Frank stayed down in the roadside ravine for nearly a mile before he came up onto the road. Unfortunately, he had to run in a direction which led him away from the base camp, so now his only hope was to try and find the village. And that wasn't going to be easy, because he had never been to the village before.

Jimmy had been to the village, and Frank had been depending on Jimmy to get them there. In fact, Frank hadn't even bothered to check the village coordinates, though that information would be useless to him now, because he didn't have a map or a compass. Frank was lost, right in the middle of an area which was crawling with N.V.N.

Frank continued to plod on, cross-checking his references with the sun, trying to work his way south, through the valley to a major road which he knew was some fifteen miles away, and which he knew was constantly patrolled by Americans. His primary enemy now was the jungle; the bug-infested, exhausting, unforgiving, all-encompassing jungle.

And so he forgot about his other enemy, the N.V.N., until suddenly he felt the angry buzz of bullets, followed by the staccato snap of an AK-47.

"*My!*" one of the N.V.N. yelled excitedly, saying the Vietnamese word for American.

Frank dived headlong behind a fallen log, then crawled several feet until he was able to roll down a slight ridge. He could hear the N.V.N. yelling and firing their weapons, but as none of the rounds appeared to come too close he knew that they were shooting in the blind. Frank began moving backward on his stomach, still looking up toward the ridge line. He felt his feet get wet, then he looked around to see a stream. He eased the rest of the way down into it.

"*My, lie dai,*" he heard a woman's voice call softly. "American, come here."

Frank looked around in gut-wrenching fear, then saw a young girl on a boat, motioning for him to come toward her. She spoke again in a soothing voice, and it allayed his fears.

"*My, lie dai,*" she said.

Frank slipped silently through the water until he reached the boat, and then pulled himself into it. He could hear the N.V.N. shouting again, and he rose from the bottom of the boat to look up the bank, but the young girl pushed him back down, shaking her head and holding her finger to her lips in the international symbol of quiet.

The girl covered Frank then, first with a straw mat, then with vegetables and finally with fish. The smell was almost unbearable.

The staccato fire of the AK-47s exploded along the bank, and Frank could hear the bullets plopping into the water near the boat. The soldiers yelled at the woman and she answered them. Then Frank could feel the boat turning and he realized that they were rowing toward the shore. She was about to betray him!

There were more exchanges between the woman and the N.V.N., then a rocking motion of the boat as one of the N.V.N. stepped on board. Frank could feel every step the soldier made, and when he poked around the fish and vegetables, Frank could even see his face through the weave of the mat. Frank could see the N.V.N. because the N.V.N. was silhouetted against the sky, but the N.V.N. couldn't see Frank, and that was Frank's salvation. Finally, the N.V.N. appeared to be satisfied, because he left, and Frank felt the boat moving again.

After several minutes the smell was beginning to get unbearable. and Frank tried to come out. But the girl shouted something which sounded like *kome* and shook her head vigorously, so Frank stayed where he was.

After what seemed like hours, the boat pulled into a small slip alongside a bamboo dock. The girl spoke softly and helped Frank up. He stepped onto the dock but the combination of his inactivity and cramped position on the boat almost made him fall on the water-slickened dock. An old man

with a wispy beard grabbed him and held him up.
Then the old man and the girl led him toward the
village and into one of the houses where they motioned for him to lie down.

The girl spoke sharply, and from out of nowhere
three or four children appeared with hand fans
and they began to fan him. Another brought a
basin of water and the girl removed Frank's flak
jacket, shirt and trousers, and began to bathe him,
being especially careful when she came across his
injuries. Frank hadn't even known that he had so
many cuts and bruises.

Frank made a motion with his hand, indicating
that he wanted something to drink, and the girl
gave another order. Within a moment a glass was
thrust before him, and when Frank tasted it, he
realized that it was a drink made from fresh lime.
He thought it was the most delicious drink he
had ever tasted.

After the drink and the bath, the girl put some
ointment on his wounds and on the many insect
bites and branch scrapes he had picked up during
his trek through the jungle. The ointment had a
soothing effect, and Frank soon drifted off to sleep.
He awoke once in the middle of the night, noticed
that a mosquito net had been put up around him
and that a delightful breeze was blowing in through
the open window. He also noticed that the girl
was sleeping beside him. Frank slipped back into
a carefree sleep.

When he awakened the next morning he saw
the girl standing there smiling at him. She had put
on a freshly laundered dress, and Frank knew that
she had done it for his benefit. She was wholesome-
looking, and Frank thought that, given a chance,

she might even be pretty. It didn't matter. She could have been a wart hog, and still have seemed to him to be the most beautiful woman in the world. She had saved his life.

"Good morning," Frank said.

The girl smiled, and thrust a slice of mango toward him. Frank suddenly realized that he hadn't eaten a bite since breakfast the previous day. "Thank you," he said, taking the mango and eating with gusto.

"I speak English," a male voice said with a noticeable French accent. Frank looked up to see a man wearing the collar of a Catholic priest.

"Where am I?" Frank asked.

"Boc Sang," the priest answered.

Frank smiled. "Well, it looks like I made it after all," he said. "This is where I was headed."

"To bring ammunition to the village guard?"

"Yes."

"You were betrayed," the priest said. "Many of the village guard are V.C. It was they who told the North Vietnamese soldiers, and arranged the ambush. They were disappointed because the fire destroyed the ammunition they would have used for themselves."

"You already know about it?"

"Yes, there was talk of it in the village last night," the priest said.

"I can't stay here."

"Don't worry, you are safe for the time being," the priest said. "However, there are many elements of the North Vietnamese army operating in this province with the V.C. now. So we must be very careful."

"Do you think you can get me through?" Frank asked.

"It would be very dangerous to move you right now. You have, I don't know how to say it . . . broken your head."

"A skull fracture? I have a skull fracture?" Frank touched his head, then gingerly pulled his hand away when he realized that what the priest said was true. He had not even realized it until this moment.

"So, as you can see," the priest continued, "moving you now would be very dangerous."

"How about getting word back to the Americans that I'm here, then?" Frank asked. "They could send a chopper in after me."

"I fear that would be equally out of the question," the priest said. "There are too many V.C. informers and sympathizers in the village. You and the helicopter crew would be in great danger. You must wait."

"It doesn't look as if I have too much choice, does it?"

The girl spoke to the priest, and the priest laughed.

"She wants to know if she can socialize with you," the priest explained. "We see very few Americans here, and she has never spoken with one. She is very curious."

"Are you serious?" Frank asked. "It seems impossible that there could be anyone left in Vietnam who *hasn't* seen an American."

"There are villages, my friend, where the villagers don't yet realize that they are Vietnamese. Their loyalty is to their family, their village, their district, and then to their country. If their country gets lost along the way then it isn't missed too badly. Is it any wonder that there are confused loyalties for the Saigon and Hanoi governments? V.C. and Republican can live side by side in pcaee until the war actually touches them, you see, because the government is the least important thing in their lives."

The girl spoke again.

"She asked if you are married," the priest translated.

"No."

"Girlfriend?" the priest translated again.

"Yes."

"What's her name?"

"Stacey."

The priest smiled at the girl's response. "She said that Stacey will be very happy to know that you are alive and well. She is very happy for Stacey."

"Tell her that I will make certain Stacey knows that I owe my life to this girl. What is her name?"

"Her name is Linh."

"We eat now," the girl said in halting English, pointing to a table which was by now laden with food.

The meal was pleasant, partially because Frank had had so little to eat since the morning before, but also because the meal was really quite tasty. Frank especially liked the fruits and vegetables peculiar to Vietnam, and he had long ago learned to handle the *nuk maum* sauce which covered the baked fish.

Frank spent four more days in Boc San, playing with the children and watching the men work the fishing nets in the daytime, and sleeping in the cool breeze beneath the mosquito net and lying next to Linh each night. At first, Frank was fearful that he would be turned over to the North Vietnamese, particularly since the priest had told him of the great number of V.C. who lived in the village. Surely some of those very men he watched work the fishing nets by day were V.C. by night, and yet, strangely, no one came for him. It was as if all the villagers had arrived at a truce, the terms of which specified that Frank would remain under their protection. What made it even more ironic was the realization that some of the villagers must have been some of the same V.C. who arranged the ambush.

On the fourth night, Linh came to Frank, offering herself to him, and they made love, not with the passion or sensuality he had known with Stacey, but it was a gentle sharing of bodies that seemed totally natural.

This village was becoming almost a paradise to Frank, and he had thoughts of the mutinous crew of the H.M.S *Bounty,* how they had revolted not so much against an evil captain as to stay in the paradise they had found. Frank was beginning to feel some guilt over not trying to leave this village and return to Remote Team Alpha headquarters.

On the morning of the fifth day, the priest, whom Frank had seen only once since the first day, returned.

"The North Vietnamese army has withdrawn," he said. "Now there is no obstacle to taking you back. If your head feels well enough, we can return today."

"Yes," Frank said. "Yes, I'm ready. When can we start?"

"Linh is preparing us a lunch. If we leave now, we should be at the main highway where you will be able to flag down an American vehicle by late this afternoon."

Linh handed a basket to the priest and when Frank offered to carry it the priest declined, saying it would be better for his head if he didn't get over-tired. They left the village with the village children chasing them, calling to them with laughter for almost two miles down the trail. Then for several more miles there was only the buzz of insects, the occasional scream of a monkey, and the fluttering wings of the many birds which were frightened into flight. Frank was struck by the surprising number of birds and didn't realize that their density was due to the fact that they were seeking refuge in the decreasing area of jungle as yet untouched by defoliants, explosives or napalm.

Their timing was just right, and they reached the highway at the precise time an American convoy was approaching.

"I will leave you in good hands," the priest said, starting back toward the jungle.

"But wait," Frank said. "Can't we give you a ride somewhere?"

"It would be best if I were gone," the priest said. "It would not be good for me to be seen in the company of so many Americans. Many of my parishioners would no longer trust me."

"Yeah," Frank said. "Yeah, I see what you mean. Well, okay, I guess this is good-bye." Frank stuck out his hand and clasped the priest's in his own. "And thanks. Thanks for everything."

The priest started to leave.

"Hey!" Frank called. "I don't even know your name!"

"Just remember me as the good samaritan," the priest called back with a chuckle.

The lead jeep of the convoy pulled over to answer Frank's wave. It was a marine convoy, and there was a major in the right front seat. Frank saluted.

"Who are you, and what the hell are you doing out here?" the marine major wanted to know.

"Sir, I'm Lance Corporal Frank Bell of Remote Team Alpha," Frank said. "My jeep was ambushed, and my partner was killed. I've been evading the enemy ever since."

"Did you say Remote Team Alpha?" the major asked.

"Yes, sir."

"Touchstone, this is Hammer. Why have we stopped?" the jeep radio suddenly blared.

"Hand me that microphone," the major said, twisting in his seat and speaking to the sergeant who was riding in the back. The major took the mike and squeezed the talk button. The power generator wheezed on, and the squelch static stopped. "Hammer, this is Touchstone. We've just encountered an individual who identifies himself as a U.S. Marine, emerging from the jungle."

Hammer's voice came back on the radio, and Frank looked at the radio with curiosity. There was something about that voice, something hauntingly familiar from long, long ago.

"Hold the convoy in place, Touchstone, I'll be right there," Hammer said.

"Do you have any identification?" the major asked.

"No, sir," Frank replied. He had been in the habit of leaving his billfold in the base camp. There was nothing he could buy in the jungle, so he didn't need money, and he didn't want to take the chance of losing any of his I.D. cards, his driver's license, or personal pictures and papers. "I don't carry my billfold with me, sir."

"Dog tags?"

Frank felt for the familiar chain around his neck, realizing then for the first time that they too were gone. He didn't know when he had lost them.

"No, sir," he said. "I don't know where they are."

"You realize we'll have to hold you in custody until you can prove you are who you say you are, don't you?" the major said. "There are TWXs out now on deserters and dopers."

"Major, I'm neither a deserter nor a doper," Frank said. "If you want to find out who I am, just take me to Remote Team Alpha. Hell, the guys there'll tell you who I am."

"We can't take you there," the major said.

"I don't mean the whole convoy. Just send me there in a jeep," Frank said.

"No, you don't understand," the major replied. "We can't take you to Remote Team Alpha, because there is no Remote Team Alpha. The camp was overrun by the enemy and everyone there was killed."

"What?" Frank asked weakly. "My God, *all* of them?"

"Yes," the major said. "I'm sorry. I'm sure they were your friends."

Another jeep arrived then, coming from far back in the convoy, and stopping just in front. The tall antenna whipped back and forth as the jeep stopped, and a full colonel stepped out and walked back toward Frank and the others.

"Is this the man?" the colonel asked, pointing at Frank. Then, when the colonel saw Frank, he stopped and smiled broadly. "Damn, Frank, is that you?" he asked, shocking the major and the others with his instant recognition and familiarity with the young marine.

"Colonel Bell, you *know* this man?" the major asked.

"Hello, Uncle Gilbert," Frank said wryly. "Long time no see."

15

F<small>ROM THE</small> *Washington Daily Standard*, late city
edition, Sunday, November 16, 1969:

QUARTER OF A MILLION ANTIWAR PROTESTERS
GATHER FOR PEACEFUL RALLY IN WASHINGTON;
VIOLENCE ERUPTS AFTER RALLY

Gathering Sets New Record

---

*Demonstrators Demand
Immediate Withdrawal*

By: Ken Ripley

W<small>ASHINGTON</small>, Nov. 15—A huge crowd of young
Americans gathered in the nation's capital in
the heart of the city today, demanding an
immediate withdrawal of American troops
from Vietnam.

Jerry Wilson, Chief of the D.C. Police Department said a "moderate" guess would place the crowd at 250,000. This would establish a new record for the number of demonstrators gathered; the previous record was 200,000 in the civil rights rally of 1963.

After the peaceful rally, a small segment of the crowd, reportedly led by Larry DeWitt and Mack Burton, moved across Constitution Avenue to the Labor and Justice Department buildings where they burned United States flags and threw cans of red paint to signify "innocent blood."

The police refused to speculate on whether the two leaders were actually Larry DeWitt and Mack Burton, or whether they were two other protesters impersonating the missing militants. DeWitt and Burton were thought to have been killed when they set fire to their own house during an attempted arrest by the police last August. Three bodies were found in the ruins of the house, two men and one woman, and though the bodies were never positively identified DeWitt and Burton have not been seen since that time.

If the men who led the militants' protest yesterday were DeWitt and Burton, that would leave a question as to who was found in the burned-out house. Some speculate that the bodies may have been those of Jerry Turner and Bill Frankel, known associates of DeWitt and Burton.

"Look at this," Larry said, laughing as he showed the newspaper to Mack. "The fuzz don't know whether to shit or wind their watches. They don't know whether we're dead or alive."

"Yeah," Burton said. "Well, they're going to know pretty soon. We can't let up now; we've got to keep the pressure on the man."

Larry sighed as he looked at the photograph of the huge crowd of demonstrators which had marched the previous day.

"I don't know, man," he finally said. "It looks to me like the whole country was out there yesterday, and he didn't hear us. Nixon didn't even *hear* us."

"He'll hear us," Mack said. "If we have to, we'll just yell louder. "But he'll hear us, my man. I promise you."

Larry walked over to the window and pulled the shade away so he could peer outside. He and Mack were in a two-room apartment over a store building, and across the street was a small black church. Church was just letting out and the minister, dressed in black and red robes, was standing on the steps, shaking hands with members of his congregation as they departed. It was a bright sunny day, though the weather was quite cold, and Larry could see the fogging breath of the people as they hurried down the street.

"I don't know," Larry said quietly, from his position by the window. He continued to look outside. A father and mother got into their car, then waited patiently while their young daughter, dressed in a pretty little white dress, picked up the Sunday school material she had dropped.

"You don't know what, man?" Mack asked.

Larry sighed and let the shade fall, shutting off the outside world. All the shades were kept pulled to prevent the possibility of anyone recognizing either of them through the window and informing the police. The interior of the apartment was dark, lighted only by a couple of lamps and two bare lightbulbs which hung from wires suspended from the ceiling. The dark furniture and woodwork and the peeling and aged wallpaper added to the gloom.

"I don't know if it would do any good to yell any louder," Larry said. "I mean I don't think it would do any good even if we went right up to Nixon's ear, cupped our hands around it and yelled, "Get the hell out of this fuckin' war! In fact, I don't know that we're doing any good at all."

"Yeah," Mack said. "We're doin' some good, man. We have to be doin' some good. Otherwise Dess, Bill, Jerry, all our brothers, man, they died for nothin'.'"

"And the guys in Vietnam," Larry said. "They're dying for nothing, too. Like Jack Hunter."

"Who's Jack Hunter?"

"Don't you remember? He's the helicopter pilot they interviewed. He's the one who said I had a right to do what I was doing."

"Oh, yeah, I remember. Was he killed?"

"No," Larry said. "At least not that I know of. I was just using him as an example. There's a man with principles, and yet he's fighting the war. I'm a man with principles, and I'm fighting *against* the' war. Now, suppose one of us dies. Which of us will have died in vain?"

There was the sound of footsteps coming up the back stairs, and both men looked toward the door apprehensively.

"Carol's not supposed to be back yet, is she?" Larry whispered.

"No, not for a couple of hours yet," Mack said. He pointed to the closet. "Get in there. I'll see who it is."

"What about you?"

"Man, down here, one more black face won't make that much difference. But if they see your white face shinin' out of here, someone's going to get curious."

Larry stepped into the closet, then pulled the door shut, but not all the way. He could still see through the narrow crack remaining.

Mack walked over and jerked the door open, revealing Carol standing there, holding a bag of groceries and fishing for her door key. Carol was a tall attractive black woman who was sharing her apartment with Larry and her bed with Mack.

"What you doing back so early, girl?" Mack asked. He leaned through the door and looked down the long, narrow flight of steps which led to the entrance on the alleyway. It was the only entrance to the apartment. He satisfied himself that no one had followed her, and then shut the door.

Larry breathed a sigh of relief and came out of the closet.

"Wow," Carol said, smiling at the two men. "You two really are jumpy, aren't you? I just decided to skip choir practice this afternoon, that's all. 'Sides, I figured if I wasn't here to fix your lunch, you'd both starve. I got a nice fat hen. How 'bout some chicken 'n dumplins?"

Carol started removing the groceries from the bag and placing them on the oilcloth-covered table across from the stove. She turned on the gas and held a match to the burner until she was rewarded with a small crown of dancing blue flame.

"Chicken 'n dumplin's, huh?" Mack said. He smiled broadly. "Shit man, this livin' on the run is all right."

"The guns at Parrot's Beak? We're going after the guns at Parrot's Beak? Colonel Mayfair, you can't be serious!" Jack said. He was in Colonel Mayfair's office, and he had just leaned forward in his chair to make certain he heard the colonel correctly.

"I'm afraid I am serious," Colonel Mayfair said. He stood up and walked over to look at the wall map. The gun position at Parrot's Beak was marked by a red-headed pin. "I put in a request for an air force strike," Colonel Mayfair said. "It was turned down, and I was ordered to launch our own strike against it."

"That's as it should be," Kramer said. Kramer was sitting on the sofa beside Colonel Mayfair's desk. "It was galling to think that the air force would be doing what should be our job."

"When do you want the strike?" Jack asked with a sigh of resignation.

"Tomorrow," Colonel Mayfair said.

Jack walked over to look at the map. "Maybe we can—"

"I've already laid it out," Kramer interrupted. Jack looked at him in surprise. "Tell him the rest, Colonel," Kramer went on.

"Jack, I'm going to let Kramer lead this mission," Mayfair said.

"All right, sir," Jack answered quietly. "I'll fly the five slot."

"No," Kramer said. "Bostic will fly the five slot. You aren't going."

"What do you mean I'm not going?"

"I'm taking A Troop," Kramer said. "I don't want any problems with misplaced loyalty or division of command."

"Colonel, you'd be the ranking officer on the mission," Jack said easily. "My men understand the structure of command."

"Nevertheless, I would prefer that you not go," Kramer said. "And as I am the mission commander, that's the way it's going to be."

"Very well," Jack said. "Might I at least be a party to the planning? How are you going to do it?"

"Here are the air-recon photos," Kramer said, opening a manila folder. "We've had Mohawks over the area several times. Now, look, do you see this stream? It winds through here, then goes right up into the valley here. I intend to come in on the deck, following that streambed right up to them. They won't even know we're there until we're in the valley."

"But, Colonel, once you're in the valley you have nowhere to go except straight ahead and then up," Jack protested. "That means you'll be sitting ducks for at least twenty seconds."

"Just twenty seconds," Kramer said.

"Hold your finger in a candle flame for twenty seconds," Jack said, "and you'll see how long twenty seconds can be."

"The plan already has approval," Kramer said. "Brigade approved it this afternoon."

"Do you have another idea, Jack?" Colonel Mayfair asked.

Jack looked at the photos and then at the map. "No," he finally said. "There is no other way, except to let the air force do it."

"Don't worry about it, Captain," Kramer said. "By this time tomorrow, the guns will be gone."

"I hope you're right, Colonel," Jack said. "I hope to God you're right. What about ordnance mix? What are you talking?"

"I thought I'd just take rockets," Kramer said.

"A suggestion, sir?"

"What?"

"Put mini-guns on every other ship. Take them in in fire-teams, at staggered altitudes. The mini-guns might keep Charlie's head down while the rockets are doing their job."

Kramer rubbed his chin with his hand, and looked at the photos for a long moment before he answered. "Yeah," he finally agreed. "Yeah, that sounds like a pretty good idea at that. I may do just that."

"I'll see Mr. Vaughan and have him start his maintenance boys on the gun kits. They'll be ready to go tomorrow."

Jack left Colonel Mayfair's office to find Chief Vaughan, his maintenance officer. He found him at the Red Bull, pulled him away from a tape-replay of the previous week's football game, and sent him to the flight line to prepare the Cobras for the next day's mission.

"Hi," a quiet voice said from behind Jack after Vaughan had left.

Jack turned around and saw Deena standing there. She was holding a can of beer in each hand.

"Hi yourself," Jack said. "Are you knocking them down two at a time these days?" Jack pointed to the two cans of beer.

Deena smiled and handed one of the cans to him. "It's a peace offering," she said. "I want to talk."

Jack looked around to see the usual crowd at all the tables, and he pointed outside. "How about the bunker?" he sugegsted.

"No, not there," Deena said quickly.

"The picnic tables?"

Jack held the door open for Deena, then followed her through. There were coals glowing in the barbecue pit, and the smell of steak still hung in the air from a cookout a group of officers had held a little earlier. They walked over to the table, then sat on the table with their feet on the seat.

"I've left a lot of messages for you," Jack said.

"I know . . ."

"You haven't answered any of them."

"I know that, too," Deena said. "Oh, Jack, why did you go back to that woman? I thought it was finished between you."

"Finished? It never started," Jack said. "Deena, there was never anything between us. Anything real, I mean. She was a . . . a sneeze, and little more."

"So what happened?" Deena asked. "Did you catch another cold?"

"What do you mean?"

"You know what I mean. The day of the awards ceremony. You were with her that day, weren't you?"

"I had to go out there to attend a reception," Jack explained.

"It's funny that none of the other officers were there," Deena said.

"I . . . I was the only one there," Jack admitted. "It was a trick. But when I found out, I started to come back, only . . ."

"Only what?"

"Only when I got to the gate, I saw you and Kramer together. You didn't waste any time getting another date, did you?"

"What did you expect me to do, sit around and twiddle my thumbs while you and Madam Dragonfly, or whatever her name is, played house?"

"Maybe not," Jack said. "But I certainly didn't expect you to jump in with Kramer, of all people. Deena, you know what I think of Kramer."

"Well, I . . . don't necessarily share your opinion of him," Deena said. "I think you and Bert just have a personality clash, that's all. Anyway, I didn't *jump* into anything with him. We went to Saigon, had a meal at the My Kahn, then came back, and that's all there was to it. Can you say your afternoon with Madam Ngyuen was that innocent?"

"No," Jack said quietly. "No, I can't." He took another swallow of his beer. "I wish I could say that, Deena. I wish to God I could. That woman, there's something about her, something evil. I hope I never see her again."

"Do you mean that, Jack?"

"Yes, I mean it," Jack said. "Of course I mean it."

"I'm glad to hear you say that. I was afraid that, well, that she might have you under some sort of spell. I was afraid I'd lost you."

"Lost me?" Jack asked, brightening. "Do you mean I was yours to lose?"

"Yes," Deena said. "That is, you could be if you wanted to."

Jack looked at Deena for a long, silent moment. "I want to," he finally said.

"Do you know what you're saying?" Deena asked.

"I think I'm saying I love you," Jack said. He smiled a crooked smile. "If it's not coming out right, you'll have to forgive me. I've never said this to another woman."

"Oh, Jack, *do* you love me?" Deena asked. "Do you really love me, or do you just feel trapped into saying so?"

Jack laughed. "I really love you," he said. "I don't think I realized how much I loved you until these last few weeks, though, when you weren't seeing me. God, how I missed you. God, how I hurt."

"God, how I love you," Deena said.

Jack started to put his arm around Deena to kiss her, but she pulled away. "No," she said. "Not here. Now I think I would like to go to the bunker."

16

"CAP'N, they're comin' back," Creech said, sticking his head through the door of Jack's office.

Since Jack didn't go on the mission, he used the morning to catch up on several reports that were due. In actuality, he did it more to keep his mind off the morning's mission than to accomplish the work. Yet, despite the work, the morning seemed to drag from the time the thirteen Cobras took off for their strike against the guns at Parrot's Beak, until the moment Creech reported that they were on their way back to the airfield.

"Thanks, Creech," Jack said, grabbing his hat and starting toward the landing pads.

Jack could feel the beat of the engines and blades of the approaching helicopters, and he looked north as they approached. There was something wrong! He looked toward Creech with an expression of confusion on his face.

"Did one element land already?" he asked.

"No, sir," Creech answered.

"There are only five in this group. I wonder why they're coming back in two groups?"

"Beats the hell out of me, sir," Creech said. "The Fly was in command. Who knows why he does anything?"

The Cobras approached in a single file over the hospital, then broke left for the final approach to the A Troop pads. Jack watched them as they hovered by. The noses of the ships were painted with shark's teeth, but there was a slightly different personality to each ship so that Jack, from the ground, could identify most of the individual aircraft. He saw his ship, the one flown by Kramer, but he didn't see Bostic's aircraft.

"That's what they did, all right," Jack said. "Bostic isn't with them. He must be bringing in the second group."

The five Cobras sat down lightly on the pads and the pilots killed the engines. Now the whine was replaced by the swooshing noise of the rotors as they began spinning down. Gradually the canopies were pushed open and the men began climbing out, coming out gingerly, as if checking the ground they had so recently abandoned to see if it was still there.

Ed Selfridge climbed out of Snake Six and started slowly toward Jack.

"Hey, Ed, why did Kramer divide you into two groups?" Jack asked.

Ed looked up at Jack, and the expression on Ed's

face caused a sudden knot to form in Jack's stomach. He felt a dizzying nauseousness. "My God, Ed," he said. "Don't tell me . . . Eight? We lost eight ships?"

"Yeah," Ed said quietly. "Bob got it. So did Mike, the slack man, Terry . . . we lost sixteen men today. Jack, you don't even have a command anymore."

"But how? What happened?"

"Cap'n, you know what it would be like if you put a bird in a food blender? Well, that's what it was like today. The shock isn't that we lost eight Cobras; it's that even five came back."

"The guns?"

"We didn't even get them dirty."

The other men started across the PSP then, two from each remaining helicopter, so that, counting Ed and Kramer, ten men had returned from the mission. Ten out of the twenty-six who took off that morning.

"Cap'n, I hope you don't have anything else for us to do today," Ed said. " 'Cause if you do, it's going to have to be somethin' a drunk can do. I doubt there'll be a man jack sober in an hour."

Ed started directly for the Red Bull, followed closely by the solemn-faced quiet pilots from the other ships. Now only Kramer remained, and he had yet to get out of the helicopter.

"Go ahead," Jack said quietly, knowing that he wasn't actually giving permission but just acknowledging a fact. He watched them for a moment, then looked back toward the field. By now every blade was still, and the crew chiefs had reached the aircraft and were tying down the blades. The crew chiefs for the ships which hadn't yet returned were standing around in shocked silence.

"Creech, go get Colonel Mayfair," Jack said quietly.

"Yes, sir," Creech said. Creech walked over and climbed into Jack's jeep, then started toward the squadron headquarters, leaving Jack standing out on the PSP alone.

"Get out of that helicopter, you son of a bitch," Jack said under his breath. "You've got to get out sometime. You can't stay there the rest of the day."

Finally Jack could wait no longer, so he started toward his ship. As he got closer he could see the damage that it and the others had sustained. There were a dozen holes in the tail cone and in the blades. The others had about the same degree of damage. It would be a week before any of them would fly again.

Jack reached the side of the Cobra and saw Kramer sitting there with a strange, almost detached look on his face. Kramer looked around as Jack came up to him.

"It was rough," he said.

"Rough?" Jack said. "You lead sixteen of my officers to slaughter and all the hell you can say is it was *rough*?"

"We ran out of ammunition," Kramer said. "If we hadn't run out of ordnance, we could have taken them out. I know we could take them out."

"You son of a bitch!" Jack swore, slamming his fist against the side of the fuselage.

"I've never seen such flak," Kramer said, not even reacting to Jack's outburst. "It was rough. It was really rough."

Jack looked at Kramer in anger and frustration. Frustration, because he knew that at this very moment, Kramer was only barely aware that he was alive. He wasn't aware of Jack at all.

Creech came back then, driving out to the helicopter with Colonel Mayfair riding in the right front seat. Mayfair jumped out of the jeep as soon as it stopped, and he looked at the row of empty pads.

"My God," Mayfair said. "We lost eight?"

"Yes, sir," Jack said.

"Bert, what the hell happened?" Mayfair said. "Didn't you have enough sense to call it off when you couldn't get through?"

"We ran out of rockets," Kramer said.

"Ran out of *rockets*? You stupid sack of shit, you nearly ran out of *men!*" Mayfair exploded.

"Colonel, we aren't getting through to him," Jack said, putting his hand on Mayfair's arm.

Kramer climbed out of the Cobra then, and without a word to anyone, started across the PSP toward the BOQs.

Jack and Colonel Mayfair stood there, watching after him until he walked between the maintenance hangar and the operations shack and disappeared behind a line of buildings.

"I'm going to ground that son of a bitch," Colonel Mayfair said quietly. "I'm going to ground him and order him into the hospital for psychiatric examination."

"I'm the last person to defend Kramer, as you well know," Jack said. "But I would imagine that an experience like today could shake up any man."

"But don't you understand?" Colonel Mayfair said. "There was no need for an experience like today. The orders gave us specific authorization to terminate the assault if it proved to be unfeasible. Shit, Kramer wasn't supposed to make more than one attempt, then pull away. I didn't want to launch this attack in the first place, but it was the only way we could get headquarters to request an air force strike."

"You mean the whole attack was a decoy?" Jack asked.

"Yes. At least it was supposed to be."

"Colonel, why the hell didn't you give me those orders and let me lead the mission then?" Jack asked. "You know how Kramer felt about calling in the air force."

"Yes," Mayfair said. "I know. That's exactly why I used him. Headquarters knew also, so if Kramer made one light pass and then came back, it would strengthen our request. If I sent anyone else headquarters may have suspected what my game was, and made us go again. Damnit, Kramer *knew* what I wanted, and he deliberately violated my orders."

"Bring the son of a bitch up on charges," Jack suggested.

"What charges, Jack? That he disobeyed my orders to disobey orders from a higher command?"

"Yeah," Jack said. "Yeah, I see what you mean."

Mayfair looked around the airfield. "Where are the others?" he asked. "The ones who made it back?"

"Over at the Red Bull."

"What the hell are they doing over there? The Red Bull won't serve any liquor until 1600."

"Wanna bet?"

"No," Mayfair said. "I don't want to bet, 'cause

I'd lose. I imagine if those guys want something to drink, they're going to get it, whether the Red Bull serves it or not."

"I feel like joining them," Jack said.

"Go ahead. I'm authorizing a thirty-six-hour stand-down for A Troop right now."

"Thanks," Jack said. "Creech, tell the men."

"Yes, sir," Creech said.

"You comin' to the club?" Jack asked Mayfair.

"No. No, I'd better get up to brigade. They're going to have to be told the news. I'm just glad I'm not the one who has to tell the families."

"Take my jeep," Jack offered. "It'll save you having to go back to your office."

"Want me to drive you, sir?" Creech asked.

"Yes, if you don't mind," Mayfair said. He looked over at Jack, and Jack thought he had never seen such sadness in any man's eyes. "Jack, I was in World War II and Korea, and I've never had a blow like this. You were even closer to the men than I was, so I know what you must be feeling. I just wish—" He stopped in mid-sentence and then shook his head. "I wish there was something I could say or do, but there's nothing."

"I know," Jack said.

The two men looked at each other for a long, awkward moment. Then Mayfair made a motion with his hand and Creech drove away. Jack watched as the jeep passed the detail of mamasans, then turned onto the road which led up to brigade headquarters. The mamasans were laughing and chattering away, totally oblivious of the tragedy which had just befallen the troop which employed them.

When Jack stepped into the Red Bull a moment

later he could smell the food being prepared for lunch. The tables were set with tablecloths, silver and napkins, while in the darkened bar area the remaining nine pilots of his company, all warrant officers, had pulled a couple of unset tables together. Open whiskey bottles sat on the table before them, and they were all drinking quietly.

"There," a Vietnamese voice said. "That's them. I told them, 'No can drink before 1600.' But they no listen. They come behind bar and get bottles anyway."

The voice belonged to the Vietnamese civilian who had been hired to oversee the other Vietnamese employees of the club. He was talking to Lieutenant Dixon, who, as a nonaviator, had been appointed the club officer.

"I'll take care of it," Dixon said. Dixon looked around the table quickly, saw that they were all warrant officers, then smiled as he realized that none of them outranked him. "Here, you men, what the hell do you think you're doing?" he demanded.

"What the hell does it look like we're doing, you dumb shit?" Ed replied. He drained the rest of his glass, then wiped his mouth with the back of his hand. "We're drinkin'."

"You can't drink in here until 1600 hours this afternoon."

"Kiss my ass," Selfridge said, pouring another glass.

"What?" Dixon sputtered, nearly choking over the warrant officer's audacity. "Listen, just because you men have wings on your chest, that doesn't give you license to—"

"Let it go, Lieutenant," Jack interrupted.

"I will *not* let it go," Dixon said indignantly. "These men have to learn that—"

"Throw him out," Jack said, and the two warrants at the end of the table nearest to Dixon stood up and grabbed him under the arms, then dragged him across the floor and tossed him through the door.

Dixon stood up and dusted himself off. "I'll be back with Major Morris!" he said, speaking of the provost marshal.

Jack walked over to sit in a chair offered him by Selfridge. He looked at his men, and at that moment he loved them more than anything in the world. There was no love which could compare with this; not love of a man for a woman, not love of a man for his brothers, sisters, parents, or country. It was a private love, shared only by those who had been in the crucible of battle, and understood by no one but them.

"Jack, you've got guts," Ed said quietly. "But I've never seen anyone quite like Kramer."

"He's beyond guts," one of the others said. "He's crazy."

"Tell me what happened," Jack said.

"Kramer was the first one in," Ed said. "We had the rockets, Mike went in with the mini-guns to cover us. Mike got hit right off. It must have hit the fuel cell because his ship blew apart right in front of me. I figured that without the mini-gun Kramer would break off the run, but we went right in. The stuff was all around us, but we didn't get hit."

"Did you fire your rockets?"

"Yeah, but those guns are so well dug in that you'd have to thread a needle to do any good. My rockets burst on the rock wall of the mountain."

"The next two ships went down," someone else said. "Then Joe and I went in, with Ollie and Fergus in the mini-gun ship. By then it was so hot that all I could think of was to get out of there. We fired a volley, but we didn't do any more than Ed was able to do."

"It kept goin' like that," Ed went on. "On the first complete pass we lost five. Five on one pass! I thought sure we would break off and come back then—hell, it was obvious we couldn't do anything. A fella'd almost have to walk up there and shove the rockets in by hand, I mean the guns are that well protected. But Kramer ordered another pass. This time, I figured I'd make sure it was our last pass, so I fired off everything we had left. Then you know what that son of a bitch did? He took us in a third time with nothing to shoot!"

"Why?"

"Why? You tell me why," Ed replied. "Because the son of a bitch is crazy, that's why!"

"What about Bob? When did he get it?"

"I don't even know," Ed said. "I tell you, Cap'n, after the second pass it was all I could do to keep from peein' in my pants. I've never been so scared in my life."

"He got it on his second pass," one of the others said. "I saw him go down."

"You know, after we lost eight ships in, oh, less than two minutes, I thought it was all over. I thought, this crazy bastard is going to keep going in until we're all gone. He has some reason to commit suicide and he wants to take all of us with him."

"I guess it finally got through to him," Jack said. "He finally gave the order to break off the attack, after eight were gone."

"No, he didn't," one of the pilots said. "That's just it, he never did give the order."

"What do you mean?"

"Hell, Cap'n, there wasn't a rocket left, there was no need for going back in there just to buzz 'em, the way he did, so the rest of us—well, we just started back."

"You mean he was going to keep you on station after you had expended all your ordnance!"

"Well, he never *said* as much," one of the other pilots said. "But when we all reported that we were out of ammunition, he didn't give us the order to withdraw either."

"That's when the crazy bastard went in again," Ed said. He grinned sheepishly. "I don't mind tellin' you, Cap'n, that I was sitting up front cussin' him out for all I was worth."

"When I saw him go in on an empty run," the other spokesman said, "I just said to hell with it and I started back. The others followed me."

"What did Kramer say about that?" Jack asked Ed.

"He didn't say anything," Ed said. "When we pulled out of the last run, he saw that the others were starting back so he just started after them."

"He didn't say anythig? Not a word?"

"Not a word," Ed said.

"Cap'n, what's going to happen now?"

"Colonel Mayfair has given us a thirty-six-hour stand-down," Jack said.

"Then what? We don't have a troop anymore. Are we going to be broken up and sent to other units?"

"I don't know," Jack said. "I hope not. I'd like to keep us all together, but I guess that's up to the ol' man. I know one thing, though—we've got to get some more pilots and aircraft before we're operational again, that's for sure."

"Cap'n, I'm going to tell you somethin', and I'll tell you right now," Ed said. "I will never fly another mission that Kramer commands. If this is sedition, then it's sedition, but I'll go to Leavenworth before I fly with that crazy man."

"That goes for me, too," another pilot said, and their declarations were echoed by all the others there.

"Oh, oh, we got company," one of the pilots said, pointing toward the door of the club. Major Morris was standing there, looking toward the table.

"Let me handle it," Jack said. "I know Morris. He's a pretty straight dude."

Jack walked over to talk to the provost marshal.

"Did Lieutenant Dixon come to you with his tale of woe?" Jack asked.

"Yeah," Morris said.

"Listen, they've been through it," Jack said. "I'd appreciate it if you'd just let 'em sit there and drink. I'll keep 'em out of trouble, I promise you that."

"Yeah," Morris said, as if distracted. "I heard what happened, and I told Dixon to back off. Fact is, when he heard about it, he withdrew his complaint anyway. That's not why I'm here, Jack."

"It isn't? Well, why are you here? What's up?"

"It's Colonel Mayfair," Morris said.

"Mayfair? What about him. Does he want to see me?"

"No," Morris took a deep breath. "Colonel Mayfair just had a heart attack," he said. "He's dead, Jack."

17

W HERE THE HELL did he go?" the marine hissed. "Sergeant Bell, did you see him?"

"He went right between those two trees," Frank said, pointing with his M-16 in the direction they had seen the V.C. flee. A V.C. sniper had fired on Frank's patrol just moments earlier. Frank and the others returned fire, but the V.C. got away into the jungle. They chased him about one hundred meters, and then lost him.

"Well, he can't just disappear into thin air," the first marine said.

"Listen," Frank ordered. "You take the others back down and tell Colonel Bell that I'm going to stay up here for a while longer. He may be hiding and when he thinks everyone is gone, he'll pop up again."

Frank had been promoted to Sergeant since running into his uncle, and was now the squad leader of the security squad which was assigned the duty of staying with Colonel Gilbert Bell's headquarters, wherever it may be.

"The colonel ain't gonna like it none, you stayin' up here alone," the marine said. "Especially you bein' his nephew 'n all."

"You don't let that bother you," Frank said. "I'll take care of my end of it, you just do what I told you."

"Yeah," the marine said. "Well, I'll tell you what, iffen the ol' man was *my* uncle, I'll be damned if you'd find me out here chasin' Charlie's ass around. I'd be his driver or his orderly or somethin' like that. Anyone that would get his ass shot at when he don't have to is crazy."

The patrol went back the way they had come, talking among themselves, and snapping twigs and breaking branches as they walked. Frank lay quietly, listening to them, understanding now how easy it was for the V.C. to set up an ambush against Americans. They announced their presence as surely as if they were preceded by a brass band every time they moved.

Frank lay on his stomach and aimed at the spot between the two trees, making certain that there was nothing in the way of his fire. He eased the safety off, then waited.

Bugs started crawling around on him, but still Frank waited, fighting against the impulse to move with all the willpower at his disposal. Finally, after a wait of nearly ten minutes, he heard something. Or felt it. Or sensed it.

Frank moved ever so slightly, laying his cheek along the stock of the weapon and peering down

the barrel. A head appeared, Frank started to
squeeze the trigger—then something told him to
hold back. He waited, and the head began to rise,
and then Frank realized that it was someone crawling out of a hole in the ground. A second and then
a third figure emerged from the ground, then all
three came through the trees to return to the place
where Frank's squad had first encountered the
sniper.

Frank squeezed the trigger and a burst of fire
hosed out from the end of his weapon. All three
V.C. crumpled under his fire, but even after they
fell he fired several more rounds at them, watching
the bark fly off the trees and the leaves kick up
where the bullets hit the ground. The sound of the
sustained burst of fire was deafeningly loud, and
after Frank let up on the trigger, he could still hear
it, bouncing back in echoes from the trees.

Frank stood up and ran in a crouch toward the
three bodies. When he got there he looked down at
them, making certain that all three were dead. His
heart was pounding, and his breath was coming in
short gasps, and he felt lightheaded, almost as if
he were out of his body watching the whole scene
from some unique vantage point.

Frank heard the snapping and popping of twigs
and branches approaching, and he swung his
weapon toward the sound.

"Sergeant Bell! Sergeant Bell, are you all right?"

"Yeah," Frank answered. "Yeah, I'm all right."

"What was the shooting? Did you get 'im?"

"Yeah," Frank answered. "Yeah, I got 'im."

Not one, but four marines were coming to his
rescue, and when they got there they stopped and
stared down at the three bodies.

"They're deader 'n shit, that's for sure," one of the marines said.

Frank turned one of the bodies over with his foot and looked down at him. Frank had no idea how old the V.C. was; he could have been anywhere from fifteen to thirty. It was hard to tell with the Vetnamese anyway, and the slackened features of death made it even more difficult to tell.

The dead man's eyes were closed. There was an old scar on his face, and an open sore on his chin. Two of Frank's bullets had caught him in the neck, and the tumbling action of the bullets had opened a large hole. He had on a black shirt, and was wearing a pin of some sort, perhaps rank, pinned to his breast pocket. His belt was leather, and the buckle said "baseball." He was wearing shorts, and one leg was pretty well damaged by Frank's bullets, but the other was unblemished, save the hundreds of bush and insect scars from living in the jungle. The V.C. was wearing sandals made of old automobile tires.

"We'd better call Hammer and tell him what happened," one of the marines said.

Frank saw that he was carrying a PRC-6 radio. "Here, give me that," Frank said, reaching for the radio. He took the radio in his hand and squeezed the talk button. "Hammer, this is Saber."

"Go ahead, Saber."

"We've killed three Victor Charlies and located a tunnel entrance. Over."

"Roger, Saber. Understand you have located a tunnel entrance?"

"That's affirmative. Over."

"All right, leave two guards and report back to headquarters."

"Roger, out."

"You, and you," Frank said, pointing to two of the marines. "You stay here."

"What about them?" one of the marines said, indicating the three dead V.C.

"Bury 'em."

"Bury 'em? What the hell for? We didn't kill the stinky son of a bitches."

Frank looked around and saw a ravine. "Drop them down there," he said. "Throw a little dirt and leaves over them."

"Drop them down there," one of the marines said. "As if they could walk themselves over there and there wouldn't be anything to it. Grab the feet, Larry."

"Why do I have to grab the feet?"

"Well, do you want to look into the son of a bitch's face?"

"No, no, I guess not. Okay, I'll grab the feet."

Frank went back along the trail until he found the road. Battalion command post was just across the road, and he saw his uncle looking at a map which was spread open on the hood of a jeep. A couple of staff officers were with him. Gilbert Bell looked up as Frank approached.

"Frank, show us exactly where you found that tunnel opening," he said.

Frank looked at the map for a moment, then he pointed. "It was right here, sir."

Gilbert drew a small red circle on the map, then he looked at the other circles he had drawn. He tapped his pencil on the map and smiled. "All right, gentlemen, look," he said. He pointed to the circles. "Here, here, here, here, here and here. They're making a great circle around . . ." He stopped and studied a moment longer. "They're making a great circle around Xuan Chi. There's no doubt in my military mind now, gentlemen. VCONGCOM is located right here."

"Colonel, I don't know," one of the staff officers said. "Most intelligence puts it closer to Phu Chat, way down here."

"I know," Gilbert said. "Believe me, I know. But I've searched every hill and stone in the whole province, and I'm convinced it's not there. Look, we know this is a main supply route for them through here, and this one here. The routes intersect at Xuan Chi."

"The B-52s have bombed that intersection half a dozen times," the staff officer said. "If there was anything there, it would have been wiped out."

"Not if the whole thing is underground," Gilbert said. "Gentlemen, we're going to Xuan Chi."

"I hope you're right, Colonel," a major said. He smiled broadly. "It would tickle the hell out of me to find VCONGCOM."

"What's VCONGCOM?" Frank asked.

"Viet Cong command headquarters," Gilbert answered his nephew. "It's the nerve center of the entire operation. If we could take it out, we'd wipe out the V.C. as an operative force."

"Damn," Frank said. "You mean get all the V.C. in the country at one time?"

"There would be V.C. left," Gilbert said. "But without a unified command, they'd be totally ineffective."

"Colonel, are we going to get support?" one of the majors asked.

"Yes," Gilbert said. "If I'm right, I don't think we could take 'em with one battalion, less heavy weapons. We'll need some augmentation, at least from the local guard commanders."

"Hell, the guard commanders are probably V.C. themselves," the major said. "I doubt that VCONG-COM could even exist in a province without them knowing about it."

"I know," Colonel Bell said. "Hopefully, the brass in Saigon will have enough sense to realize that, and send us American reinforcements."

"When are you going to ask?"

"I'm going to ask right now," Colonel Bell said. "It'll take two days to get an answer."

Jack folded the menu shut, then looked across the table at Deena, who was still studying hers. He laughed. "What's the matter, can't you make up your mind?"

"It's such a change from ordering at the Red Bull," Deena said. "There, you either want steak or you don't. And if you don't, you take whatever else they have."

"You've been to the My Kahn before," Jack said. "You were here with Kramer."

"I thought we weren't going to bring that up," Deena said. She folded her menu and laid it on top of his. "Anyway, that time doesn't count. I was disappointed that I hadn't come in with you and I let Bert order for me."

"What did he order?" Jack said. "I'll be sure I don't order the same thing."

"I don't know exactly what it was," Deena said. "But it was some kind of glazed chicken."

"Then I'll order *het ba ting goy* for the both of us," Jack said.

"What is that?"

"Literally, it's beef with vegetables. Don't worry, you'll like it. And we'll start off with *my ton* soup, and spring rolls."

Jack gave the order to the waiter, then looked out over the rail of the boat at the Saigon River. A small skiff was passing by, with a Vietnamese woman standing in the rear of the boat, stoically tending the tiller with her foot. The front of the boat was loaded with baskets of vegetables.

"It's hard to believe there's a war on when you're right here, isn't it?" Deena asked.

"Not always," Jack said. He let out a small, ironic laugh. "In the early days of the war this was a favorite target of the V.C. They used to hit it about once every six months. It's been quite a while since they've hit it, though."

Deena shivered and looked around. "I hope that doesn't mean they're due," she said. The waiter brought the soup, then disappeared again, leaving the two of them alone at their table by the railing. "Uhm, it's good," Deena said after her first taste.

"This is what the G.I.s call Chinese noodle soup," Jack said. "You've seen the old men pushing the soup carts down the streets?"

"Yes," Deena said.

"The carts are actually portable kitchens. There are several cauldrons in specially designed holes in the cart, one cauldron filled with steaming broth, another with vegetables, and a third with noodles. When you order a bowl of soup you can have it tailor-made to your taste, more or fewer noodles, and so forth. As the vendors push their cart, they have young boys running ahead of them banging two sticks together, like the percussion sticks of a Latin band. The rhythm of the sticks is very distinctive, according to the soup vendor, so if you like one guy's soup, you learn to listen to the rhythm of the sticks. That way, even if you're inside you'll know when your man is coming. The Vietnamese all have their own soup bowls, and they carry them out to the vendors to be filled."

"Have you ever done that?"

"Yeah," Jack admitted sheepishly. "I had an apartment downtown when I was here for my first tour."

"Did you have a live-in girlfriend?" Deena asked.

"No, not really. But I did party a lot. It was the thing to do then. A lot has changed since those early years."

"Like what?"

"The war was more fun then," Jack said. He laughed self-consciously. "I know that's not the proper way to express it; no war should ever be fun, and people were being killed then as well. But there seemed to be more of a purpose to what we were doing, and we had a sense of camaraderie then that doesn't quite exist now. There was no problem with the dopers, and no one had ever heard of the term *fragging*."

"Fragging? I haven't heard of it yet. What does that mean?"

"It's a term the enlisted men use when they talk about throwing a hand grenade into a BOQ or an officers club," Jack said.

"My God, Jack, are you serious? GIs would do that to their own officers?"

"It's been done a couple of times. Mostly by someone who's so spaced out on drugs that he doesn't know what he's doing."

"Oh," Deena gasped. "I guess in a way that was what Springs was doing with Bert, wasn't it?"

"If he had gone through with it," Jack said. "I don't think Springs ever really intended to go through with it. But Kramer is just the kind of officer who invites that sort of thing. He's self-centered and intractable and doesn't give a damn about the men under him."

"And now he's your commanding officer," Deena said.

"Yeah," Jack replied solemnly. "Now he's my commanding officer."

"I was so sorry to hear about Colonel Mayfair." Deena put her hand across the table on Jack's. "But there were so many that day that he sort of got lost in the shuffle."

"Now I know how Custer would have felt if he had stayed home that day," Jack said.

"How are the new pilots coming along?"

"They're coming along fine," Jack said. "We've had the in-country orientation flights, and they went well."

"And Bert? How's he doing?"

"As a technical commander, he's doing a fine job," Jack admitted. "But commanding officers have to show a little compassion ever so often, and Kramer doesn't make it there."

"Jack, you're so full of bitterness against him that you can't see around the wall you've built. You may have him wrong."

"Deena, as far as I'm concerned, that son of a bitch killed my men."

"He was just doing his duty."

"No, he wasn't. He went beyond duty, beyond sanity even."

"But isn't he up for a medal?"

"Yeah," Jack said. "He's up for the Distinguished

Flying Cross. They wouldn't put him up for anything any higher than that, because they were afraid an investigation would show that he should be in the looney bin."

"Let's not talk about Bert anymore," Deena said. "It just gets you upset."

"A most astute observation, my dear," Jack said. He smiled. "Besides, I don't remember inviting him to have lunch with us, do you?"

"Not at all," Deena said, returning Jack's smile.

Jack heard whistles and sirens out on the street, and he looked over to see what was going on. Two motorcycle policemen, dressed in white and with very wide leather belts, crash helmets and large sunglasses, led a motor procession. They were followed by a jeep, then a large black Mercedes, then another jeep and two more motorcycle policemen. In addition to the whistles and sirens, there were flashing red and blue lights, clearing the way for the convoy.

An old woman had spread a bamboo mat out near the curb by the *My Kahn*. She had several wicker cages and the cages contained live ducks and chickens. The approaching procession made no effort to avoid her, and at the last moment the old woman had to flee for her life. The vehicles struck the wicker cages, killing some of the fowl and freeing most of the others.

The ducks and chickens began beating their wings wildly, trying to get away. For the crowd, the chickens and ducks became fair game, and the birds were gathered up in a matter of seconds as men, women and children dashed away carrying a duck or chicken under their arms.

The convoy proceeded without acknowledging

the old woman or the damage done to her. Inside
the Mercedes, looking straight ahead as if totally
unconcerned with the havoc that had been caused,
Jack saw the Black Dragon and Madam Ngyuen.

"Yes, I saw it," Colonel Ngyuen said to his wife,
as their car sped away from the My Khan.

"You saw it?" Madam Ngyuen replied. "You saw
what?"

"I saw the jeep. Your American captain's jeep was
at the My Kahn. It is quite distinctive, you know,
with all the yellow. Surely you saw it as well?"

"No," Madam Ngyuen said. "I didn't see it."

"You just didn't want to see it, my dear," Colonel
Ngyuen said. "If he was at the My Kahn, he was
probably with the American nurse they say he has
been seeing. What is her name?"

"I have no idea," Madam Ngyuen said.

"Bell," Colonel Ngyuen said, answering his own
question. "Her name is Lieutenant Bell. She's quite
a lovely thing too, fair and blonde and lovely, as
fair, blonde American women are wont to be."
Ngyuen rubbed himself without shame. "It is too
bad we could not arrange a small get-together, you
to keep Captain Hunter entertained, and I . . ."
Ngyuen smiled in appreciation of his fantasy. "I
would keep the young lady entertained."

"I'm sure they would enjoy that," Madam Ngyuen
said sarcastically.

"Oh, but Americans do such things frequently,"
Ngyuen said. "They are called swap parties."

Madam Ngyuen didn't reply to her husband's
comment; she didn't want him to see how appealing
the idea really was to her. Instead, she looked
through the car window to avoid his gaze, hoping

to prevent him from seeing the sudden hunger which had leaped into her eyes at his suggestion.

"Ah, here is USARV Headquarters. You wait in the car, my dear. I shan't be too long. After all, I'm not *asking* permission to conduct an operation. I am telling them that I *intend* to."

"Where are you going to conduct your operation?" Madam Ngyuen asked.

"At Phu Chat," Ngyuen said. "I am going to destroy VCONGCOM."

"You know that VCONGCOM isn't at Phu Chat," Madam Ngyuen said.

"Yes," Ngyuen said, smiling broadly and flashing his gold tooth. "But the Americans are convinced that it is there. And they will gladly assist me with air support. And even though VCONGCOM isn't there, Colonel Duong's provincial headquarters *is* there, and the colonel is beginning to get a bit too much power to suit me. After Phu Chat, Duong will be reduced to little more than a guard officer."

"You are planning to use this operation to mask your own consolidation of power," Madam Ngyuen accused.

"Yes," Ngyuen said. "After Phu Chat, I will control every province around Saigon; Phu Chat, Phu Loi, Di An, Cu Chi, Ben Chat, Xuan Loc, and of course Saigon itself. I can move into the presidential palace and there will be no one to stop me."

"Do you think the Americans will allow you to conduct a coup and do nothing?"

"The Americans did nothing when Diem was killed, and they did nothing about the series of coups which followed that. They have an official hands-off policy with regard to Vietnam's internal affairs. No, my dear, they will do nothing about this. Soon you shall be the wife of the President of the Republic of Vietnam."

"Wouldn't the term *republic* be somewhat of a misnomer?" Madam Ngyuen asked.

Colonel Ngyuen laughed. "It's a misnomer now, my dear, but one which is accepted by our good friends and allies. Now, wait here while I discuss the operation with our friends."

Colonel Ngyuen got out of the car and was met immediately by some of the American press photographers who hung around the United States Army Vietnam headquarters. They started firing questions at him, and he smiled and responded in such a way as to keep their attention, though not give them any more information than he wanted to give them.

Madam Ngyuen felt such a hate for him at that very moment that she wished with all her might she could will someone to dart out of the crowd with a pistol and kill him. What an arrogant, pompous ass he was. How much better off all her people would be when the corrupt Saigon government and all its pretenders were thrown out, and the country was united under the government in Hanoi.

Madam Ngyuen had been working toward that goal for four years. She would rather be an ordinary citizen in a United Socialist Vietnam than be the first lady in a government headed by Ngyuen Thom.

18

G ENTLEMEN, the commanding officer," the adjutant announced, and all the officers who had gathered in the Fifth Air Calvary's enlisted mess hall stood as Kramer entered the room.

Jack was surrounded by the officers from his own troop, most of whom were newly arrived in-country, and all of whom were new to him. Ed Selfridge was the sole member of the original bunch who was still with Jack. One of the first things Kramer had done after taking command was to break up A Troop, so that the remaining officers of his old bunch were gone.

"If I don't break up your troop, Captain Hunter, there will be a clique formed by those men who were with the original bunch, and the new men will be out in the cold. It would not be good for morale."

Jack hated to admit it, but he knew that Kramer was right. It seemed a cruel thing to do, and it was hard to break friends apart, but there was some validity to the move. As long as they were together, there would always be the memories of those sixteen men who were killed.

"Gentlemen," Kramer said, "please be seated." There was a scrape of chairs as the officers sat again. Most had coffee and cigarettes, and they began drinking as they listened to Colonel Kramer give them their briefing.

"Gentlemen, this is big," Kramer said, rubbing his hands together. "This is very big. In fact, if we're successful, and I see no reason why we shouldn't be, we could end the war with the operation we're about to conduct."

Kramer's bold statement was met with a surprised gasp and outbreak of conversation from the officers in the room. Kramer smiled for a moment, then held his hands up for quiet. He laughed. "I know that's quite a declaration, but in a nutshell, gentlemen, what we're going to do today is destroy the command headquarters for the entire Viet Cong army. That would be the equivalent of wiping out Hanoi for the North Vietnamese."

"Colonel, are you saying we've located VCONGCOM?" a major who was the commander of one of the other troops asked.

"That's exactly what I'm saying," Colonel Kramer said.

"How did we find it?" the major asked. "Hell, we've been looking for it for seven years."

"We have three separate sources of verification," Colonel Kramer said. "The first source is by air recon. An interpretive study of a series of photos from the area has shown a definite increase in activity just prior to any major V.C. operation. The second source has been by ground recon, most recently from a reduced combat battalion of the United States Marines." Kramer laughed. "In fact, the marine colonel who's in command of the battalion asked for heavy weapons augmentation so he could conduct the operation himself. He's still waiting for an answer, and while he's waiting, we'll be acting. The Marine Corps will have all their press photographers and T.V. cameramen standing by, but this is one time they won't be getting any publicity, because this is an army show, gentlemen, not a marine show."

The officers laughed and applauded Kramer's statement. Then Kramer resumed with the briefing. "The third verification is probably our best source of information, and it comes from Colonel Ngyuen of the Lightning Force. Colonel Ngyuen has had operatives in the field, and he's penetrated the VCONGCOM headquarters. Ngyuen actually has a man on the staff of the senior V.C. commander."

"Where is VCONGCOM?" the major asked.

Kramer smiled. "It's right where we thought it was, all along. VCONGCOM is located very near the village of Phu Chat."

"Phu Chat?" Gilbert exploded when the message came back to him. "The idiots are going to attack Phu Chat?"

"Yes, sir," his adjutant replied. "We got the TWX from Saigon about an hour ago."

"But VCONGCOM is here, not in Phu Chat," Colonel Bell said. "What the hell is the matter with them?"

"The operation is a joint one, with the U.S. Army supplying the air support and Colonel Ngyuen furnishing the ground forces," the adjutant explained. "Colonel Ngyuen has definitely located Phu Chat as the headquarters for VCONGCOM."

"Bullshit. Ngyuen couldn't locate his ass with both hands and a compass if there weren't something in it for him. I don't know what his reason for wanting to attack Phu Chat is, but it definitely isn't to take out VCONGCOM."

"Should we TWX them back, sir?" the adjutant asked. "Maybe they didn't understand that we found VCONGCOM."

"No," Gilbert said. "No, never mind. We'll take on Xuan Chi without help. We'll just do it by ourselves."

The adjutant smiled. "Yes, sir!" he said. "I'll alert the commanders."

Gilbert looked at his watch. "Have them at the C.P. for a briefing at 1930 hours tonight. We'll move out at 0530 in the morning."

"Cap'n, you want to meet with our officers?" Ed asked after Kramer's briefing was concluded. Ed was a chief warrant officer, grade two, and was now, by virtue of a chain of events, the senior warrant in Jack's entire troop. There had been no commissioned officer to replace Bob Bostic, so Ed was also acting as an unofficial executive officer, a situation that was working out very well because Ed knew Jack well enough to anticipate his wishes.

"Yeah," Jack said. "We'll meet in Bostic's Bar."

"Roger," Ed said. He walked over to tell the others, while Jack stepped up to the front of the mess hall to talk to Colonel Kramer.

"Well, Captain Hunter, tomorrow is the first major operation for most of your boys. Do you think they're up to it?"

"Colonel, this is all a big mistake. I think you should call off this operation," Jack said.

The smile left Kramer's face, and he glared at Jack. "What do you mean, call it off? Have you gone crazy?"

"Colonel, can we speak in your office for a few minutes?" Jack asked.

"I think we'd better," Kramer said. He closed the manila folder on the table in front of him, then dropped it into an envelope which was marked Top Secret at the top and bottom. He tied the envelope flap down, then slipped it into another manila folder and carried it with him.

Colonel Kramer's office was the same one Colonel Mayfair had used, and when Jack followed Kramer into it, he felt a sense of painful regret over the death of his friend. The office was the same, but the furniture had been completely rearranged, so that now the desk was at the opposite end of the room, and the comfortable old couch was missing, replaced by two hardback chairs and a bookcase. The informal meetings Colonel Mayfair used to hold with his commanders and staff officers had been eliminated. Kramer conducted briefings, but no informal meetings.

The office which used to be Kramer's was now occupied by Major Fentress, recently arrived from the States. Jack realized that Kramer could very well have given A troop to Major Fentress, and moved Jack into the office as Squadron Executive officer. Because all the troop commanders would have ranked Jack, his function would have been administrative only, with the senior troop commander actually taking over the squadron in Kramers absence. That would have been a dead-end job for Jack, and he was glad, and a little surprised, that Kramer hadn't done it to him.

Kramer dropped the envelope on his desk, then looked back at Jack. "Now, Captain Hunter, what do you have on your mind?"

"It's this operation, sir," Jack said. "I knew this afternoon that it was in the works. We stage at 0600 hours tomorrow, Colonel Ngyuen will have two battalions at the line of debarkation, and two companies in reserve.

"Where did you get all that information?" Kramer asked.

"I got it from the same person who also told me that the whole thing is a farce. Colonel, the Black Dragon is just using us to consolidate his own power. VCONGCOM is not in Phu Chat province."

Kramer laughed. "Hunter, what are you trying to do?"

"I'm just trying to keep us from dancing to the Black Dragon's tune, that's all."

"I see," Kramer said. "And would you mind telling me the source of all your information?"

"I'd rather not," Jack said.

"You have no choice, Captain," Kramer said. "Now, what is your source?"

Jack sighed. "Madam Ngyuen told me."

Kramer smiled slyly. "Oh, so you're seeing her again, are you? Have you broken things off with Deena?"

"My relationship with Deena is none of your concern, Colonel. Nor is *any* of my personal life," Jack said sharply.

"On the contrary, Captain. It is of much concern, especially now that you're coming to me with this cock-and-bull story."

"It isn't a cock-and-bull story," Jack said. "I was told by Madam Ngyuen that her husband is just using us, and I believe her."

"When did she tell you this?"

"This afternoon," Jack said.

"Where did you see her?"

"I saw her at police headquarters in Di An. I got a call from the Vietnamese police that they had stopped one of my supply trucks, and I would have to come sign a release for the driver. When I got down there, I found out that Madam Ngyuen had had the truck stopped, just to get a chance to talk to me. That's when she told me everything."

"I see," Kramer said. "And why didn't you come to me then?"

Jack paused for a moment, and looked down toward the floor. Finally he sighed. "I didn't believe her," he said quietly.

"You didn't believe her?" Kramer said. He laughed again.

"I thought she was just using that as an excuse to see me again. I thought she just wanted . . ."

"Your body?" Kramer laughed.

"Yes," Jack said.

"Oh, my," Kramer said sarcastically. "It is difficult to be a sex symbol, isn't it?"

"There's more to it than that, Colonel Kramer," Jack said. "But I'd rather not go into all the personal aspects of it. Anyway, I had no intention of falling into any of her traps, whatever they might be. I'm in love with Deena, and I don't want to see her hurt."

"Well, now, there we agree, Captain," Colonel Kramer said. "I don't want to see you hurt Deena, either. I think she's quite a lady. But apart from that, if you didn't believe her when she told you this afternoon, what makes you believe her now?"

"When you held the briefing tonight and told us where we were going, then I knew she wasn't fooling me. And if she was telling the truth about the fact that there was going to be a mission against Phu Chat, then I think she was also telling the truth about the fact that VCONGCOM wasn't there. Colonel, call USARV and get us out of this."

"Captain Hunter, use your head," Kramer said. "I can't do that. Do you think that the Black Dragon's word is the only information on this operation? My God, man, they've been flying recon over that area day and night, using infrared photography. There have been long-range patrols—American patrols, I might add—who have spotted activity there. And there are agents in the field who are on our payroll who have confirmed VCONGCOM. And most damning of all, there was a request from an American marine colonel, just two days ago, requesting permission to attack VCONGCOM. His information is that he's found tunnel entrances all around the place. Now, against all that, you're going to have me call USARV and say, 'Hold it, gentlemen, the mistress of one of my officers says we're all wrong.'"

"The mistress?" Jack said. "I would hardly call her that."

"Well, would you rather I said you've been sleeping with the Black Dragon's wife and that *she* told you?"

"You could at least quote the source," Jack said.

"You would not have to editorialize about our relationship."

Kramer pinched the bridge of his nose for a long moment before he spoke again. When he did speak, he spoke in a lower, friendlier tone of voice. "Listen, Jack," he said. "I know that you and I got off on the wrong foot when we came here. I don't know, maybe we were both hotshot officers, vying for the old man's attention. Well, *I'm* the old man now, and I don't feel the same sense of competition with you that I did then, so I'm willing to let bygones be bygones. Hell, I got a new major in, and don't think he doesn't want your troop, but I've kept you over there."

"And I appreciate it, Colonel, really I do," Jack said.

"I know the business at Parrot's Beak hit you hard. Hell, it hit all of us hard. But you have to realize that this is war, and men get killed in war. You just have to accept it, that's all. You can accept it, can't you? You aren't letting it color your judgment, are you?"

"I'm not sure I'm following you, Colonel."

"All right, I'll put it in a nutshell. Except for Mr. Selfridge and yourself, everyone in your troop is green. Could it be that you're concerned that what happened to Lieutenant Bostic and the others might happen to these new men as well?"

"Well, as you said, Colonel, this is war, and those things happen in war. Of course I'm concerned. Isn't everyone?"

"Perhaps so, but not everyone allows that sense of concern to make them so overly protective that their judgment is impaired. Perhaps you believe Madam Ngyuen because you *want* to believe her."

"Kramer, are you calling me a coward?" Jack asked, a biting edge to his voice.

"No, of course not," Kramer said. "Jack, you're as good and as courageous an officer as I've ever known, and despite our differences, I really do feel it has been a privilege to have you serve under me. But the loss of more than half your command had to have some effect on you. Hell, it would have some effect on anyone. I'm just suggesting that it may have had the effect of clouding your judgment without you even realizing it."

"I see," Jack said.

"Look," Kramer went on, "I'll tell you what. I'll send a DD 95 up to USARV, detailing the information you've given me here tonight. It's too late to stop the operation now, even if I wanted to. But if what you say is true, if Ngyuen is attempting to use this to consolidate his own power in some way, then USARV will at least have been warned, and they can take action. Is that fair enough?"

"If that's all I can get, I'll take it," Jack said.

"I appreciate your concern, Jack, really I do," Kramer said, still speaking in a friendly though almost patronizing tone of voice. "But after all, what could go wrong tomorrow? If you are right, and there is no VCONGCOM, then the worst we'll get out of it is we'll waste a little fuel poking holes in the sky. If there are no V.C. there will be no battle, and if there's no battle no one can get hurt. And if you're wrong, then that means that VCONGCOM *is* there, and it's the battle we've all been looking for."

Jack smiled sheepishly. "Yeah," he said. "Yeah, I guess you are right at that."

"I'll see you tomorrow morning then," Kramer said.

"I've got my pilots waiting for me in Bostic's Bar. I guess I'd better go talk to them."

"Jack, your troop will be in reserve tomorrow," Kramer said as Jack started out the door.

"Reserve?" Jack asked, turning back toward Kramer. "You mean we have to sit on our ass at the staging area?"

"No, you can go aloft," Kramer said. "But I want you to orbit at the IP until—and in case—we need you."

"All right," Jack said. "But my guys aren't going to like it."

"You make them like it."

When Jack stepped into the A Troop officers' lounge a few moments later, everyone was talking and laughing, and the very atmosphere was charged with an electric excitement, akin to that in a locker room before a football game.

"Hey, Cap'n Hunter, what's the skinny?" one of the younger warrants asked. "Are we going to win the war tomorrow?"

Jack walked over to the refrigerator and opened the door before he answered. There was only one beer left, and he hesitated for a moment.

"It's yours, Jack," Ed said quietly. "I threatened to bust the head of anyone else who took it."

"Thanks," Jack said, smiling and taking the can. He made a mark by his name on the tally sheet, then opened the can and looked around the lounge. The lounge had been built by Bob Bostic the second month he was in-country. It had been fairly easy to do; Bostic just stretched walls between two existing buildings, added a floor and a roof and the lounge

was born. The lounge was a nice, quiet place to
write letters, read or have a few beers, if you didn't
want to go over to the Red Bull. There had been a
few half-hearted attempts to name it when it was
first built; someone had suggested the name Snake-
Pit, another the Wet Mouse. Now it was called
Bostic's Bar by everyone, and Jack had even had a
sign painted, identifying it as such.

"This will be the first operation for most of you,"
Jack said. "Some of you were in another company
before you came here and you have an operation
or two under your belt, but it will be your first
with the Fifth Cav. You'll all have a weapons mix
tomorrow, half mini-gun and half rockets. Get a
good night's sleep tonight, and make a thorough
pre-flight before you take off in the morning."

"Which element are we, Cap'n, do you know?"
Ed asked.

Jack sighed. "Yeah," he said. "We're being held in
reserve.'"

"Reserve?" a half dozen pilots said disgustedly.

"Yeah," Jack answered. He smiled. "But at least
we don't have to sit it out at the staging area, so
that means we can go aloft and wait targets of opportunity."

"But what if a target of opportunity doesn't come
along?" one of the warrants asked.

"I believe in making my own opportunities," Jack
said.

"All right!" his officers answered, cheered by the
fact that they were guaranteed by their commander
that they would see some action tomorrow.

"Ed, you want your own ship tomorrow, or do
you want to be my gunner?"

"I'd better be your gunner, Cap'n. You couldn't

hit a bull in the ass with a bass fiddle without me."

"Good," Jack said. "I was hoping you'd say that."

"Oh, I saw Deena over at the Red Bull a bit earlier. She wanted to know if you were going to stop
by."

"Yeah," Jack said. He looked at his watch. "It's
only 2100. I thought it was a lot later than that."

19

DEENA was still in her bed when she heard the helicopters taking off the next morning. At first she turned and pulled the pillow over her head to drown out the noise, but there were so many of them that the whine of their engines and pop of their rotors couldn't be shut out.

Suddenly Deena was wide awake. Jack was in one of those helicopters!

Deena got up quickly and ran to her window, then looked out toward the field. The helicopters were leaving in one long line, passing just a few feet over the top of the hospital, and she could see them approaching, growing larger and larger, then suddenly whipping by over her head, only to be replaced by another, and then by another.

Deena and Jack had gone to the bunker the night before. They had gone to the bunker but they had not made love. It had been a strange evening. Jack was quiet and introspective, and yet, rather than feeling shut out, Deena had felt very much a part of his thoughts.

They had not made love, but they had held each other, and exchanged long and hungry kisses. Deena had somehow felt closer to Jack last night than she had at any time in the past, even when they had made love.

A chill passed over Deena, and after the last helicopter was gone she went back to her bed. She hoped the almost spiritual closeness she had felt with Jack last night was not some sort of omen, that it did not mean that Jack was going to be hurt today . . . or worse.

Deena closed her eyes and mouthed a quick prayer. She had seen many wounded young men since coming to the Second Field Hospital, and she never saw one without feeling that it could be Jack or Frank. Every one of them was someone's brother, husband, son or lover, and she tried to imagine what it might feel like to be the one closest to a wounded soldier.

Last week there had been a handsome, muscular young man who had lost both legs below the knees to a Claymore mine. The soldier had been an All Big-Eight Conference football player who had been drafted by the Denver Broncos. Everyone was talking about him, and someone commented to the soldier about what a shame it was that he, a football player, should lose his legs.

"I know you feel bad, man," the soldier had replied. "But I want you to understand something. My legs would have been just as important to me if I hadn't been a football player, so don't feel any extra sorry for me. Feel sorry for *anyone* who has to go through this, no matter who he is."

It had been particularly moving for Deena, because the soldier spent all his time trying to make everyone else feel better. She wished she could have just a little of his strength.

Deena tossed around and tried to go back to sleep, but she was unable to. Finally she got up, dressed and went to the hospital mess, where they were already serving breakfast. After downing a cup of coffee, she reported to her ward, two hours earlier than she was scheduled to go on duty.

"Colonel Bell, all the demo squads are in position," Frank reported to his uncle. Frank was on the radio, coordinating the demo squads.

Gilbert looked at his watch, then at his adjutant, who was on another radio in communication with the company commanders who were deployed around Xuan Chi. "Are the commanders all ready?" he asked.

"Yes, sir," the adjutant replied. "They're all in position, ready to go."

"Okay, Frank, tell 'em to drop the charges," Gilbert said. "That'll send everyone in toward the middle. Then, when they figure out that all the entrances were hit at the same time, they'll have a hint that something's going on. That's when they'll come out, and that's when we'll have them."

"This is Hammer. Drop your charges," Frank said into the radio.

The C.P. was surrounded by a series of stomach-jarring thumps as the explosions went off.

"Send in the companies," Gilbert said to his adjutant, and that order was passed on as well.

A moment later, they heard the first sporadic sounds of rifle fire. Gilbert looked at the others and smiled broadly. "Gentlemen, we are engaged," he said.

The sound of rifle fire grew more sustained, until within a matter of a few moments it was obvious that all along the line the battle was joined.

"Colonel, we're encountering much stiffer resistance than we thought," the adjutant said. "Captain Miller estimates that there may be two battalions of V.C. in position to guard the tunnel complex."

"Where's he getting the most resistance?" Gilbert asked.

"On his north flank," the adjutant said.

"Give me the map," Gilbert replied. He spread the map out on the hood of his jeep and looked at the sectors of responsibility he had assigned. He reached for the microphone.

"Touchstone, this is Hammer. Can you move one thousand meters to your right and advance up that ravine?"

"Negative, Hammer," Touchstone's voice answered. Frank could hear the sound of rifle fire over the radio, as well as in the distance. Touchstone's voice sounded high-pitched and excited. "There's a mine field between our right flank and the ravine."

"You've got to get over there," Gilbert said. "There's a possibility that Bravo Company will have their flank turned if we don't get into a blocking position."

"We can't cross here, Hammer, but I'll find a way to get over there."

"Do it as quickly as you can," Gilbert said. He

set the microphone back down on the hood of the jeep, then looked around the C.P. area. There were twenty men here, including the security squad and the battalion staff. It took less than a second to make up his mind.

"Lieutenant," he said quickly, taking the map off the hood of the jeep and tossing it into the front seat.

"Yes, sir?"

"Get the men together, We're going up the ravine."

"*We* are, sir?" the young lieutenant gulped.

"That's right, Lieutenant, *we* are," Gilbert said. "We've got to set up a blocking position before Charlie turns Miller's flank. Now let's get a move on!"

Frank started the jeep with a big grin, and looked at his uncle. "You better hang on," he said. "I'm going to drive this son of a bitch right up to Charlie's front door."

"That's what I'm paying you for," Gilbert answered.

Frank slipped the jeep into four-wheel drive, then started right up the ravine, which offered a tortuous though continuous path to the edge of Xuan Chi. The jeep bounced and tossed, and the engine strained and protested, but both the jeep and the two three-quarter ton trucks behind it moved the twenty men into position much faster than they could have walked the distance.

Suddenly there was a loud twanging, then a swishing sound as wire whipped by each side of the jeep. The V.C. had tied a wire between two trees, stretching across the ravine at about neck height. It was one of their favorite tricks, and early in the war there had been a few hapless soldiers decapitated as they drove under it. Now, all vehicles were equipped with a wire cutter, a piece of angle iron welded to the front bumper, sharpened on the front, designed to cut through any such wires. Frank's cutter had just done the job for which it was intended.

"I'll tell you," Frank said, breathing a sigh of relief, "whoever thought that little gimmick up is a smart man. If I ever meet him, I'll buy him a drink."

"I imagine there are quite a few men who would like to buy him a drink," Gilbert said.

The machine gun which was mounted on the jeep opened up right over their heads. Frank watched the tracer rounds whip into the trees at the top of the ravine.

"What is it?" Gilbert asked.

"There's someone up there, Colonel," the young man at the machine-gun ring said. "He was just watching us."

"Did you get him?"

"No, sir, I don't think so."

"We'd better hurry," Gilbert said, "or they'll be at the other end of this thing, waiting for us."

"If I go any faster, I'm liable to hit a rock and bust open the oil pan," Frank said.

"Never mind about that," Gilbert said. "If you knock a hole in the pan, just keep going until the engine freezes. We've got to get up there."

Frank went as fast as he could go and still maintain control of the jeep. Now the rifle firing which had been in the distance was right on them. The hair stood up on the back of Frank's neck, because he was certain that an entire V.C. platoon was waiting just ahead. They would be trapped in the ravine, and the V.C. could shoot them like shooting ducks in a barrel.

Then they were through the ravine, and at the edge of the rice paddy. Frank whipped the jeep into a turn and stopped behind a dike.

"Take up positions behind the dike!" Gilbert shouted to his men. He stood up in the jeep and pointed to the dike, in the way he wanted his men to go.

A bullet smashed through the windshield of the jeep and buried itself in the seatback cushion. It passed right between Frank and his uncle, miraculously hitting neither of them.

Frank looked up and saw more than a hundred V.C. coming across the rice field toward them.

"Jesus Christ, look at that!" he said, pointing toward the advancing figures.

"Take 'em under fire!" Gilbert shouted. "Take 'em under fire!"

The machine gun on the jeep opened up, but after a burst of less than two seconds, the machine gunner was hit, and he pitched over the back of the jeep with a bleeding bullet hole in his forehead.

Frank crawled up behind the machine gun.

"Frank, no, that position's too exposed," Gilbert warned.

"It's the heaviest weapon we have!" Frank answered, and he started firing toward the advancing V.C., hosing the tracer rounds up and down along the line, feeling a gut satisfaction every time he saw one of the black-clad men crumple.

Gilbert came back to the jeep then and took the microphone. "What's the marine air push?" he shouted to Frank.

"It's preset by channels," Frank called down to him. "Channel one is marine air, channel two is navy, channel three is air force, and channel four is army."

Gilbert turned to channel one.

"Hello, any air, any air ,this is Hammer. Come in."

A bullet careened off the machine gun ring, and pieces of it shaved off and hit Gilbert in the face, stinging in a dozen different spots.

"Any air, any air, come in," he called again. He switched to the navy channel and tried three times there, but without success. He switched to channel three.

"Hello, any air, any air, this is Hammer. Come in."

"Hammer, this is Dawn Patrol, over."

"Dawn Patrol, can you give ground support assistance?"

"Where are you, Hammer?"

"I'm near Xuan Chi, in Alpha sector. I need—"

"Sorry, Hammer, we must have an atmospheric bounce on the signal. I'm over two hundred miles away. It'll take twenty minutes to reach you. Can you hold out?"

"We don't have much choice," Gilbert said. "Get over here as fast as you can."

"Roger," the air force pilot said. "I'm on my way."

Frank was hit then, once in the leg and once in the shoulder. The bullets made a hollow, thocking sound as they hit him, and blood squirted from both wounds. Frank slumped in the gun ring, but he grabbed hold, then pulled himself back up.

"Get down from there," Gilbert ordered.

"I heard the air force," Frank answered. "They're twenty minutes away. This gun is all that's keepin' those bastards back!" Frank started firing again, and the V.C. who had jumped up when they thought he was out of action now dropped back to the ground.

"I'll try the army," Gilbert said. "I don't know what they could possibly have that'll do us any good, but I'd call the Girl Scouts if I thought they could help." He turned the preselector to channel four.

"Any air, any air, this is Hammer, come in."

"Any air, any air, this is Hammer, come in."

Jack heard the call, and he changed his transmitter to match the receiver. "Hammer, this is Snake Six, go ahead."

"Snake Six, where are you? Do you have ordnance?"

"Affirmative, I have a flight of Cobras."

"Cobras? Outstanding. I need ground support urgently."

"Who are you, Hammer? I have no code on Hammer."

"Brass Monkey, Snake Six," the voice said. "Brass Monkey."

Brass Monkey was the code which identified one branch of service requesting assistance from another branch. The words were to be used only in an extreme emergency, and a Brass Monkey report was to be filed with the Military Assistance Command, Vietnam, as soon as practical after the incident.

"Roger, Hammer, understand Brass Monkey. Where are you? What do you need?"

"Xuan Chi, sector Alpha. I have one marine battalion, and we're being opposed by brigade-strength Victor Charley."

"Brigade strength?"

"Roger. How soon can you get here?"

"About ten minutes," Jack said.

"I'll pop smoke when you're here."

"All right!" Ed said from his position in front of the Cobra. "It looks like we're going to see a little action after all."

"That's a rog on that," Jack said. He flipped channels. "Snake Flight, this is Snake Six. Follow me out, we have a fire mission." He flipped channels again, then called Colonel Kramer.

"Tiger Six, this is Snake Six. Over."

"Go ahead, Snake Six."

"Tiger Six, request permission to answer a call for ground support."

"Negative, Snake Six," Kramer replied, and Jack could hear the irritation in his voice.

"It's a Brass Monkey," Jack said. He was already enroute to Xuan Chi, despite Kramer's disapproval. Kramer didn't answer, so Jack said again. "Did you hear me, Tiger Six? It's a Brass Monkey."

"Wait, Snake Six," Tiger Six said, and Jack waited for the reply while continuing toward the call for help. About seven minutes later, he still had no answer, but he saw Xuan Chi and a couple of burning huts, and then he saw a firefight in progress.

"Look, over there," Ed said, pointing to an open field. There were a handful of Americans behind a dike, and several black-clad soldiers inching toward them.

"Snake Six, this is Tiger Six," Kramer's voice came back.

"Go ahead, Tiger Six."

"Negative on the Brass Monkey. I checked with MACV, and the air force is on their way. They should be there one-zero minutes from now."

"I'm here now, Tiger Six, and there's going to be a slaughter down there if I don't respond."

"Negative, Snake Six. Return to your station at once!"

Jack flipped the selector switch off. "I didn't hear a word he said, did you?" he asked Ed.

"Who's that, Jack?" Ed replied. "Were you talking to someone?"

"Not a soul." Jack called the others in his flight. "Arm," he said. He saw a pillar of green smoke rising from the group of Americans behind the dike.

"I have green smoke," he said over channel four.

"You got it, Snake Six," Hammer's voice replied. "I never thought I'd say this about the army, but you guys look beautiful."

"Hey, I know you Marines are a bunch of macho bastards," Jack teased. "But it looks to me like you just let your alligator ambition overload your hummin'-bird ass. I never saw so many damn V.C. in one place before."

Jack made a pass over the rice paddy, firing rockets and mini-guns. There was another Cobra right beside him, and between the two of them the entire rice paddy was under fire.

Jack pulled up at the end of the strafing run, loading the rotor disc and feeling the G-force of the turn. He twisted around in his seat and looked behind him to see the third fire team making their pass.

"Hey, you guys did that pretty good!" Hammer's voice said. "You've stopped them cold."

"Let's go around again," Jack said to Ed. "And get it right this time."

"Roger," Ed replied. He selected his weapons mix and freed the sight, preparing for the next run.

"Here we go again," Jack said, and he dropped the pitch and rolled the cycle forward to start his second strafing run. Now he could see dozens of bodies lying in the paddy, and the formation which had been advancing so confidently against the handful of marines was starting back toward the woodline on the opposite side of the field.

"All right!" Hammer's voice said. "You got 'em on the run. I want to thank you for a job well done."

"You need another couple of passes?" Jack asked.

"Negative, I just heard from the air force and they're on station. They're going to napalm the woods."

"All right, Hammer. By the way, do you have a friendly element on your left?"

"Yes, they're attempting to link up with us," Hammer said.

"They've about got the job done," Jack said. "I'd say they're no more than two hundred meters away."

"Thanks, Snake Six. I owe you," Hammer said.

"Snake Flight, return to station," Jack said.

"Look at that," Ed said, pointing back toward the woodline. A Phantom was just climbing out of its bombing run, and a sheet of fire was spreading behind and below as the napalm exploded. "They don't screw around, do they?"

"I'll say they don't," Jack said. He flipped the

selector switch back to the Tiger frequency. "Tiger Six, this is Snake Six. I'm reestablishing contact, over."

"Snake Six, return to base at once," Tiger Six said angrily. "Report to me as soon as you land."

"Roger, Tiger Six."

"Cap'n, I'll swear the radio wasn't working," Ed said.

"Let 'im do his damndest," Jack said. "Let's go by Phu Chat and see what's going on. My hunch is that the whole thing is a wash-out. That's probably why he's so pissed off."

"I wouldn't doubt it," Ed said.

It was about a ten-minute flight back to Phu Chat, and during that ten minutes Jack wondered what Kramer would say. If there had been no firefight at Phu Chat, there wasn't much Kramer *could* say. He would have to try and balance a disobeyed order against the rescue of the Marines, and Jack was pretty sure that Hammer, whoever he was, would come to his defense if it ever came to that. The truth is, it would probably never come to that at all. Kramer would make an ass of himself if he tried to press it. At worst, Kramer could see to it that Jack's troop got the short end of every assignment, but that wouldn't be any different from what it already was.

"Hey, Cap'n, what the hell is that?" Ed suddenly asked.

"What?"

"Look down there, between those hooches and the river! What is that? What's going on?"

Jack banked around so he could see where Ed was pointing, then he saw, too. A group of villagers, men, women and children, stood huddled together while a line of black-clad soldiers were standing off to one side. There was a winking of muzzle flashes from the black-clad soldiers, then the villagers began falling to the ground.

"Son of a bitch, those are V.C. down there, executing villagers!" Ed said.

"Tiger Six, Tiger Six," Jack called. "This is Snake Six. Where are you?"

"Snake Six, this is Tiger Six, five miles South of Phu Chat, returning to base."

"Negative," Tiger Six said. "Phu Chat is cleared. Return at once!"

"Jesus, they just brought in another bunch," Ed said.

Jack hit his parrot identifier, and punched the ident response code. If the troops on the ground were friendly, they would have responded to his coded inquiry, but there was no response.

"No squawk on parrot," Jack said. "Let's hit 'im! Snake Flight, V.C. are killing villagers down there. Let's take 'em out!"

Jack whipped the Cobra around in a tight turn, then dropped pitch and rolled forward, coming down as swiftly as the German Stuka dive-bombers of World War II.

Ed started firing the mini-guns. The rate of fire was so fast that the guns buzzed like drills, and the soldiers began crumpling.

"Fire on them," Jack said to the others in his flight. "Use mini-guns only, no rockets. Watch out for the villagers."

Two more Cobras after Jack's made a pass at the now-disorganized soldiers, and within minutes their bodies littered the ground, along with the bodies of the villagers who had been executed.

"Snake Six, Snake Six, cease fire, cease fire! They're friendlies, they're friendlies!" Jack recognized the voice of one of his pilots.

"What?" Jack shouted.

"I've picked them up on Fox Mike, and they squawked my Parrot!"

"My God," Jack said, feeling sick.

"Snake Six, I've got a follow-up report," the pilot said quietly. "We've just killed two American Advisors, fourteen ARVN troops, and Colonel Ngyuen."

20

ITEM IN *Newstime magazine:*

There will be two trials going on in Saigon next month. One will be the court-martial of a U.S. Army captain, and the other, a Vietnamese military tribunal's trial of a Vietnamese national for espionage. The two trials, though separate, are linked together in a fashion which has all the earmarks of an international scandal.

The American being tried is Army Captain Jack Cavalier Hunter, a helicopter pilot. (See *Newstime*, The Nation: "The Reluctant Hero," August 9, 1969). Captain Hunter is accused of dereliction of duty and willfully disobeying an order from his commanding officer.

The Vietnamese national to be tried by military tribunal is Madam Ngyuen Ly, widow of the late South Vietnamese strongman, Colonel Ngyuen Thom. (See *Newstime*, The World: "The Dragon is Slain," November 26, 1969). Madam Ngyuen, regarded by many as one of the most beautiful women in the world, is being charged with espionage. Should Madam Ngyuen, who is also known as the Dragon Lady, be found guilty, she could face death by firing squad.

Madam Ngyuen's husband, Colonel Ngyuen, was killed during an operation against the long-sought VCONGCOM (Viet Cong Command). It has been disclosed that Colonel Ngyuen was actually killed by American helicopter gun-ships commanded by Captain Hunter, when he allegedly mistook Colonel Ngyuen's troops for V.C. (Colonel Ngyuen's troops were dressed in black uniforms, the traditional color of the V.C. guerrilla.)

The U.S. Army charges against Captain Hunter are based on the fact that, against specific orders to the contrary, Captain Hunter left his assigned station during the operation, then returned and, again against specific orders, led the attack against what he had reported as V.C. troops.

According to informed military sources, there are no other charges yet filed, but Captain Hunter's relationship with Madam Ngyuen will figure heavily in the Saigon government's spy case against the Dragon Lady. The Vietnamese military tribunal which has jurisdiction in all cases of treason, even those involving civilans, has heard testimony from two witnesses who have sworn to the fact that Captain Hunter and

Madam Ngyuen were sexually intimate. One is a hotel maid who reportedly witnessed Captain Hunter and Madam Ngyuen bathing together, and the second is a house-girl employee of the Ngyuen villa, who actually saw Captain Hunter and Madam Ngyuen having intercourse. The house girl's testimony is most damaging, even though she is only eleven years old, because whereas the hotel maid could only put them together in a bathtub, the house girl testified to having actually witnessed the two having intercourse, watching them through a one-way mirror which Colonel Ngyuen had installed in his house as part of an elaborate security system.

It is being suggested by the Saigon government that Madam Ngyuen exercised her considerable sexual influence over Captain Hunter and convinced him to attack her husband's troops in order to allow the hardcore cadre of VCONGCOM to escape. Reportedly, there are letters and documents as well as eyewitnesses attesting to Madam Ngyuen's espionage activity, and the case against her seems fairly strong.

The case against Captain Hunter is, by the prosecution's own admission, not yet strong enough to ask the United States to submit Captain Hunter to the Vietnamese courts for trial.

One possibility: Vietnam military law allows the tribunal to return a verdict of guilty against Captain Hunter, even though he is not tried directly. Should that happen, the South Vietnamese government could request that Captain Hunter be turned over to them for sentencing. Under the law, that could be death by firing squad.

American servicemen have at times been remanded to host nations for sentencing in the past. One American was sentenced to life imprisonment by the government of Japan in 1957 for shooting a pilferer while he was on guard duty, and an American lieutenant, "The Autobahn Torso Killer," was sentenced to thirty years by the Federal Republic of Germany in 1965 for murdering his mistresses. However, it seems highly unlikely that Captain Hunter would be surrendered to the government of South Vietnam, regardless of their finding.

"We've got 'em, Mack," Larry DeWitt said, putting the magazine down on the table. He smiled broadly and pounded his fist into his hand. "By God, we've got 'em!"

"We've got who, my man? What are you talkin' about?" Mack asked.

"Did you read this article on Captain Hunter? I mean did you *read* this shit, man?"

"Yeah," Mack said. "Yeah, I read it."

"Well, that's it," Larry said. "That's how we're going to make Nixon hear us."

"Hey, man, you've lost me. I don't know what the hell you're talking about," Mack said. He laughed. "Fact is, I don't think you know what you're talkin' about yourself."

"Oh, but I *do* know what I'm talkin' about," Larry said. He pointed to a photograph of Captain Hunter. "When you see him, what do you think about him?"

"I think it's some dude who has his tail in a crack," Mack said.

"I see a symbol," Larry said.

"What kind of symbol is he?"

"Any kind of symbol you want him to be," Larry said. "Now, dig, he's a hero, right? He's spent three tours in 'Nam, he's won all kinds of medals, flown all kinds of missions, killed V.C.—I mean John Wayne himself would be proud to go to an American Legion barbecue with him, right?"

"Yeah . . ."

"But this is also the same guy who had balls enough to say in public that he had questions about the war, and he applauded those whose dissent kept the government honest. He even named me by name, if you recall."

"Yeah," Mack said. "It gave you a big head, too."

"Well, I've got to get my press where I can," Larry said, smiling. "I never had the ability to break quarterbacks in half. Anyway, when Hunter said that, he sent out a lot of good vibes to the protesters, man. There've been a few letters to the editors about it, and I've heard people talk about what a gutsy thing it was for him to do. So I don't think he'd be lynched at an ADA meeting either, would he?"

"Probably not, man, but what are you getting at?"

"Just this," Larry said. "Captain Hunter is a symbol to the right and a symbol to the left. That makes him more than a symbol, that makes him the pivot point of this entire war. Mack, public opinion is going to turn upon this man, like a vault door turns open on a fine-jewel bearing. Captain Hunter is the beginning of the end of the Vietnam War. The long nightmare is coming to an end."

"Fine, fine," Mack said. "Now, tell me how he's going to bring all this about."

"He isn't," Larry said. "We are."

"We? You mean you and me?"

"No," Larry said. "I mean the entire nation. Look, for the last several years there have been demonstrations against the war and demonstrations for the war, but there has never been one united demonstration for the same goal. Not until now, that is. But with this guy. . . ." Larry tapped his fingers on the picture of Captain Hunter. "With this guy we can do it. Don't you see? Here we have an opportunity to bring it all into focus. Here's what the war has done to a genuine American hero. Captain Hunter has played by their rules, and he's getting it stuck to him. If the system will go against him, it will go against anyone, and everyone has to see that. I think we should mount a demonstration in support of Captain Jack Hunter. We could get ten, twenty, maybe thirty thousand people together and march against the White House. When Nixon looks outside those gates, he's going to see hard hats and hippies, ADA and American Legion, peace symbols and the American flag. See, it's not a narrow interest anymore. It's not just a handful of people protesting the war because they don't want to fight; it's an entire nation protesting a war that's gone haywire."

"You're really serious about this, aren't you?" Mack said.

"Yeah. In fact, I'll tell you how serious I am. I'm so serious that I intend to surrender to the FBI in front of the White House on the day of the demonstration."

Mack smiled. "That's where we came in, my man, remember? You were going to surrender the night the police burned our house."

"Yeah," Larry said. "Then I was the only one of us the FBI wanted, and you convinced me what a good thing it would be for the cause. Now, you're wanted, too. Do you still think it's a good idea?"

"Yeah, for you," Mack laughed. "Not for me."

"I'm not going down alone," Larry teased. "I'm going to name names."

"You know what they do to stool pigeons in the slammer?" Mack asked. "They break their heads."

Larry winced. "I'm your best friend, remember? Surely you wouldn't make me go through something like that."

"I guess not," Mack said. "I guess the only thing I can do is go down with you. All I can say is, I hope this idea works. If it does, you're a brilliant man. If it doesn't, I'm stupid."

"Why are *you* stupid if it doesn't work?"

"For going along with your dumb-ass idea."

"Go ahead and give her what she wants, man," a voice said.

"Yeah, Romeo? Well, what does she want?"

"Man, she wants to get in the back seat of that car and get laid."

"Don't worry, William Holden's my main man. If the broad wants to get laid, he'll take care of her. Don't forget, he's tryin' to get into her sister's britches, too."

Frank could hear the strange conversation even before he opened his eyes, and he lay there listening, trying to figure out where he was. Under his face he felt the crisp, clean feel of bed linen, and the coolness of an air-conditioned environment. He tried to turn over, and he felt a pulling of skin and a sharp pain. He winced, and groaned aloud.

"Hey, the marine's coming out of it," one of the voices said.

Frank opened his eyes. He was lying in bed, and right across from him was another bed, a hospital bed with the top half cranked up so that the occupant was nearly in an upright position. That occupant was looking at him.

"Hey, my man, how do you feel?"

"Where the shit am I?" Frank asked.

"See, I told you he wouldn't know," the man said over his shoulder to another bed beyond him. "These dudes never know. They wake up in here and they're surprised as hell." He looked back at Frank. "You're in the Second Field Hospital, man, in Phu Bien. Hey, you got one good-lookin' sister, you know that?"

"Sister? You mean Deena? Is she here?"

"I bet she's come in here ten times this mornin' to see if you were awake yet. My name's Pete, this here is Morgan. We flipped a jeep out on 13."

"He's going to get her now, Petey. They're going to the picnic, and that's when he's going to get her."

Petey laughed. "We been watching *Picnic* on the T.V. You ever see it? It stars William Holden and Kim Novak."

"I don't know," Frank said. "I'm not much into television shows."

Petey laughed. "It isn't a television show, it's a movie. They're just showin' it on AFN."

"Man, would you look at Kim Novak?" Morgan said. "I'd soak my pants in gasoline and run through hell just for the chance to spend one night with her."

"That movie's fifteen years old," Petey said. "Kim Novak's an old broad now."

"Are you kiddin'?" Morgan asked. "I seen a picture of her not too long ago. She ain't changed none. I'd do it fifteen years from *now*, even."

Frank managed to get turned enough to see the T.V. mounted on a bracket on the hospital wall. "I can't even hear it," he said.

"There's no sound," Petey said. "We don't want to get bogged down with the story, we just like to look at the pictures." He laughed.. "Besides, it's better when we make up our own story."

The three men heard the click of shoes on the floor, and they looked toward the sound.

"Here she comes again," Petey said. "Is she really your sister? She's a lot prettier than you are, man."

Frank grinned. "Yeah," he said. "She's my sister."

Deena walked up to Frank, smiling broadly. She leaned over and kissed him. "I told you not to do this," she said.

"Not to do what?"

"Not to get wounded just to get down here to see me."

Frank laughed. "Hey, you didn't have anything to do with it, sis. I just wanted some clean sheets and an air-conditioned room. It's nice down here. You live like this all the time?"

"Well, sure," Deena joked. "Doesn't everyone?"

"I wish."

"Ah, it's not all that nice. Room service after eleven at night is lousy." The smile left her face, and she became not a nurse, but a sister who has gone through the anguish of seeing her brother brought in more dead than alive. "Oh, Frank, I've been so frightened for you," she said. "The doctors didn't give you much hope at first."

"What happened to me?"

Deena looked surprised. "You mean you don't even remember?"

"I remember driving a jeep up a ravine," Frank said. "I don't remember anything after that. What happened, were we ambushed or what?"

"I don't really know," Deena said. "I know you fought in a big battle." She smiled. "Uncle Gilbert said he was putting you in for a medal. He was very mysterious about it."

"Uncle Gilbert," Frank said. "Is he all right?"

"He's fine." Deena reached up and brushed some hair away from Frank's forehead. "Frank, do you remember some army helicopters coming to help you out?"

"No," Frank said. "I don't remember anything about the med-evac."

"I don't mean med-evac," Deena said. "These were Cobras."

"Cobras? No, I don't remember anything about any Cobras. Why?"

"Oh, it's just someone . . . I know . . . is in trouble because he came to help you instead of doing what he was supposed to be doing."

"Hey, if we needed help, how can he be in trouble for helpin' out?"

"I don't know for sure," Deena said. "It's all very complicated and frightening. It's like they're out to get him or something."

Frank smiled. "This is someone you just know, right? I mean there wouldn't be any more to it than that, would there? Like maybe you're sweet on the guy?"

"Well, maybe I am, just a little," Deena admitted, returning Frank's smile. "But you've no room to talk, brother. I happen to know that there's a girl who managed to get herself transferred from

Da Nang to Phu Bien, just to be able to see you when you can have visitors."

"Stacey?" Frank asked. "Sis, is Stacey here?"

"Yes."

"You've . . . you've met her?" Frank asked anxiously, looking into his sister's face for her reaction.

"We've had dinner together at the Red Bull a couple of times," Deena said. "That's the officers' club."

"What do you think?"

"I think she's a beautiful girl, a lovely person, and one smart chick. Wait until you hear what she did to Captain Morrow."

"Captain Morrow? What about him?"

"It seems that your ex-commander got rid of you just so he could move in on Stacey." Deena laughed. "Stacey said Morrow thought it was the days of the old plantations, with massa callin' in his wench. Anyway, she set up a meeting, pretending she would go along, then she stole his clothes and he had to walk from the back of the generator shed all the way to his hooch, absolutely naked. Everyone got quite a kick out of that."

"Sis, what do you think about. . . ."

"About the fact that Stacey is black?"

"Yeah."

"I think you're both asking for a lot of trouble," Deena said. Then she smiled. "But I don't know any two people who would be better able to handle it."

"Then you approve?"

Deena laughed. "Hey, big brother, since when have you ever needed my approval for anything?

It isn't my place to approve or disapprove. It's only my place to wish you happiness, and that I do."

Frank reached out and took Deena's hand in his own. "You know, sis, you didn't grow up to be such a pain in the ass after all."

21

TERRY K. KANODE was more than just a good lawyer. He was, as he liked to say, better than Perry Mason. Perry Mason got his innocent clients off despite the odds against them. Terry K. Kanode could often get his clients off even if they were guilty.

Kanode had been hired to defend Jack Hunter by the Citizens' Alliance for Justice, an unlikely coalition of liberals and conservatives who wanted to see that Captain Hunter received the best defense possible.

The Universal Code of Military Justice supplies military lawyers for all the accused, but it does make allowances for civilian lawyers, should the defendant desire one.

It had been easy to get authorization from the Judge Advocate General's office to have a civilian represent Captain Hunter. It had been a little more difficult to get permission from Captain Hunter. Kanode had to use his most persuasive arguments just to convince Jack that he would be better off with a civilian attorney. Kanode even enlisted the aid of Deena Bell to plead his case, and under all that pressure, Jack finally relented.

Kanode looked like anything but a lawyer. He was a veritable giant, at least six feet four, with an enormous frame, from which was suspended a huge belly. The belly was the end result of one of his hobbies, cooking. Despite the large belly, he was covered with inches-deep layers of muscle, all of which combined to give him the bulk of a mountain. Kanode flew around in the States in his own private jet. Here, in Vietnam, he would be able to move only at the sufferance of the U.S. Army. When he represented a client in the States, he stayed in the most expensive suite in the best hotel in town. In Vietnam, he was assigned a plywood-enclosed B.O.Q. room, just like everyone else. Kanode ate in the finest restaurants in the States; here he would have to take his meals at the Red Bull. In the States, his suits were tailor-made for his large frame. Here he was dressed in jungle fatigues and canvas boots.

"But I have no problem with any of that," Kanode explained to Jack. "My boy, you have become a *cause celebre*. I have here a copy of Monday's Washington paper. Read this article."

They were in Bostic's Bar, and Jack took the paper from Kanode, then settled back in the green vinyl couch to read while Kanode pulled a beer from the refrigerator and made a tally-mark by Jack's name.

"God, how does anyone keep enough liquid here?" Kanode asked, wiping the perspiration from his face before he started to drink. "I feel like I'm melting away in a pool of sweat."

"You get used to it," Jack said.

"Lord, I hope not," Kanode answered. "I don't want to be here that long."

Jack read the news article.

THOUSANDS MARCH HERE TO SHOW SUPPORT FOR CAPTAIN HUNTER

Doves and Hawks in Unprecedented Show of Unity

Thousands of demonstrators thronged Pennsylvania Avenue yesterday as they marched from the Capitol Building to the White House. In a city grown used to war demonstrations, this one attracted a great deal of interest because of its unique composition of formerly opposing forces. A long banner stretched across the front of the marchers, bearing a peace symbol on one end, and an American flag on the other. Veterans of Support for America marches walked arm-in-arm with veterans of protest marches, all asking that Captain Jack Hunter be cleared of the charges facing him.

The Vietnamese tribunal has already found Madam Ngyuen guilty of espionage, and, in that same hearing, tried Captain Hunter *in absentia,* returning a guilty verdict against him as well. Both Madam Ngyuen and Captain Hunter were sentenced to death by the tribunal. Because Madam Ngyuen is a world-famous personality, and because the government of Saigon wished to show "its compassion and awareness of world interest in the case," Madam Ngyuen's sentence was reduced to twenty years' banishment, which means she will be free if she can find a country to accept her.

France has already made the offer, and it is believed that Madam Ngyuen will go to Paris, where Madam Nhu, sister-in-law to the late President Diem, is now living. Captain Hunter's sentence was "remanded to the United States Army for disposition in a way which is to the best interests of both countries."

At the conclusion of the march, ADL activists Larry DeWitt and Mack Burton, accompanied by two members of the American Patriot's Committee, voluntarily surrendered themselves to the FBI. They did this, they said, in order to "call attention to the miscarriage of justice which has brought Captain Hunter to trial."

"I hope DeWitt and Burton made out all right," Jack said, folding the paper and laying it to one side.

"Don't worry about them," Kanode said. "They can't even get them for draft-dodging. It turns out they're both 4F."

"Burton is 4F? I thought he was an All-American Football player."

"They're the kind who have the hardest time passing the physicals," Kanode explained. "By the time they've had four or five years of footabll, they've got all kinds of injuries. Anyway, the government's case against them will never stand up. I'll have 'em both out, protesting again before you know it. You're the one we have to worry about now."

"Yeah," Jack said. "You know this other business, this spy business, is so ludicrous that I don't even know how to approach it."

"It's not as ludicrous as you think," Kanode said.

"What do you mean?" Jack laughed. "You don't really think the army's going to turn me over to them, do you?"

"No," Kanode said. "But in light of the findings of the Vietnamese court, the army has added another charge. The JAG officer notified me this afternoon."

"What's the other charge?"

"Article 118 of the UCMJ," Kanode said. "Murder."

"Murder?" Jack said in a shocked voice. "Did you say murder?"

Kanode opened his briefcase and pulled out a charge-sheet. He cleared his throat, then began to read: "In that Captain Jack Cavalier Hunter, ASN 02214390, did at Phu Chat, Vietnam, on or about 0830 hours, 19 November, 1969, murder Colonel Ngyuen Thom, Sergeants Filmore Addison and Mark Cavindish, and fourteen South Vietnamese soldiers, members of an allied military force, by means of shooting, or causing by his command to be shot, by strafing with an armed helicopter."

"Damn!" Jack said. "Damn, I can't believe they're actually charging me with that."

"I'd rather have it now than get you off on the dereliction of duty charge and then have to go up against this one later. Better to get it over with while sentiment is on our side."

"Do you think the sentiment will help?"

"I don't know," Kanode said. "I honestly don't know."

"Who's the trial counsel?" Jack asked.

"Major Fred Albright," Kanode said. "He's sharp. The army brought in a big gun for this one; Albright has an outstanding record, and he recently published a brilliant article in *The American Bar Association Magazine* on the legal responsibility of the military to the judicial system of host nations. I took the time to read those articles, Jack. Albright will have all the advantages in this case. He's in his home territory, he knows his way around a military court, and he's the recognized expert on this particular kind of case."

"Mr. Kanode, you don't really think he has a chance of . . . I mean, he couldn't really get a finding of guilty, could he?"

"He has so much of a chance that I visited with him after I picked up the charges, to see if there was a chance to plea-bargain involuntary manslaughter, and accept guilty to disobeying an order and dereliction of duty."

"You're not leaving me much of a career, are you?" Jack said.

"Career? Captain Hunter, I'm trying to save your life," Kanode said.

Jack stood up and walked over to the door of the lounge. He looked through the plexiglass window, out across the compound. He could see the roof of the building where the trial would begin the next day. He could also see the Red Bull, where he knew pilots were reflying today's missions, and doctors and nurses were unwinding from the day's tensions. And he was no doubt the subject of a dozen or more conversations. He wished none of this had happened, he wished he could just close his eyes and turn the clock back to before Phu Chat, to the days when he was like the others, marking off one more day at the tables of the Red Bull.

Jack was no longer commander of A Troop. Major Fentress had his troop now. In fact, Jack had no official position at all. He had been relieved of command, even before the charges were filed, and assigned to the Squadron S-4 as an assistant supply officer. He had no real duties as assistant supply officer, for which he was thankful because it gave him time to aid in the preparation of his defense. It also gave him some time with Deena. That was the only bright spot.

Major Albright was sitting in the BOQ room which had been assigned to him. He dropped a manila folder on his desk and scooted his chair back. He pushed his dark-rimmed glasses up and pinched the bridge of his nose, the pink of the inside of his palms contrasting sharply with the deep black of his face.

Major Frederick Douglass Albright was thirty-four years old, five-foot-three and 135 pounds. He looked a lot like Sammy Davis, Jr., and had even been mistaken for him on one or two occasions.

Albright picked up the *Stars and Stripes* which was folded on the desk before him and read the banner-line concerning the trial:

KANODE TO DEFEND HUNTER

The prospect of facing Kanode had been both

exciting and frightening to Albright. Kanode was a legend among lawyers, and Albright was going to meet him in the arena of the courtroom. He felt as he imagined the gunfighters must have felt in the days of the Old West when they got a chance to go up against the top gun.

Albright had once had the ambition of becoming not just the greatest Negro lawyer, but the greatest lawyer in the country. Unfortunately, acquiring his law degree wasn't enough. Even though he attempted to go into private practice, he found that those people who could afford lawyers' fees, black as well as white, preferred to take their chances with a white lawyer. After a year of frustration, Albright applied for a commission in the Army Judge Advocate General's Corps, where, within the Army's particular social structure, he had become an officer first and a Negro second. There he was given interesting cases to try and fascinating legal problems to solve. He found a home, and like many an ambitious and professionally dedicated Negro before him, he decided to make a career of the army.

And now the army had given him the opportunity to go against the best. Albright smiled. He was ready for him. Let the trial begin.

It seemed to Jack that every news service Vietnam had a representative at Phu Bien. They were lined up along both sides of the plank walk which led to the front door of the courtroom. The courtroom was actually an administration building which had been cleared of desks and file cabinets, and converted over for this purpose. Cameras snapped and whirred, and reporters stepped up to him, thrusting microphones into his face. There were all sorts of microphones, the larger ones belonging to the mobile T.V. crews, and the smaller ones to the hand-held cassette tape recorders. A half dozen reporters shouted questions, all at the same time.

"No comment at this time, gentlemen," Kanode said as he put his arm on Jack's elbow and continued to walk him through the crowd.

"Just one question, Mr. Kanode, please?" one of the reporters shouted.

"Please, gentlemen, I promise you a statement later in the day, but none now."

"Can we get a photograph of the two of you?"

Kanode stopped and turned toward the photographers with a big smile. "You may take a picture, but we won't answer any questions."

Jack stood nervously as the newspaper photographers and the television cameras ground away at them. After a moment Kanode smiled and said, "We'll see you later, gentlemen."

Inside the building, the sun streamed in through the plexiglas windows, and the bright beams picked up a million dust motes which floated in the still air of the quonset-hut type building. The air conditioners hummed and rattled, and the one nearest the defense table was dripping water. Jack watched the drops fall into a little puddle, spreading concentric circles, while the court-martial board was sworn in.

After the swearing-in ceremony, Jack looked at the board, and his eyes fell on Colonel Gerald Youngblood, the president of the court. Colonel Youngblood had bushy eyebrows, smoothly combed hair, and a beakish nose. It was almost a hawk nose, and because his name was Youngblood, Jack thought of *Youngblood Hawk,* the Wouk novel. As Jack looked down the board at the other officers, he wondered about the background of these men who were met to determine his fate, There were only three aviators out of the seven board members, and, Jack noted disappointedly, the board president was one of the four who was not an aviator.

There was more ceremony, much of it incomprehensible to Jack, until finally Major Albright was able to call his first witness. Albright called Lieutenant Colonel Bert Kramer.

Those in the room watched the door through which the witness would enter. There was an expectant air to the court, like the collective pause of breath at a football game just before the opening kick-off.

Colonel Kramer came in, a formidable figure in his ribbon-splashed khakis, saluted the board president, was sworn in, and took his seat on the raised platform in the center of the room.

Colonel Kramer was approached by Major Albright and asked to explain in his own words the events leading up to the tragedy of November 19.

Colonel Kramer told the operational plans, including the intelligence report of the enemy situation. He told of the overwhelming amount of evidence which had been gathered in support of the contention that Phu Chat was headquarters for VCONG-COM, and then he told of Captain Hunter's visit on the night before the operation, during which time Captain Hunter tried to get the mission cancelled.

"And how did you handle Captain Hunter's request?" Major Albright asked.

"I submitted a DD-95 to USARV Headquarters," Kramer answered.

"A DD-95?"

"You know, a memorandum," Kramer said. "It was too late to actually do anything about it, other than report to headquarters that Captain Hunter had made the request."

"Colonel Kramer, why did Captain Hunter try to cancel the mission?"

"I can only tell you the reason he gave me," Kramer said. "He said that he had information that VCONGCOM was not at Phu Chat."

"And where did he get this information?"

"From Madam Ngyuen," Kramer said.

There was a buzz of interest among the courtroom spectators, but it died quickly under Colonel Youngblood's piercing gaze.

"No further questions," Major Albright said.

Kanode stood up, but he didn't leave the defense table. "Colonel Kramer, did you locate VCONGCOM?"

"No, sir," Colonel Kramer replied.

"Thank you," Kramer said, sitting down.

"Redirect?" Colonel Youngblood asked of Major Albright.

This time Major Albright stood up from his table without approaching the witness. "Colonel Kramer, how would you classify the mission, other than the fact that VCONGCOM wasn't located?"

"There were 129 of the enemy killed, and we took eighteen casualties; seventeen killed and one wounded. I believe we would have located VCONGCOM had it not been for the strafing death of Colonel Ngyuen. Captain Hunter is responsible for—"

"Objection," Kanode said quickly. "Colonel Kramer is usurping the authority of the court in his statements. It is for the court to assess the responsibility."

"Objection sustained," Colonel Youngblood said.

"Colonel Kramer," Major Albright said. "Even without locating VCONGCOM, knowing what you know now, would you still have conducted the operation?"

"Of course I would," Kramer said. "Any time you achieve a kill ratio that large, you have had a successful operation."

"Then you believe the information Captain Hunter came to you with on the night before the mission was false information? Now, bear in mind I'm not asking what Captain Hunter's motivation was. I'm only asking for your assessment of the quality of the information."

"The information Captain Hunter gave me on the night before the operation was totally false," Kramer said.

"And again, just so I'm sure about things, where did the information come from?" Major Albright asked.

"Defense will stipulate that the information came from Madam Ngyuen," Kanode said easily.

"Ah, yes, Madam Ngyuen," Major Albright said. "For further identification, would defense agree that it is the same Madam Ngyuen who was found guilty of espionage by a Vietnamese tribunal?"

"The same," Kanode said.

"Thank you," Major Albright replied. He smiled broadly at the long table of officers who comprised the court-martial board. "No further questions of this witness at this time. I would like to reserve the right to recall."

"Very well. Call your next witness."

"The court calls Specialist Five Benjamin Adams," Major Albright said.

Adams was a small, wiry enlisted man who was nervous, and who sweated profusely despite the air conditioners. Adams was an avionics maintenance man, someone who worked on radios. He testified that the transponder was inoperative in aircraft number 84195. That was the tail number of the helicopter Jack had flown that day. The transponder IFF was the devise whereby a coded signal would identify friend or foe.

"What was wrong with the transponder?" Major Albright asked.

"The parrot wouldn't squawk," Adams answered.

"The parrot wouldn't squawk?"

Adams smiled. "That's the code receiver, sir," he explained. "When you get the identifying code, it makes a squawking noise. That's why they call it a parrot."

"Did Captain Hunter know that his parrot wouldn't squawk?"

"It was written up on the dash-thirteen, sir," Adams said. "I made the entry myself."

"Is there any way he could have missed it?"

"I don't see how, sir. That's the first thing a pilot looks at before he starts to fly."

"Thank you, Specialist Adams," Major Albright said. "Your witness, Mr. Kanode."

"Specialist Adams, when did you make the entry about the transponder?" Kanode asked.

"I checked it out when we were arming the aircraft, sir, just before the mission," Adams said.

"How long before the mission?"

"Maybe fifteen minutes," Adams said.

"Was that *after* Captain Hunter had pulled his pre-flight?"

"Well . . . yes, sir, it might have been," Adams said.

"Did you *tell* Captain Hunter about the transponder?"

"No, sir," Adams said. "I couldn't. He was at a mission briefing. But I wrote it up."

"Thank you, Adams," Kanode said.

Albright stood up again. "Specialist Adams, did Captain Hunter look at the log book before he took off?"

"I don't know, sir," Adams said. "He's supposed to. All I can do is write it up."

"Thank you," Albright said. "The court calls Specialist Six Thomas Deckheart."

"Major Albright, if you call the next witness now, I shall have to limit your time. Would you prefer adjournment?"

"Yes, sir," Major Albright said.

"Very well," Colonel Youngblood said. "This court stands adojurned until 1300."

"Well, what do you say, Captain, shall we go to the Red Cow for lunch?" Kanode asked Jack.

"That's the Red Bull," Jack said. "And unless you want to eat C rations, that's the only place an officer can eat on this base."

"Then let's go," Kanode said. "I'm starved."

"I'll go with you," a woman's voice said, and Jack turned quickly to see Deena standing behind them.

"Deena! What are you doing here?"

"Major McGee has given me leave for the duration of the trial," she said. "Are you happy to see me?"

Jack smiled broadly and held his arms open, inviting Deena to come to him. She did and they embraced, just as half a dozen cameras clicked from the back of the room.

"Smile," Jack said. "You're on candid camera."

"If you don't mind," Deena said, "I have a guest who's going to eat lunch with us."

"I don't mind at all," Jack said. "Who is she?"

"It isn't a she," Deena said. "It's a he."

"Oh?" Jack said. "Then maybe I do mind," he said archly.

Deena laughed. 'He's my uncle, Jack, and you won't mind at all. You've met him before . . . sort of."

"I've met him before?"

"You only know him as Hammer," Deena said.

"Hammer? You mean the marine colonel . . ."

"The marine colonel you helped is my Uncle Gilbert," Deena said. "He's come down here to, in his words, 'pull your ass out of the fire.' "

22

WHEN COURT reconvened after lunch, Specialist Six Thomas Deckheart was sworn in as a witness for Major Albright. Specialist Deckheart was a linguist, assigned to the American advisory team which was attached to Colonel Ngyuen's unit. Deckheart was the only American who survived the strafing incident, and he was just completing his story of what happened.

". . . Addison went down with the first pass," Deckheart said. "And Cavindish, he couldn't believe it. He kept saying over and over again, 'Doesn't the son of a bitch have his radio on? Doesn't he know what he's doing?' Then, he got his. He . . . he died in my arms."

"And then what happened?" Major Albright asked.

"I'd been squawking the IFF ever since the first pass," Deckheart said. "Finally it got through to them. They broke off the attack and flew away . . . but it was too late for Addison and Cavindish. And for Colonel Ngyuen and several of his men."

"Tell me," Major Albright said, "what was Colonel Ngyuen doing during the strafing?"

"He was amazing, you know? He moved right out into the opening and started waving his flag at them."

"His flag?"

"Yes, sir. It was his personal flag. He carried it everywhere he went. He figured that if the pilots saw that, they would recognize it, and break off the attack."

"Do you think they would have recognized it?"

"Yes, sir," Deckheart said. "Colonel Ngyuen's flag was so well known that everyone knew it. It was very distinctive, yellow, with a large red diamond in the center, then a white circle in the center of the diamond and a black dragon in the white circle."

"Do you think the pilots did recognize it?"

"Yes, sir," Deckheart said. He looked toward the table where Jack sat with his two defense attorneys. "The leader of the group sort of zeroed in on it, like he wanted to make *sure* he got him."

"Objection," Kanode said.

"Sustained," Colonel Youngblood agreed. "Specialist Deckheart, you will answer only such questions as you can answer from personal knowledge. Your opinions are not admissible, and you may find yourself subject to conduct-unbecoming charges should you persist."

"I'm sorry, sir," Deckheart said.

"Specialist Deckheart, who was the first person killed in the strafing?" Major Albright asked.

"I don't know, sir. But Colonel Ngyuen went early."

"Thank you," Major Albright said. "Your witness."

Kanode stood up and tapped his pencil in the palm of his hand for a long moment before he spoke. Deckheart, who had finished his testimony before Major Albright with a sense of defiance, wilted under the extended period of silence, and he broke off his challenging glare to look at the floor.

"You liked Colonel Ngyuen, didn't you?" Kanode finally said.

"Yes, sir."

"Why?"

"Because he was a fighter," Deckheart said. "He didn't pussyfoot around like so many others. When he went after something, he didn't hold back."

"What do you mean, he didn't hold back?"

"Well, like if he was in pursuit, and Charley left Colonel Ngyuen's sector, he didn't bother getting permission from the province chief or ARVN headquarters or anything else. He just went about his job."

"He never checked with the village mayors or police or anything?"

"No, sir,'" Deckheart said proudly.

"And you thought that was good?"

"We're supposed to be at war over here, sir," Deckheart said. "To Colonel Ngyuen's way of thinking, war is total. He said once that if you made war unpopular enough, there wouldn't be any wars."

"A noble statement," Kanode said. "No doubt he used it as justification for attacking villagers. He did attack villagers on occasion, didn't he?"

"Mr. Kanode, I beg your pardon, sir, but you don't know shit from shinola."

"Specialist Deckheart!" Colonel Youngblood barked in an angry tone of voice, but Kanode held up his hand.

"If it pleases the court," he said quietly, "I would like to allow this witness the freedom to express what's on his mind in his own words."

"Very well," Colonel Youngblood said. "However, Specialist Deckheart, you are cautioned about the propriety of this court, and the respect due its officers."

"Yes, sir," Deckheart said sullenly.

"Specialist Deckheart, would you go on, please?" Kanode asked. "Would you explain why you think I don't know shit from shinola?"

There was nervous laughter now from the spectators of the proceedings.

"It's not just you, sir," Deckheart said. "It's anyone who hasn't been in the bush. The straphangers and the civilians, they think the war is soldier against soldier. But I've seen twelve-year-old kids blow a guy away. I've seen pregnant women throw hand grenades, and I've seen old men and old women trigger punji stakes. When you see that, sir, then you know there ain't no such thing as villagers. There's just dinks, and it breaks down to the dinks who are trying to kill you and the dinks who aren't."

"How do you know the difference?" Kanode asked.

"Well, sir, it sort of becomes us against them," Deckheart explained. "If he was one of Ngyuen's soldiers, he was us . . . if it wasn't one of Ngyuen's soldiers, it was them."

"And the operation of Phu Chat, was it us against them?"

"Yes, sir," Deckheart said.

"Specialist Deckheart, do you believe VCONG-COM was there?" Kanode asked.

"I can't answer that question," Deckheart said. "I'm only supposed to answer the questions I have knowledge about."

"Did you have knowledge that VCONGCOM was there?"

"We had reports," Deckheart replied.

"What sort of reports?"

"Air recon, intelligence, verification from an American marine unit."

"Did you actually *see* any of that information?" Kanode interrupted.

"Well, no, sir," Deckheart said. "I just heard. . . ."

"What was the basis of *your* information?"

"Colonel Ngyuen said VCONGCOM was there," Deckheart said.

"Did you believe him?"

Deckheart looked over at the court.

"Answer the question," Colonel Youngblood said.

Deckheart looked back at Kanode, then down at the floor. "No, sir," he mumbled.

"I beg your pardon?"

"No, sir," Deckheart said again. "I didn't believe him."

"Why didn't you believe him?"

"I speak the language," Deckheart said. "I overheard Ngyuen laughing and talking with some of the officers and noncoms on his staff. He told them he was using VCONGCOM as an excuse for the operation."

"Did you tell any of your superiors what you heard?"

"He *was* my superior," Deckheart said.

"I mean did you tell any of your American superiors?"

"No, sir," Deckheart said. "That is, no one except Cavindish and Addison. I told them."

"And what did they do?"

"They didn't do anything. They figured one operation is pretty much like another and it didn't really make any difference."

"Was this operation like the others?" Kanode asked.

"What do you mean?"

"Did you make a habit of rounding up civilians for execution?"

"Objection!" Major Albright shouted.

"Sustained," Colonel Youngblood said. "Mr. Kanode, watch the direction and content of your questions, sir."

"I withdraw that question, sir," Kanode said. "Specialist Deckheart, how many of the enemy were killed on this operation?"

"One hundred and twenty-nine, sir."

"And how many enemy weapons were recovered?"

"One, sir."

"*One*? One hundred and twenty-nine enemy soldiers killed on the battlefield, and only one weapon was recovered? Isn't that a little unusual?"

"No, sir, not really," Deckheart said. "You see, the V.C. put a great premium on the weapons. They'll save a weapon before they'll save one of their own wounded."

"I see. And how many casualties did Colonel Ngyuen's force sustain?"

"I . . . I don't know, sir," Deckheart said.

Kanode went back to his table and picked up a piece of paper. "I have it right here," he said.

"There were a total of eighteen casualties. Seventeen killed, and one wounded. Would that sound right to you? One hundred twenty-nine of the enemy and only eighteen friendlies?"

"Yes, sir," Deckheart said. "We fought a good fight."

"How about the enemy? Did they put up much resistance?"

"I don't know what you mean."

"Did you get a lot of return fire? Was there an organized resistance at all?"

"I don't know," Deckheart said. "I guess there must have been. I mean we had eighteen casualties."

"Did you observe a vigorous return fire?" Kanode asked. "You're a man of the bush, you say. Surely you can recognize whether or not you're in a firefight?"

"Well, I . . . I thought we had pretty good control of the situation," Deckheart stammered.

"Eighteen casualties to one hundred and twenty-nine would seem to indicate that you had control," Kanode said. It becomes even more significant when you realize that seventeen to eighteen were killed by the American helicopters . . . and not by the enemy at all. The eighteenth casualty, the soldier who was 'wounded,' suffered a sprained ankle when he left the helicopter." Kanode dropped the paper on his desk. "It doesn't sound like much of a fight, does it? Only one weapon recovered, and no casualties sustained. But there were one hundred and twenty-nine of the 'enemy' killed. Were they soldiers?"

"I beg your pardon, sir?"

"The one hundred and twenty-nine who were killed, were they soldiers?"

"They were V.C.," Deckheart said.

"But were they soldiers?"

"They were V.C.," Deckheart said again.

"Oh, yes, I'd nearly forgotten. Being a civilian, or a straphanger, I was ready to make a distinction between soldiers and non-soldiers. By your definition, there is no distinction, is there?"

"No, sir."

"So, some of the dead enemy could have been villagers?"

"V.C. villagers," Deckheart said.

"V.C. villagers who might have been, let's see, a twelve-year-old kid, I believe you said, a pregnant woman, an old man or an old woman."

"I . . . I don't know," Deckheart said. "There may have been."

"In fact, Specialist Deckheart, couldn't it be said that the *entire* one hundred and twenty-nine dead were composed of villagers of all ages and sexes, including one infant not yet able to walk?"

"It . . . it could have been," Deckheart admitted nervously. "There was so much shooting going on, there was so much confusion . . . I really don't know. One moment we were in a mopping-up action, and the next moment we were being attacked by our own helicopters."

"While Colonel Ngyuen was mopping up, as you say?"

"Yes, sir."

"Now, I ask you, Specialist Deckheart, isn't it possible that the mopping up, given the unique construction of the V.C. enemy so that it included villagers, isn't it possible that someone flying over might mistake Colonel Ngyuen's troops, who were dressed in black, as Viet Cong who were murdering villagers?"

"They weren't murdering, sir, they were mopping up," Deckheart insisted.

"But isn't it possible that from one thousand feet it might look like murder?"

"I . . . I guess it's possible, sir," Deckheart said. "I just don't know."

"No further questions," Kanode said.

The courtroom sat in stunned silence for a long moment, and finally Colonel Youngblood asked Major Albright if he had any redirect.

"No, sir," Major Albright replied. "I would like to recall Colonel Kramer, however."

Bert Kramer was recalled, and he took the stand as confidently as he had earlier in the day.

"Colonel Kramer, what specifically were Captain Hunter's orders on the day of the incident at Phu Chat?" Major Albright asked.

"His orders were to orbit at the holding station, to be ready in case he was needed in support of the operation."

"And did he remain on station?"

"No, he did not," Kramer said. "He requested permission to answer a request for a fire mission from a marine colonel."

"And did you grant him this permission?"

"No," Kramer said.

"Why not? Wasn't the request put in the form of a high priority code which must be answered?"

"Yes, it was," Kramer said. "And I was going to allow him to answer the request, even if it meant placing our own operation in danger of being without reserves, but when I questioned MACV I learned that an air force flight was enroute to answer the request, and would arrive on station at approximately the same time. I felt that Cobra helicopters being on the scene at the same time as air force Phantom jets would cause utter chaos and confusion. It was conceivable that the confusion would do more harm than good, so I refused Captain Hunter's request. Captain Hunter took it upon himself to disregard my refusal, and he took the mission anyway."

"Colonel Kramer, is it possible that Captain Hunter's absence from your operation could have led to the confusion he encountered when he returned? Had he remained on station, would he not have known the whereabouts of Colonel Ngyuen's troops at all times?"

"I can't see that it could have made that much difference," Kramer said. "He was thoroughly briefed before the mission. He knew such things as the radio frequencies, the plans for the attack."

"Would he have known that Colonel Ngyuen's troops were dressed in black?" asked Albright.

"Oh, absolutely, sir," Kramer said. "He had supported Colonel Ngyuen's forces many times in the past."

"And would he have recognized Colonel Ngyuen's personal flag, do you suppose?"

"Everyone knew Ngyuen's flag," Kramer said. "Ngyuen was such an egomaniac about it that he had a flag bearer with him practically everywhere he went."

"But given all this, isn't it still possible that things happened just as Captain Hunter said? Isn't it possible that he mistook Ngyuen's troops for V.C.?"

"Major, with the thoroughness of Hunter's prestrike briefing, the familiarity of Captain Hunter with Colonel Ngyuen's operating procedures and with the radio equipment and safeguards before any attack, I can only say that it would be inconsistent with Captain Hunter's demonstrated ability to make such a mistake."

"That leaves only one alternative, doesn't it?" Major Albright said. "If Captain Hunter did not strafe Colonel Ngyuen by mistake . . . he had to do it by design."

"Yes, sir," Kramer said. He looked over at Jack, fixing him with a cold stare. "I suppose that is correct."

"No further questions."

Kanode stood then, and walked around to the front of his table, then leaned on it for a moment. "Colonel Kramer, did you honestly believe that VCONGCOM was located at Phu Chat?"

"Yes, of course," Kramer answered.

"Despite all the evidence to the contrary?"

"Evidence to the contrary?"

"Colonel Kramer, I have here a copy of the operations orders, authorizing the attack at Phu Chat. They specifically say—"

"Those orders are classified secret," Kramer said quickly. "What are you doing with them?"

"Mr. Kanode, this court will not be a party to the compromise of classified material," Colonel Youngblood said quickly. "I will not allow you to introduce that document, and I am ordering you to tell this court how such a document got into your hands."

"Colonel Youngblood, this document has been officially declassified, and I have a letter to that effect from the commanding general of U.S. Forces in Vietnam. And as to how I received this document, I shall shortly call as a witness for the defense the man who not only provided me with the document, but managed to get the document declassified." As Kanode spoke, he crossed over to the long table and handed the document and the letter of declassification, along with copies of both, to each member of the board.

"Very well, Mr. Kanode," Youngblood said, putting the letter and the document down. "You may proceed."

"Now, Colonel Kramer, I have in my hand the operations order authorizing the mission against Phu Chat. Is it from this document that you drew your information for the prestrike briefing?"

"Yes," Kramer said.

"I would like to read a paragraph," Kanode said. He cleared his throat, then began reading aloud. " 'While there is strong evidence to refute Colonel Ngyuen's contention that VCONGCOM is located at Phu Chat, it is felt that token cooperation with Colonel Ngyuen at this time will be in the best interest of the counter-insurgency effort, because it will, by its very failure to turn up VCONGCOM, justify renewed efforts to locate the headquarters in other provinces. All U.S. commanders will be briefed accordingly, and cautioned to avoid situations which may be compromising to U.S. forces.'

"Now, I ask you, Colonel Kramer, does that sound like a total endorsement of the idea that VCONGCOM was located at Phu Chat?"

"Colonel Kramer," Colonel Youngblood said. "Did you receive a copy of this secret order before you briefed your officers?"

"Yes, sir," Colonel Kramer said.

"And yet, in your briefing, you led them to think

that our government actually believed VCONGCOM existed just where Ngyuen said it was?"

"Yes, sir," Kramer said.

Youngblood looked at the document a moment longer, then he sighed and ran his hand through his hair. "Colonel Kramer, the very purpose of this document was to inform the American commanders of the truth in order that they might act accordingly. It was classified secret so as not to damage relations with the government of the Republic of Vietnam, but certainly it would have behooved you to exercise some command judgment on its contents. You were most imprudent, Colonel—in fact, one might say you were incompetent. I intend to launch a thorough investigation into your whole performance of duty with regard to this issue. Now, Mr. Kanode, what I don't understand is why this was kept away from us this long? And how did you come by information which the court didn't have?"

"If it please the court, I should now like to call a witness for the defense," Kanode said.

"You may call your witness, for I would like to get to the bottom of this," Colonel Youngblood said. "But as president of this court, I am saying here and now that as soon as we hear the testimony of this witness, I am dismissing the defendant as improperly charged, and I am dissolving this court."

Colonel Youngblood's words stunned Jack for a moment, then, suddenly, they sank in. He was free! A smile broke across his face and he turned to tell Deena, but she had understood Colonel Youngblood's statement as quickly as he had, and she was already upon him, embracing him before the buzz of excited voices from those in the court.

So intent was everyone upon Jack's reaction to his sudden and unexpected victory, that no one noticed as Colonel Kramer, with his head hanging in shame, sneaked out through the back door of the building.

23

COLONEL YOUNGBLOOD could have ordered the court to quiet immediately, but he allowed the buzzing to go on for several moments without interfering. He lit a cigarette, then leaned over to talk to the major who was sitting next to him.

"I'm going to let it go for a few moments," he said, "to let the tension ease."

"It's a good idea, sir," the major replied automatically, though he would have just as enthusiastically supported the colonel had the court been ordered into silence. Finally, the buzzing died of its own accord, and the spectators and the reporters took their seats, then looked expectantly toward the front of the court to see who Kanode's next witness would be and what he had to say.

Colonel Youngblood butted his cigarette, and the others on the board who had begun to smoke did the same, including one major who had just lit a fresh one. Colonel Youngblood looked at Major Albright, and Major Albright stood and called the court back to order.

"Now, Mr. Kanode," Colonel Youngblood said. "You may call your witness."

"I call Colonel Gilbert Bell, of the United States Marine Corps," Kanode said.

Colonel Bell, a tall, fine-looking officer with a crop of closely cut, silver hair and a chest full of ribbons showing not only Vietnam but also Korean War service, took the witness seat. He was a man at ease with command and totally in control of himself.

"Colonel Bell, would you identify yourself for the court please, and explain your connection with this case?"

"I'd be glad to, counselor," Gilbert said. In a smooth voice which could only be said to be commanding, Gilbert told the court of his connection with the case. He told of encountering VCONG-COM, and of requesting support for an attack against the Viet Cong headquarters. He told of the actual attack, and of running into more V.C. then he had bargained for, then of his request for assistance, and the answer of that request by a team of U.S. Army Cobras, led, he later learned, by Captain Jack Hunter. Those Cobras, he insisted, had saved many from his command, and possibly his own life. The air force jets did arrive, but without the support from the Cobras, the air force jets would have been too late to be of much help.

"What about this document?" Kanode asked.

"Oh yes, the operations order," Gilbert said. "I received a copy of this document, along with a cover letter saying that after this operation I would get the support I needed to attack what I thought to be VCONGCOM. Unfortunately, there was an error in transmission and the first report I got said only that Phu Chat was being attacked. It was twenty-four hours before I received all of it. Had I received it on time, I would have delayed my own attack. Later, when I heard of the trouble Captain Hunter was in, I went to MACV and requested that this document be declassified. It was a sensitive document, because its publication would prove that the U.S. had conducted a ruse against its allies by pretending to go along with Colonel Ngyuen only to use that as a lever for our own attack later. Because of that sensitivity, we had to go all the way to Washington for approval. It just came back this morning."

"Colonel Bell, I want to thank you personally for taking an interest in this case," Colonel Youngblood said. "You are to be commended for your efforts in preventing a miscarriage of justice, and you have not only my appreciation, but the appreciation of the United States Army as well."

"And that of Captain Jack Hunter," Jack said and though he had spoken out of turn, it was such an obvious comment that it brought a comic relief to the proceedings, and everyone, including Colonel Youngblood laughed.

"This board, convened under the provisions of the Universal Code of Military Justice, is hereby dissolved, and all charges and specifications are revoked," Colonel Youngblood said.

The audience cheered, and all rushed to congratulate Jack.

"Jack, here is someone else who wants to congratulate you," Deena said a short time later, after most of the people had left. Now there was just Jack, Terry Kanode, Colonel Bell and a few of the court officers, who were so busy putting papers into briefcases and preparing to leave that they were totally separated from Jack and his little group.

Jack looked toward the man Deena was with, and he smiled broadly, for he recognized Frank, Deena's brother. Jack had visited with him a few times during his convalescence in the hospital.

"I'm glad you beat it," Frank said. "After all, I'm told that if you hadn't come when you did, I would have bought it."

"There's no doubt about it," Gilbert said. "The way you hung on to that machine gun, you were the number one target of the entire V.C. brigade."

"I don't remember that," Frank said. He laughed, a small, self-deprecating laugh. "The fact is, it's hard for me to believe I'd do anything that dumb."

"That wasn't dumb," Jack said. "That was brave. When we arrived, you had them all pinned down. It was like shooting ducks in a barrel for us."

"I'll say it was brave," Gilbert said. "It was brave enough to earn you the Medal of Honor."

"What'd you say?" Frank gasped.

Gilbert smiled. "The declassification of these documents wasn't the only news I got from Washington this morning," he said. "I also got word that the Medal of Honor has been approved for award to Sergeant Frank Bell. Congratulations, Frank."

Deena hugged her brother then, and the tears of happiness which she had finally been able to stop over Jack's victory started again over the news of her brother's award.

"Damn," Frank said. "Damn, that's really somethin', isn't it?"

"I'll say it is," Jack said, smiling and offering his hand in congratulations to Frank. "It's going to be hard to live up to a Medal of Honor winner as a brother-in-law."

"A brother-in-law?" Frank said. He looked at Deena. "What's this crap? I haven't given my approval yet," he teased.

"You might as well give it, big brother, because with or without your approval, I'm going to marry Jack."

"In that case, you have my approval," Frank said. "As long as he understands that a captain in the army is below a sergeant in the marines, I see no prob—" Frank broke off when a shout came from the front door of the administration building.

"Jack, come quick!" Warrant Officer Ed Selfridge yelled. "It's Kramer!"

"Kramer?" Jack said. "What about him?"

"He's gone crazy!" Selfridge said. "Operation just got a radio call from him. He's going after Parrot's Beak, single-handed!"

"What?" Jack said. "What does he expect to do at Parrot's Beak? The air force hasn't even been able to take it out in two strikes."

"Hell, I don't think Kramer expects to, either," Selfridge said. "If you want to know the truth, I think the son of a bitch is trying to commit suicide."

"Let's go," Jack said, starting toward the door.

"Jack, what are you going to do?" Deena called in a frightened voice.

"I'm going to try and catch up with him before he gets there."

"And then what?"

"I don't know," Jack said. "Stop him somehow, if I can."

"Jack, no, that's not your responsibility," Deena said. "Please, don't go!"

"Deena, I've—"

"Let 'im go, sis," Frank said, putting his hand lightly on Deena's arm. "He's doing what he has to do."

Jack and Ed ran to the nearest Cobra, then leaped into it and started it, without even so much as a perfunctory pre-flight. Jack saw by the gauges that the fuel tanks were full, and for that he was thankful. The ship wasn't armed, but weapons would only make it heavier and rob him of a few extra miles of speed. Without them, he might have enough speed to catch up with Colonel Kramer before he did whatever it was he intended to do.

Jack pulled the ship off the ground even before the engine instruments were stabilized, and cut across the field without bothering to use the normal exit pattern. He rolled the nose forward and flew at full power and optimum angle to get as much speed as he could.

"Tiger Six, Tiger Six, this is Tiger Four," Jack said. Using the code Tiger Four for his own call letters sounded awkward and unfamiliar, but the number six was used only for a commanding officer, and Jack was no longer a commanding officer. He was now an assistant supply officer.

"Well, well, well," Kramer's voice said, coming back over Jack's headset. "Merry Christmas, Jack. Didn't Santa Claus bring you a nice Christmas present?"

"Colonel Kramer, where are you?"

"Little Jack Horner, sitting in a corner, eating your Christmas pie. Are you eating your Christmas pie? Only six shopping days left till Christmas, you know."

"Where are you?" Jack asked again.

"I'm at Parrot's Beak," Kramer answered, "just where I told ops I would be. I'm doing my Christmas shopping early. Do you know what I'm going to give everyone for Christmas? I'm going to give them the guns at Parrot's Beak. All gift-wrapped and everything."

"Colonel Kramer, wait," Jack said. "Wait for me."

"Jingle bells, jingle bells," Kramer started, singing in a strange high-pitched voice.

"He's gone crazy," Ed said. "The son of a bitch has gone off the deep end."

"Colonel Kramer, listen, I want you to think about what you're doing. You can't take those guns on by yourself. Come on back, and let's plan a strike against them."

"Ah, are you going to talk me out of this now, little Jack Horner?" Kramer asked in a singsong voice. "You talked Springs out of blowing us all up with a grenade remember? You're good at talking people out of things. You even talked yourself out of a murder charge."

"I was innocent," Jack said. "You would want me to get off if I were really innocent, wouldn't you?"

"Dear boy, I had no wish to see you off the hot seat only to find myself in it."

"You'll make out all right," Jack said. "Listen, Youngblood's not your next higher, anyway. What the hell can he do?"

"What can he do? He can keep me a lieutenant colonel for the rest of my career," Kramer said. "Or worse, he can end my career. Then what would I do, Jack? Sell used cars somewhere?"

"Listen, don't just give up," Jack said. "Don't just give up without a fight."

"There it is," Kramer said. "Parrot's Beak. Are you anywhere close yet? I want you to . . . ah, there you are. I see you."

"I'm right on you now," Jack said. He could see the Cobra in front of him, orbiting just outside the valley entrance to Parrot's Beak. When he drew closer, he could see that there was no gunner with Kramer, who was flying solo. Kramer waved at him.

"Come on back now, Bert," Jack said.

"Why the hell should I come back?" Kramer asked. "It's all over, you know."

"But it's not all over. Hey, you know what? Kanode would be a good man for you to know. Let me talk to him, he'll—"

"I don't mean just my career," Kramer said. "It's all over. The whole thing. Don't you see?"

"No," Jack said. "No, I don't see. I don't understand what you're talking about."

"I'm talking about the American dream," Kramer said. "You know, the great hope of mankind, the cradle of Democracy, the invincible duty, honor, country, American dream. I've tried to build a career out of shadow and smoke. What kind of army have we become that we let clowns like Ngyuen dictate strategy to us? We have half a million men in this godforsaken place. Why don't we just start at the southern tip and move north, until we've cleaned out the whole friggin' country?"

"Because we aren't fighting that kind of a war," Jack said.

"Then we have no business being over here at all."

"Maybe we don't," Jack replied. "On that one

point, at least, Ngyuen was right. We have no business, as soldiers, trying to make policy. Our only business is to follow that policy, whatever it may be."

"You do that," Kramer said. "You're the reluctant hero. You're the one who understands, and you've understood all along. What's your secret Hunter? How are you able to cope? We aren't going to win this war, you know. What's going to happen then?"

"We're going to win, Bert," Jack said. "Maybe not like you said, not by turning this country into a parking lot. But is that what we really want? Wouldn't it be better to have a victory of the spirit, a testing of what America is all about, and a new strength from this crucible?"

Kramer laughed. "Spoken like the true reluctant hero," he said. "I can't do that. I can't face any of it. I can't face the defeat of being a warrior without honor, in an army without victory. It's better to let it end here. Merry Christmas, Jack."

Kramer broke out of his orbit then, and plunged his Cobra down toward the valley opening. Jack dived after him, following him down as if he were a fighter plane on the tail of an adversary in a dogfight.

"Ed, if he goes up the valley, I'm going after him," Jack said.

"I'm game," Ed said. "I sure feel naked up here without anything to shoot, though."

"I'll break off before the guns have an angle on us," Jack said.

"What does that crazy son of a bitch think he's doing?" Ed asked.

"Bert," Jack called. "Bert, break out now. Another twenty seconds and they'll have the angle on you!"

"Do you suppose there are any warriors in hell?" Kramer asked in a calm voice.

The guns opened up then, and flak began bursting all around. The bullet sensor counted dozens of shrapnel strikes, and the helicopter jumped up, like a car hitting a bump in a rough road.

"Damn, we've got to get out of here!" Jack said, shoving in a pedal and throwing the cyclyc around, forcing them into a tight turn. Jack held the turn until he was out of the valley and clear of the angle of fire from the guns.

"He's firing at them now," Ed said, and Jack looked toward Kramer's Cobra, slipping quickly and darkly up the valley, spewing plumes of fire as the rockets slashed forward.

"They're bursting on the rocks," Ed said. "Just like before."

"He's not turning away!" Jack suddenly shouted. "My God, he's . . ."

They heard nothing. Their own engine and transmission noise blotted out all outside sound, so there was nothing to accompany the rosette of fire which suddenly bloomed just at the opening which housed the guns. At first there was only a small bubble of fire, so small that Jack felt cheated, as if the death of a pilot and a helicopter deserved more. Then, as he and Ed watched in stunned silence, a larger bubble of fire burst out from the point where the helicopter had gone in, and then the fire began racing all along the side of the mountain, from side to side and up and down, erupting in a series of bursts, like someone setting off a string of firecrackers. Now they could feel the shockwaves from the explosions, and their helicopter was thrown around as if they were in severe turbulence. Fire and smoke boiled from the mountain, towering high into the sky.

"Son of a bitch!" Ed said in awe. "Secondaries! He got 'em! He got the damn guns!"

"Yeah," Jack said. "He got 'em."

Jack turned away and started back toward Phu Bien. He tuned his radio to Paris Control to monitor his flight. He could hear other traffic.

"Paris, have we got artillery firing at Parrot's Beak?" said a voice on the radio.

"Negative artillery," Paris Control replied.

"Then it must be a volcano. The whole top of Parrot's Beak just blew up."

"Too bad the whole country can't just blow up," another voice said. "After we're out of it, of course."

"We're never going to get out of it," still another voice said. "Haven't you heard? Nixon's new pull-out plan calls for the last American to leave in the year 2000."

"This is Paris Control. Cease all unnecessary radio traffic at once!"

"Paris, Tiger Four," Jack said when the airwaves were clear.

"Squawk," Paris replied.

Jack hit his squawk switch on the transponder.

"I.D. confirmed. Destination?"

"Phu Bien," Jack said.

"Proceed at your discretion."

Jack started his descent then, and as he came closer to the A Troop flight line, he was able to make out Deena sitting in his jeep, waiting for him to return.

"Lookie there," Ed said. "Just like having a wife meet you at the airport when you come home from a business trip, isn't it?"

Deena was out of the jeep and running under the blades of the Cobra even before Jack shut down the engine. Jack climbed out as quickly as he could, then took her and held her in his arms while the blades whished over them, spinning fast at first, then slowly turning down until they came to a complete halt. Still, Jack and Deena were locked in an embrace.

"Kramer—" Jack started to explain.

"I know," Deena interrupted. "We were monitoring the radio."

Jack sighed. "Listen, I hope you hadn't planned on anything special tonight, like a party or anything. I'd like for us to be alone together, if you don't mind."

"I'll shoot anyone who disturbs us," Deena said. "Your place or mine?"

"How 'bout the bunker?"

"I can't think of a better place to hole up," Deena said. "The bunker it is."

Arm in arm, Deena and Jack walked toward the bunker in the middle of the flower garden of the Red Bull. Overhead, two Phantom jets, their wings laden with bombs and rockets, screamed by, heading for a bombing mission over North Vietnam. In the distance, someone was listening to the radio. It was a program of Christmas carols, and they heard the silken voice of the singer.

"Peace on earth and mercy mild. . . ."

Don't miss
these other exciting
titles in
The Freedom Fighters *Series*